MASOUD

To Rev. Phil,
cheers and
blessings!

Steven Maines

MASOUD

BOOK III OF THE MERLIN FACTOR

STEVEN MAINES

Purple Haze Press

MASOUD
BOOK III of THE MERLIN FACTOR

Purple Haze Press books may be ordered through booksellers or by contacting:
Purple Haze Press
PBM 167 2430 Vanderbilt Beach Road, #108
Naples, FL 34109
www.PurpleHazePress.com

This is a work of fiction. All characters, names, incidents, organizations and dialogue in this novel are either the products of the author's imagination or are used fictitiously.

FRONT & BACK COVER DESIGN:
Jeffrey Bedrick

ISBN 978-0-9773200-5-9

Library of Congress Control Number: 2011906485

Printed in the United States of America

1. Fiction   2. Historical Fiction   3. New Age

ACKNOWLEDGEMENTS

I wish to express my deepest appreciation to the following people:

Michele Genovese-Maines, Liam Maines,
Genavee Maines, Mattea Maines.

Vashali, Elliot Malach.

Ann Maines, Chris Maines, Sharon & Fred Morales,
Lita Fice, Manuel Fernandes.

DEDICATION

This book is dedicated to my children;

Liam, Genavee & Mattea.

I love you with all my heart and soul.
May you always know your
Self and always find your song.

PROLOGUE

Rapturous beauty. Peace of soul. The bosom of the Divine. I nested in these things and more. And less. For, it is all of the One, all in the One, divine Principle. Such were my spirit's musings. In that instant I was not in my body, though I had one. My consciousness wafted to its Source, and then to my spirit's linear, physical experiences. I had occupied several bodies over what is known as terrestrial time. Those bodies, those lives and the feelings and experiences associated with them impinged themselves upon my individualized soul consciousness. I relived each experience of each life——each challenge, each triumph, each lesson, each love——in an instant. I was Gaius Cassius Longinus, the Roman Centurion who stabbed the Christ while he was tortuously hanging from his cross. Irena; my heart, my soul, my love of that life flashed before my spirit's consciousness. The spear, my Centurion's spear——the instrument I had used to stab the Anointed One——was my companion in that life, teaching me, speaking to me with what I took to be *His* voice: the voice of the Crucified One whom I stabbed.

Then another of my lives entered my awareness. I was a powerful one of the Old Ways, a Druid of great renown and fame. *Myrriddin* is who I had been. *Merlin* is who I had become. Irena had been in that life too, though in the form of another, Igraines. We had loved but shortly, each of us having other purposes then. But someone else shared love with me instead: Nimue by way of Camaroon from my life as Longinus. Obviously, our souls had not completed our journey of learning and growth together in the previous life.

As Myrriddin or Merlin, I had achieved a level of understanding of the One and existence that most *seekers* would envy. But that type of judgment is circular. Besides, there is no judgment of the One by the One. There is only the experiencing of Itself through the individualized expressions of Itself in form, material; human and otherwise.

The Spear was with me as Myrriddin as well, guiding me and aiding me once again. It was disguised as my Druid Staff. It was powerful, or so I believed for a time. But I let it go.

Another of my soul's lives came into focus. I was not a Centurion or a Druid in this life. I was a Christian, a crusader in the third misguided crusade by the Christians on the Holy Land. And, in the images of this life that came into the eye of my consciousness, in my hand I held the same Spear that had been with me in those two previous lives.

I felt myself drifting, falling away from the comfort of viewing and re-experiencing these lives from the Divine bosom.

I suddenly slammed back into physical form——my current physical form. Violence and the sound of screaming male voices and clashing swords were all around me. I was the Christian crusader from the last images I had seen while out of my body. The memory and the images of my past lives I had just witnessed began to fade. I lived once again in the now. Liam Arthur Mason was my Christian and Sir-name. But my Muslim captors called me Masoud.

ONE

"In the name of Christ, the Lord!" yelled the commander. Others around him, clad in similar armor and helmet, but with white tunic emblazoned with a red cross on its front, Templar knights, repeated the call as one. I was among them as a common crusader and soldier. We brandished our swords as we invoked the Lord to the side of the righteous: our side. It was our battle cry, or at least one of them, as we prepared to engage the *infidels'* army.

They stood before us no more than fifty paces away from our front line. Arrayed before us dressed in black from head to toe, save for the brown leather chest plates of much of their infantry. They appeared a formidable foe. They, too, had a battle-cry. "Solom Allah!" they yelled, or something like it. The infidels' army would scream their battle-cry on the heels of ours, thus invoking their Lord's name to the side of...what? Heathens, they were. Or, so I believed.

"Did you hear?!" exclaimed Henry as he turned to me. My friend, Henry Tobiason Andrews, and I had come on this crusade together, enamored with thoughts of glory and a place in history as being among those who helped rid the Holy Land of the Muslim invader. We would also, Henry and I thought, be fulfilling a sacred duty to the Church. The crusader army was made up of volunteers, volunteers of a sort, truth be told. Many crusaders were the cut-throats and thieves of society, but all of us were promised eternal salvation by the Pope for coming here and freeing the Holy Land. "Did you hear?" my friend said again, his long, flaming red hair spilling out from beneath his too-small helmet. Henry was in the line of soldiers in front of me, both of us in the fifth and sixth lines respectively behind our front line. The two armies, ours Christian, theirs Muslim, faced each other, only yelling battle-cries for the moment.

"Hear what?" I asked.

"They have it," he said, pointing in the direction of the opposing army, eyes dancing nervously. "It's been seen!"

"Have what, damn it? I don't know what you're on about," I retorted.

"It just came down the line and..." Henry began.

"'Tis true!" said the man next to me, a boy really. His tunic and helmet were much too large for his small stature. His wide, boyish eyes peered at me from beneath his helm's brim. He could not have been more than thirteen years of age. "My mate saw it this morn, he did!" the boy proclaimed.

"The Rood, Liam," Henry said to me. "The wood from the actual cross our Lord perished on. And the Great Spear of Longinus too, the very weapon that pierced our Lord's chest! Think of it!"

"Yes, yes," I said doubtfully, nearly shouting to be heard over the chorus of yelling voices, invoking Christ and Allah in turn.

"The infidels paraded it before some of our men this morning to taunt us," Henry insisted.

"They did, they did," added the boy-soldier.

"They know it to hold the power of our Lord, but the fools know not how to use it. They can't, the devil spawns!" Henry said, laughing. "They have the Grail and the Spear of Longinus too, just as King Richard said. I truly believe it now."

"I'm sure you're correct, Henry," I replied sardonically. *Ridiculous*, I thought to myself. There was a time I believed these things existed. In point of fact, I had sold all of my possessions, even indentured myself for a time to a local blacksmith in order to supply myself with weapons, armor and the tunic I now wore in ser-vice to the Crown——which most crusaders had to supply for themselves. I did it to join this idealistic quest for the Holy relics of Christendom and the *liberation* of the Holy Land. When first I became part of King Richard's army bound for

Jerusalem, I was indeed an idealistic crusader with noble intent. No more. The blood of others I had shed, the innocent lives I had taken, the fact that Christians and Muslims know the same God but by different names——for want of a better word——had shown me disillusionment as to the purpose of this farcical quest. The madness of this venture had even led me to the point of heresy; the so-called Holy relics are naught but wood and or metal and nothing more, if they existed at all. Such was my heretical line of thinking. A part of me envied my friend's continued passionate belief. "I'm sure you are correct, Henry," I repeated, with less sarcasm in my voice.

The poor boy-soldier never saw it coming. None of us did. We heard a soft thud which seemed to come from the boy. Henry and I turned our eyes upon the lad. The arrow had entered his left shoulder on the top, having descended from a high, arcing line of flight. It penetrated down into his body with only the guide feathers and notched end protruding out just behind his collar bone. The boy said nothing. He simply stared dumbly at the thing in his shoulder.

"By the Christ!" Henry exclaimed. The boy looked at us then, realization dawning on his face, tears of sadness——not of pain——filling his eyes: a young life denied. He crumpled and died at our feet.

Suddenly, the yells of our battle-cry became screams of agony and chaos. Arrows rained down on us all, hundreds of them, finding their marks in crusader flesh, spreading fear, confusion and death. Some in our ranks tried to lift their shield for protection. My friend and I had no shield. Many of our fellow crusaders had them——either because they could afford to purchase one or were issued one because they were part of the King's regular army——but some of us did not. Regardless, our close proximity to one another proved, at least for the moment, to render any shield all but useless. Bedlam ensued as the arrows came down in wave after wave, forcing all the lines of our men to collapse in a mass of crowded bodies, each man hunching and huddling against those next to him in an attempt to protect himself. The closely packed bodies thus made it all but impossible to draw one's shield as a protective umbrella.

"Hold the lines, damn you!" bellowed our commander of the moment from atop his white steed. Sir Jonathan James was his name. He was a handsome, gruff man with short cropped grey hair and a cropped grey beard (unusual for a Templar Knight, which he also was, for the Templar knight was never supposed to shave) who never wore a helmet in battle. Approximately forty-five years of age and a veteran of many bloody campaigns, rumors told that he was not only a warrior but a priest in the Church as well. Intriguing. At the moment, however, Sir Jonathan James was our commander and none-too-happy with his troops' performance. "Stand up and re-form the lines, now! Those with shields get them up high. Make the shell! Those without, get beneath the shell. Move, move, move!" Commander James yelled, his horse prancing anxiously beneath him.

The men, all of us, obeyed, such was Commander James' sway. He was a strong man and a charismatic leader. He was the type of leader that all men would follow, the type of man that every man wanted to be. Almost as one, every crusader in our ranks——nearly four centuries by the old Roman way of counting and categorizing troops——stood and formed disciplined, tight lines despite the fact the there were dead and wounded lying at our feet. At the same moment, shields came up and over most of our heads, held flat above by their owners, thus creating a protective barrier between many of us and the deadly flock of arrows still coming down. Ideally, all of the shields would overlap, creating a solid ceiling above us, with those in the front lines holding their shields in front of them, thus utilizing an age old defensive technique: a Tortoise Shell, as the Greeks once called it. Unfortunately, there were many gaps in our shell. Many of the feathered missiles still got through. Crusaders were still hit by the arrows and dropped dead or severely wounded. Still maintaining our line, Henry and I moved to two nearby fellow crusaders holding shields above their heads. In the process, I tripped over the body of our boy-soldier, slamming hard on my knees. I winced as the pain shot through my leg and body. I glanced at the boy's face. It now looked more blissful, more peaceful than sad, and I had the fleeting thought that boy was better off this way; he had avoided the carnage that was sure to come. I quickly got to my feet and joined Henry under the shields. We crouched there, swords drawn, waiting for the attack from the sky to end. But a moment later, the worst began.

A thousand and more voices in front of our ranks rose in the fevered pitch of battle frenzy. The Muslim army surged forward and slammed into our front lines.

The first few lines of crusaders were utterly crushed and killed in an instant. As a common foot soldier, I was not usually in a vantage point to know exactly how many of the enemy we faced on a given battle field. Of course, we would hear rumors of what the scouts had seen, but would not truly know how many we faced until engagement. Such was the case here. But the force of the enemy's initial charge left no doubt that they had overwhelming numbers. I was knocked down, the weight of many bodies nearly crushing the life out of me. The fetid stench of these dirty, sweating bodies, loosed bowels and fear permeated my nostrils. Add to that the coppery smell of spilt blood mingled with dust kicked up in this barren place by so many feet and so much violence, and it was enough to nearly make me vomit. Most of those who had fallen into me were alive and trying to get up and out of the crush themselves. Some were not alive. Indeed, as I got to my feet I found that my sword was caught in something. I looked closer. It was hilt-deep in the back of a crusader. I was horrified. I pulled the sword free and rolled the man over as best I could in the crush of everyone. His dead eyes stared back at me from a face I did not recognize. He had obviously fallen into my weapon or had been pushed into it during the attack. Guilt seeped into my mind. *If I had only held my sword higher*, I thought. Nay. It was a part of war. I thanked God then, as horrible as it may seem, that it had not been my friend Henry. I looked for my friend then. He was nowhere that I could see. "Henry!" I called, trying desperately to be heard over the din of battle. I could not see him.

Man-to-man combat was breaking out all around me. The whoosh of a sword's blade came deadly close to my face. From the corner of my left eye I saw several thick strands of my own light brown hair fall away. It was then I realized that my helmet was gone, fallen or knocked off in the melee, no doubt, and that the sword which had just swung dangerously close to my head had lopped off some of my own shoulder-length hair. I turned but saw no specific assailant. He had either moved passed me or had been cut down in the crowd. Suddenly, the press of fighting bodies to my left separated. An also helmet-less Henry, long flaming red, tousled hair whipping about with his movements, was defending himself against two Muslims who were hacking at him with their scimitars—— large, curved bladed and wide-ended swords. Our swords were straight and approximately four feet long and double-edged. They were not as formidable as those the Muslim army used, but our fighters were inherently more skilled in swordsmanship. It was something one started at an early age. I was proud of my friend. He was the best of the best, an expert swordsman. He was dancing around his opponents, confusing them and easily parrying their attacks. But I could see two more of the enemy coming up from behind Henry, about to join the fray against him.

"Henry! Behind you!" I called as I began to run toward him. The blow came so suddenly that I had no time to react. Pain exploded on and through the right side of my head about three inches above my ear. Intense bright light flashed before my eyes as I felt myself crumple to the ground. Then, all went black.

TWO

I dreamt. I dreamt of being in a cavernous space where the tall walls and high ceiling were made of crystal stones and gems, millions of them. The place was bright, as though the crystals expanded a small amount of natural light into the brightness of a mid-day sun. The place was also sacred; a sanctuary for the spirit, for *my* spirit. This place was my home, had been my home at some point in time. I felt it. But I had never been there. Or, rather Liam Arthur Mason had never been to this crystal sanctuary. No matter. I took comfort in being there now in my dream. I knew I was dreaming, felt it in my soul, knew it in my mind. But this place had been real, was still. I felt that too.

Someone else was with me in my dream, in the crystal cavern. The person was an old man dressed in a flowing blue robe. He had long white hair, a white beard, and the oak staff he leaned on had intricately carved symbols on it; symbols of an ancient religion. The old man looked like a powerful wizard from legend, perhaps even the great Merlin himself. And, his staff was clearly a wizard's staff. Or, as my mother would call it: a Druid's Staff. My mother, though a pious and devout Christian woman, still, on occasion, made reference to the "Old Ways"——the the Old Ways being the ancient religion, for want of a better word, of our peoples headed by the Druids. Depending on the company she happened to be with at a given moment, the reference was either in praise of the Old Ways and its Druids combined with sadness that the Christians had all but destroyed them, or condemnation of them as evil. But one thing she often said to me when I was a lad was, "Be upright and true as a Druid's Staff."

The man, the wizard, the Druid standing before me in my dream looked to be wise——it was in his eyes. I wanted to ask him about this place, this crystal sanctuary, and why it felt like home. And then the answer came. I looked deeper into his hazel colored eyes, into his very soul and saw...myself.

ڶ   ڶ   ڶ

I awoke, my eyes opening onto the actual world. My head throbbed horribly. I lay flat on my back and had no idea where I was. The guttural sound of the Arabic language, a language I had come to understand a little and despise a lot over the past year that I had spent in this region near Jerusalem, was all around me. It came back to me then: the battle, Henry fighting two——or had it been four——Muslims, and the blow to my head. I stared at the thick cloth or canvas ceiling some ten feet above my face. I was clearly in some kind of field tent. I listened more closely for a moment to those nearby. I heard no English, only Arabic. Not a good sign, for it meant that I had been captured.

I reached out and touched the right side of my head. Wet warmth greeted my fingers. Blood, no doubt. But I also felt something beneath that: cloth wrapping. Someone had bandaged my head. That surprised me. Most of us in the Christian army had been under the impression that the Muslims took no prisoners, let alone bound the wounds of the enemy. Perhaps I had not been captured after all, for, *would they not have left me for dead if they saw I was unconscious, and killed me if they saw I was alive?* I wondered.

"Do not touch!" came a scratchy male voice next to me, as the stranger slapped my hand away from the head-wound. His words had been in English, but heavily accented with Arabic. "La, la. No, no. You must let it heal, you see," he said.

I turned my head to the right until it hurt too much to do so. But it was enough to see the man who spoke to me. He was dressed in black from head to toe——from his wrapped headdress on down. His face was exposed and was very dark, even for an Arab, with the start of wrinkles around his eyes. I guessed him to be near thirty-five years of age. His slightly hooked nose and furrowed brow gave him the look of a vigilant hawk. His eyes were too close together, thus he seemed perpetually cross-eyed. Despite that, his dark eyes twinkled with the delight of one who was in a constant state of happiness. Interestingly, his dark beard had streaks of red in it and was parted oddly down the middle, from his chin to his collar bone——such was its length——ending in two points.

"I thought..." I began, finding it painful to speak. "I thought you killed any who lived...any of the enemy, is what I speak of."

"La. No," he said in Arabic. "*We* are not the...how you say...barbarians in this, you see."

"Your king executed a-thousand captured crusaders I heard."

"Our *Sultan*," he began, emphasizing my incorrect use of the word *king* for their leader, "did so in retaliation for your generals' and king's slaughter of our people," he said patiently, as if speaking to an ignorant child. "But such is not always the case, you see. *You* live, as do some others of your kind."

I looked at my surroundings. I was indeed in some kind of field tent. Its sides were open. Sleeping pallets, approximately two feet high, with wounded crusaders on them, filled the nine-hundred-some-odd square foot insides of the tent. I saw Commander James on one pallet, but saw no sign of Henry. The commander's chest rose and fell with breath, but he was unconscious. I was surprised that he had been allowed to live given that he was a high ranking officer. But, perhaps the Muslims were unaware that he was a commander. His outer tunic with colors denoting his rank was missing; it was not on his person. Commander Sir James lay on his back in his grey under-tunic and leather breeches. The under tunic was stained red on the side facing me, his right side, where it covered his lower ribs. And his head was bandaged, another red stain decorating the right side.

There were eleven of us wounded crusaders on pallets that I could see. "Is this all?" I asked.

"I do not understand," said the Arab.

"Is this all that you took prisoner?" I asked with a motion of my hand, indicating the others lying about.

"Oh, la, no, no. Many have already been sent to God, or your devil, you see," he replied.

"You make my point," I said, anger seeping into my voice.

"But...you live," the Arab said, apparently perplexed by my attitude.

"For now," I said.

He was silent for a moment.

I suddenly became aware of the sounds of moaning from inside the tent and bustling activity outside the tent.

"I am called Alhasan," said the Arab.

I said nothing, did not offer him my name.

"And you?" he finally asked. "What are you called?"

Still, I said nothing. *There is no harm in it*, I thought after a moment of silence between my captor and myself. "Liam Arthur Mason," I said.

His brow crinkled as he attempted to say it. "Lum Arter Masoud?"

"No. Lee-um Ar-ther May-sun," I repeated slowly, phonetically.

"We have several names as well. Perhaps just one is best, you see," said Alhasan.

"Mason," I said.

"Hmm. *Masoud* is close, no?"

"Not really. But close enough, I suppose," I replied, too tired to argue.

"Most excellent! You rest now, Masoud." With that, he turned and left the tent.

ل   ل   ل

I slept. I dreamt. I dreamt again of the Crystal Sanctuary——though I could not say exactly what about it I had dreamt this time around. I dreamt of other things too: of ancient places and ancient times, of ancient people and their lives. All were strange to me, Liam Arthur Mason. Yet, at the same time, they were all oddly familiar to me on a deeper level than I knew how to explain. For example, a mentor from a by-gone era whose name was Jacobi or Moscastan or something in between, I could not recall. A Christian priest from many centuries past came into my dream too; Pretorius was his name.

I also had dreams of questing for Holy things, relics of our church. At least, in my dreams I knew them to be holy relics. However, I could not remember what the relics were, save one. It was an ancient weapon; a spear. This relic, this spear was a part of me, I could feel it, at least in my dreams. Yet, at that time, most of my dreams made no sense. But dreams often make no sense.

I awoke slowly, my eyes adjusting gradually to the dimness of my surroundings. Oil lamps and candles now lit the interior of the tent, whose fabric walls had been unrolled to seal the tent from the outside world. These curtain-walls had ornate designs; scenes of things and battles, of people and their lives and what I took to be their spiritual leaders, which were all completely foreign to me.

Across from the pallet on which I lay was an opening through which one could enter or leave. It was the height of a man. Beyond the entryway, the dark of night speckled with the flicker of nearby torches. Though I could not be sure, I sensed that the hour was late. I must have been asleep for quite some time. I also saw that the entryway on the outside was partially flanked by two very large guards, each dressed in the black and brown of the Muslim army. I could not see their faces, of course, because their backs were to me and the interior of the tent. I did notice something else about them, however; they each wore a black, silk sash around their waist, the end of which dangled equal length off of their right hip. I had never seen such before.

Soft moans came from a nearby pallet, one to my left. A crusader moaned softly, but fitfully, in his sleep. His torso was wrapped in cloth even over his outer crusader tunic. Whoever wrapped this man did so hastily, not even bothering to remove the man's battle tunic. The upper portion of the red emblazoned cross on the tunic he still wore stuck out of the top of the blood-soaked cloth bandage he was wrapped in. The sight gave the illusion that the cross was drowning in blood. *How appropriate*, I thought. I shook off the thought and turned my attention back to the wounded man. It was obviously a stab wound he was suffering from, a large one judging from the amount of blood, perhaps even from a spear. The man's moaning subsided only to be replaced by whimpering from elsewhere in the tent. It came from the other side of him, from the pallet next to him and further from me.

I lifted my head to see over the stab-wounded crusader to the one who made the whimpering sounds. This one did not wear the red cross emblazoned tunic of a crusader, but a plain grey tunic with a brown cross on it. His garb denoted that he was a servant to one of our officers, perhaps even to Sir Jonathan James himself. He was young, sixteen years at most. I saw no indication of injury to his body, but he was whimpering and looking around with wide frightened eyes, lifting his head off his pallet and swiveling it side to side as if he was expecting something or someone to be there next to him. There was no one near him. It looked odd, only his head lifting and swiveling. *Why is he not sitting up?* I wondered. But then I saw why. He was strapped to his pallet. Grey leather straps ran over his chest and through the pallet. His wrists and ankles were bound to the pallet as well.

"Mon Dieu! Mon Dieu!" he whimpered in the Franc tongue. He suddenly looked at me, or rather, through me. His eyes were unnaturally dilated. "Ils viennent pour moi!" he said in French.

"What? Who is coming for you?" I asked. "En English, s'il vous plait. My Franc is not so good."

"Les Démons viennent pour mon âme!" he cried.

"Demons? Is that *demons* you say? Demons are coming for your soul?" I ventured, confused. The boy put his head back down and continued his whimpering. I began to think that the lad was not right in the head. But there had to be more to it; his pupils were too large to be that way for no reason. Then it dawned on me. We had heard stories of the Muslim army drugging captives with the "Satan's Brew", as crusaders called it, and thus driving the prisoner mad, forcing them to confess even beyond their knowledge, then killing them. That was enough proof for many of us that these Muslims were indeed spawns and pawns of Satan. I admit that I too had let that notion slip into my belief about these people. But I had begun to doubt all the tales regarding the enemy of late.

I looked closer at the area around the lad's pallet, which also happened to be in the center of the tent. Near the head of his pallet was a waist-high, wooden table. On this table were a few items——rolls of white cloth, for wrapping wounds I presumed, metal instruments for cutting and clamping by the looks of the blades and pincers, and several small bowls with some kind of liquid within. Each bowl had a small cloth soaking in it, part of which draped over the edge of the bowl. *What's in those bowls*, I wondered. *Just water, or something a little more intoxicating?* Curiosity got the better of me. I looked around the tent. There were fewer wounded crusaders lying about than earlier. There were now several vacant pallets. That was disturbing. What happened to them? I would find out later, I decided. But, I was not looking around the tent to see how many men were left. I was looking around for any of our Muslim captors. None were present. That too was odd, but with the two guards just outside the entrance, well, none of us who remained were going anywhere, especially in our condition. No matter. For the moment, I simply wanted to know what was in the bowls.

Slowly, quietly, I got up from my pallet and stood. Pain shot through the right side of my head. But to my surprise, it was a tolerable, dull pain, not an intensely sharp one as I expected. I felt dizzy, but able. Cautiously, I walked to the table near the whimpering lad. The table was much longer than it had appeared to be from the low angle perspective on my pallet. On the other side of the instruments and small bowls were five larger bowls, all containing liquid as well. In two of them the liquid was clear. In the other three the liquid was tinged red. These five larger bowls were wash basins, I assumed. I dipped a finger into one of the large bowls with clear liquid and tasted it. Indeed, water. It was obvious, then, what the red tinge was in the other three bowls. That left the initial mystery of what was in the smaller bowls.

I picked one up. The liquid within was not clear. It was cloudy and had a thickness to it that was beyond mere water. It was almost creamy in its consistency. I held it to my nose. A sickly-sweet odor wafted to my nostrils. As with the larger bowls, I dipped a finger into the substance and brought it to my mouth to taste it.

"Don't, my son," whispered the voice of Sir James. He stared at me from his pallet with pain-filled, yet vigilant eyes. "If you wish to keep your wits about you, do not so much as taste it."

"Is it...the 'Satan's Brew'?" I asked.

He started to laugh, but stopped from the pain of it. "Fools and the ignorant call it that," said Sir James. "Opium is what it is. Or, some opium concoction."

"Are the stories true then? They use it for torture and to get information?" I asked.

"Don't know what stories you speak of. It's medicinal. They," said the commander, lethargically waving his hand toward the outside, indicating the Muslims, "use it in here to dull our pain. But, if one is not careful, one begins to have a need for it at all times. I've seen it, lad. Our own surgeons use it to help our wounded. Comes from a plant. Chew it, smoke it, stew it. Satan's got naught to do with it."

I said nothing, trying simply to take in all that the commander just told me. I looked in to the small bowl again and the cloth therein, and began to understand. The cloth was soaked in the opium concoction then probably placed between the lips of the patient to drip into the mouth. What Commander Sir James just told me also explained other things I had observed during my time as a soldier. For example, I had noticed more than one previously wounded veteran crusader gnawing on a specific kind of plant stalk, or smoking from a hose pipe. Perhaps it even explains why my dreams have been so vivid and varied while being in this tent.

"Come, lad," said Sir James. "Dawn approaches. Rest some more."

The moaning crusader and whimpering servant had ceased their laments and were both sleeping soundly. My head was beginning to throb with intense pain. More rest was good advice. I walked back to my pallet and lay down. I stared at the tent's ceiling for a moment in contemplation. "Why do they keep us alive, sir," I finally asked, not really expecting a reply.

"I'm not sure, but I believe it must have something to do with what you did," answered Sir James.

I was utterly confused. "What I did, sir?"

"You don't remember," he said, more by way of a statement, than a question, but clearly surprised.

I thought for a moment, but drew nothing from my memory of what Sir James could be speaking of. "I...I was hit in the head in the battle, lost my senses and woke up here, is all I remember, sir."

"Hmm. Well, you shall find out soon enough," he said.

Fear and confusion shot through my being. I desperately wanted to ask him what I had done, but decorum and fatigue won out. I remained silent.

"Rest now, soldier," commanded Sir James.

"Mason, sir. My name is Liam Arthur Mason," I offered.

"So be it. Rest, Liam Arthur Mason."

THREE

I slept through part of the next morning and awoke to the sounds of bustling activity outside the tent; the sounds of a military camp in full active detail. But there was more. As I lay on my back listening, it became clear that there was more going on in the camp than just the normal routines of an army preparing for the day. There was none of the organized, chaotic urgency to the sounds that would indicate preparation for an impending battle, yet there was something. Perhaps, then, the Muslims were preparing to break camp and move on. Muslim army camp or Christian army camp; the sounds of the specifics were not that dissimilar. Were we, Christians and Muslims, that dissimilar as a people, then?

My trite musings were abruptly interrupted by the crashing and shattering of what sounded like a large, ceramic bowl. The shattering sound was immediately followed by an angry voice shouting in Arabic. I glanced to my left and saw a very young, eleven years old at most, Arab boy being chastised by an older Arab man for dropping what I now realized by the smell of it was, or had been, a ceramic pot full of urine. Though I could not completely understand what the Arab man was saying, his tone of voice, hand gestures and angry facial contortions made his meaning clear. Finally, he pointed to the shards of the pot on the ground and slapped the young attendant on the side of the head. The wounded side of my own head throbbed in sympathetic harmony with the boy's.

I brought my attention back to my immediate surroundings and noticed that the pallet next to me was now empty. The moaning crusader who had been on the pallet the previous night was no longer there. In fact, several more of the pallets that on the previous night had still held wounded crusaders now lay unoccupied. A sense of sadness mingled with foreboding washed over me. *Henry.* I thought once again of my friend. Still, he was not in the tent and I had not seen him since the battle. Perhaps he had been killed in the fighting after all, or worse; killed after being captured. Or, perhaps he had escaped the battle's obvious outcome and was even now on his way home to Britain. Not likely, that, but the thought lifted my sadness a bit. The tent's walls had been rolled back up and the outside air, as dry and hot as it was, flowed freely through the interior of the tent.

The reprimanding Arab ceased his berating of the lad, which allowed me to now hear another voice. This one was also a male, but it was speaking in Latin and at the level of a murmur. "The Divine Essence of All permeates my soul..." the voice said.

I looked to its source. Sir James. He lay on the same pallet as last night. His eyes were closed, but he shook and sweated as one in the throws of fever. His voice went down to a whisper, then only his lips moved, mouthing the words over and over.

After a moment his voice rose again, but to no more than the level of the previous murmur. "The Divine Essence of All permeates my soul...and brings forth...and brings forth..."

"He's been muttering that for two hours now," said yet another voice; Alhasan's. He stood next to my pallet. "Do you know Latin?" he asked me. "I do not know Latin but for a small amount. It resembles a prayer or chant to me; an incantation, perhaps."

I had not seen Alhasan enter the tent nor sensed his presence. But I listened again as Sir Jonathan James continued his unconscious repetition. I did know the Latin language, and indeed, what the commander was uttering sounded like a prayer or chant or fragment thereof. Oddly, though I had never heard this particular prayer before, it felt familiar to me. The commander's words fell to a mumble again, then to an inaudible nothing. Only the lips moved mouthing the words as before.

"You see?" said Alhasan. "Repetition is one part of an incantation."

"I would not know," I professed.

"Oh come now, Masoud. I am sure you know the nature of spells and magic," he insisted, "you demonstrated as much before us all."

I had no idea of what he spoke. I thought back to what the commander, Sir James, had said the previous night; that I had done...something. *Was Alhasan speaking of the same thing?* I wondered.

"Masoud? You look as though you are in confusion. You must remember, no?" He paused, but I made no reply. "Ah, you clearly don't. Well, such is the way of these things at times."

"What things?" I demanded. "Comman——that is, my friend there," I began, nearly revealing that Sir James was a senior officer, "mentioned something of my actions upon capture. I remember nothing."

"As I say, such is the way of the Mystery at times," replied Alhasan. "I am not surprised by it. You were with Allah at the time," he explained.

"What say you?!" I exclaimed indignantly.

"Forgiveness, Masoud," he began.

"Mason," I corrected.

"Maasoon," he attempted, feigning difficulty with the pronunciation of it, I was sure. "Masoud is, *close enough*, as you said, no? Do you not wish it? It is an honorable name. It means, *happy, lucky*, you see."

I sighed and gave in. "As you wish, Alhasan. You were saying...?"

"Ah, yes. You were deep within God, if you prefer," he said.

"That is no help at all," I replied.

"One may say, then, that you were deep in...trance, I believe is your word for it. When in trance you, your everyday mind, slips aside and your soul connects to the loving bosom of the One God, you see," he finished, obviously proud of himself for having explained it so perfectly. Or, so he thought.

"Your interpretation of what a trance is...is interesting. But it doesn't explain anything about what I'm supposedly not remembering," I countered.

"I understand," said Alhasan. "But, forgiveness, please. It is not for me to inform you, but for one far greater than I to do so."

"Oh, come, Alhasan. You can tell me. I won't reveal any knowledge obtained through you," I said, somewhat pleadingly.

"Ah, Masoud. There would be no honor in that, you see," he said nicely, but firmly. "You will be given council with His Greatness in short time. That is, if you feel well enough."

"And who is *His Greatness*?" I asked, annoyed.

"Why, Sultan Salah al-Din, of course," Alhasan said as if there could be no other.

"Salad...what?" I asked, cross sarcasm seeping into my voice.

"Have respect, Masoud," Alhasan said with a harsh tone. "Salah al-Din, or Saladin, as your people are coming to call him. *Salah al-Din* means *Righteousness of Faith*," Alhasan stated dreamily, "and he is a great Sultan and General and leader of our army, you see."

"And my captor," I said.

"Your host," Alhasan corrected.

"As a guest, then, I can go if I please," I stated flatly.

Alhasan smiled almost wryly. "Yes, yes you could, but it would greatly displease Salah al-Din," he said, his words dripping with implied consequence. "He has been most generous to you."

"How so?" I asked.

"You live, do you not?" Alhasan replied, pausing briefly. "Salah al-Din will meet with you later if you feel able. You and your muttering commander," he said indicating Sir James.

So, they know his rank after all, I thought. "I feel well enough," I said.

"Excellent!" exclaimed Alhasan. "I will come for you both shortly, when the sun reaches his zenith." With that, he turned to leave.

"The...commander may *not* feel well enough," I pointed out.

Alhasan stopped and looked at Sir James. The latter had not muttered for a few moments, but his lips continued to move in silent recitation. Alhasan then faced me once again. "Your commander will attend if Salah al-Din bids it, you see," he declared with finality. "Until the zenith, then..." Alhasan bowed his head slightly in my direction then strode from the tent.

ل   ل   ل

The sun's zenith came quicker than I wished. "Rise, Masoud," said a deep male
voice contemptuously. Still lying on my pallet, I rolled my head to my right, toward the sound of the voice. Four large, darkly clad Arab soldiers flanked a short,
stocky dark man robed in grey. His head wrap was burgundy and his black beard
was cropped short. His brown eyes were intense as he jutted out his chin, causing him to look down his stubbed nose at me in a manner that spat pretentious
importance and condescension. "The Sultan will hold audience with you now.
He commands it," the stocky Arab said arrogantly in perfect English.

"Where is Alhasan?" I asked.

"Silence and on your feet!" he bellowed.

"I don't feel well enough to-"

"Do as he says, Liam," said Sir James.

I immediately sat upright and looked at my commander. He slowly sat up as
well, looking weary and pale, but alert. "We may yet live. Do as he says, I order it."

"Yes. And you, commander. You are to come as well," added the stocky Arab.
"Bring them," he ordered to the soldiers with him. The darkly clad men——
curved scimitars at the ready——stepped forward; two toward me, two toward
Sir James. Without further preamble, my commander and I rose from our pallets.
The Muslim soldiers tied our hands in front of us with leather thongs, leaving one
long strand of the chord tied to each of our individual bindings, thus tying us to
each other, as well. We then gingerly walked with our escort out of the tent.

FOUR

The sun was indeed at its——or *his*, as Alhasan had said——zenith. It beat down with the intensity of fire, but I was not uncomfortable. It was simply good to be out of the hospital tent. My head still throbbed, but not nearly as much as on the previous day. I inhaled deeply. The hot and dry air burned my lungs as it entered. No matter. I was glad to be walking. The four Muslim soldiers surrounded Sir James and I with the stocky Arab leading the way. I glanced at Sir James. He was clutching his side and doing his best to keep the pace of our cross-camp march, which was brisk and set by our handlers. The camp was large. I didn't see tents as such for the common Muslim soldier. Instead, I noted many large, cloth canopies held aloft by poles. There were no sides to these shelters. Many men could fit beneath the protective canopy. Sir James quietly grunted in pain. I touched his arm and made a slight motion with my head when he looked at me, silently asking him if he needed to stop and rest, not that our captors would have allowed that, but I would plead his case if I had to. But that would not be necessary, for, courage and defiance filled his eyes. Sir James shook his head and we carried on.

The camp was full of Muslim, Arab soldiers going about their duties. Some stopped and stared, even pointing at us as we walked by. I saw no other crusaders, prisoners or otherwise. Again, the question as to the fate of my friend Henry briefly entered my mind.

"Move aside!" our stocky Arab leader shouted in Arabic. There were several platoons of soldiers in our path. They parted and I was able to see our apparent destination; the largest and most ornate free-standing field tent I had ever seen. It was dark in color and its front sprawled before us and it seemed to be the size of a castle. There were no turrets, of course, as on an actual castle, but the top of the tent went up into several high peaks. "Holy Christ!" I mumbled in awe.

Sir James let out a small laugh at my surprised uttering. "No doubt the size of this thing is a match to Salah al-Din's high opinion of himself, eh lad?" he quipped in a whisper.

"Quiet!" said the guard on Sir James' right, hitting my commander in the back with his sword's pommel, causing Sir James to stumble forward. He did not fall, though, and he did not let out a cry of pain. He recovered his step quickly and we walked on.

The closer we came to the tent the more dwarfed I felt by it. And, the more detail I could make out on its tall sides, sides that seemed to reach for the sky by some thirty feet. Large mural-type scenes adorned the sides of the tent. They almost looked embroidered, such was their quality, and depicted conquest and battle, Sultan-ness and Muslim piety. The whole of the tent's exterior was dark in color. The scenes, though clear as to what they were when up close, had been created with muted tones of the earth, thus blending in with the tent's overall color from a distance.

We halted before a long tunnel entryway flanked by two guards. The tunnel was made of the same material as the tent. It was approximately six feet wide and ten feet tall with a covered roof, and arched the whole way leading into the tent proper which was some twenty feet in length. The tunnel's sides were dark as well as straight and vertical, and extended from the roof down to approximately one foot off of the ground, thus leaving an open space near the ground, presumably for ventilation. In fact, as I looked once again at the whole of the large tent itself I noticed that its sides' bottom was the same as the tunnel's; extending from the top down to about a foot off the ground. I suddenly noticed something else too; there were Muslim soldiers, guards, positioned about every twenty feet all along the tent's outer wall, guarding the ventilation space so that no one could slip under it and into the tent, no doubt. I hadn't seen the guards until now because their uniforms were the exact same coloring as the tent itself, thus causing them to blend in to the tent's wall. Interesting, that. Someone nudged me in the back and we moved forward into the tunnel.

It took a moment for my eyes to adjust to the darkened interior. We were still being led by the stocky Arab and flanked by the guards, but we were now cramped shoulder to shoulder in the relatively narrow tunnel. The body stench of our captors nearly overwhelmed my sensibilities. But, then again, it was probably at least in part my own foul un-cleanliness that I smelled.

"Be respectful and stay alert, lad. God willing, we may yet get through this. 'Tis up to you, Liam," whispered Commander James.

Up to Me? What in hell does that mean?! I thought, wanting to scream.

The tunnel opened into a small room; an annex of sorts, or a waiting vestibule. Indeed, one of our guards grunted and shoved my commander and I hard in the back, shoving us to the ground. We both landed on our knees. I immediately attempted to stand.

"No, Liam," whispered Sir James urgently, as he reached out a hand to keep me down.

But it was too late. I was already nearly back on my feet when I saw bright white light splashed before my eyes from the stinging blow I received in the back of my head. I crumpled back to the ground, landing in the arms of Commander James. "They want us to stay on our knees, lad." he said.

"How was I to know? You've had more experience at being captured, commander, no doubt," I replied, slurring my words from the pain. I did not lapse into unconsciousness, but nearly so. I swooned for a moment then heard the sound of voices frantically speaking in Arabic around me and about me. The one speaking the most frantic was directing his words at the guards and stocky Arab, reprimanding them, it seemed. He then turned to me. It was Alhasan.

"Achh! Masoud," he began in English, apologetically as he helped me to my feet. "A thousand pardons, please. They are oafs, these guards, hemorrhoids on the asshole of a cow. That is why they are usually given mindless duties. They were not to harm a hair on your crusader head, you see. But, one cannot give gold to a mindless pig, you see?"

"I think you mean pearls to swine," I said, attempting to correct his reference.

"Eh?" he replied, confused.

"Nothing," I said.

"You treat these things as equals? These are the pigs!" said the stocky Arab defiantly and again in perfect English, pointing to Sir James and myself.

Alhasan whirled on the short man, jutting his hooked nose into one of the man's eyes. "You dare defy His Greatness, the Sultan?! For this is from where the orders come, my small one!" shouted Alhasan. The stocky Arab said nothing. "I thought as much, you see. Your job here is done." Alhasan stepped back and pointed back down the tunnel. "You and your...men are now to leave."

Hatred bore into Alhasan from the eyes of the stocky Arab. Clearly, this was not the first confrontation these two have had. Indeed, something told me that this was an ongoing discord and that the only thing keeping Alhasan from the grave by this one's hands was his proximity to *His Greatness*, Sultan Salah al-Din. The stocky Arab and his guards suddenly turned on their heels and marched back down the tunnel to the outside.

Alhasan turned to me once again. "Come, Masoud. And you, as well, Masoud's commander," he said to Sir James. "The Sultan awaits you both."

ﻢﻟ   ﻢﻟ   ﻢﻟ

We entered what appeared to be the main area of the tent. The space was huge, large enough to hold seventy or so people. It was richly appointed with fine rugs on the floor and tapestries on the inside walls of the tent. There were a dozen or so people, some richly dressed in dark robes and turbans, some soldiers, officers in the Muslim army judging by their attire and bearing. They were engaged in intense conversation with a black robed figure sitting in a high backed, hand carved, wooden chair. This person also had plain brown, military breastplates on his upper torso. Though he wore a black turban, tuffs of grey hair spilled from beneath, dropping in ringlets about his neck. His black and grey beard was neatly coiffed. He appeared to be approximately forty years of age. His demeanor at present seemed to be one of annoyance, impatience, toward the men chattering before him. Then, he looked at me.

His gaze was intense, so much so that I briefly averted my own gaze partly out of fear and partly out of a sudden sense of awe I felt toward the man before me. When I looked back at him, his gaze still held fast upon me, but I mustered the courage to return his look. His eyes were dark and conveyed a depth of spirit, an infinite intelligence and strength of character that belied ruthlessness when pushed. I sensed that he was a man that could be trusted, but should also be feared. Salah al-Din. The man before me in the high backed chair had to be the Sultan himself.

He suddenly shot up a hand and all before him fell silent. They then followed their Sultan's gaze to me. One of the military men who had been speaking to Salah al-Din became angry, stepping toward me and raising hand to strike. "Eyes to the ground, you heathen!" he yelled at Sir James and I in English as he approached.

"Stay your hand, Commander Hakim, and command what you have captured. He is Crusader Mason, or Masoud, as our beloved Alhasan has named him," said Sultan Salah al-Din. His voice carried a smooth, authoritative power to it. It was more than just the power of authority, however. It was the power of inner stillness, the power of inner righteousness. Not arrogance, but Righteousness: the kind that comes from a profound, singular and personal inner connectedness to the One Most High, and the knowledge or perception that what you do in the outer world of men with this Righteousness is naught but Good, regardless of the fact that it might be in the form of war and destruction.

"You honor this crusader dog with a Muslim name?" Commander Hakim spat at Alhasan. The Muslim commander Hakim was a slight man of perhaps thirty summers. An angry scowl crossed his features. It was one that I guessed had been there for a long time, judging by the permanent creases they had already created in spite of his apparent young age. His head was bare, turban-less, and I was surprised to see short-cropped red hair adorning the top of his head, and a closely trimmed red beard clinging to his face. Save for his dark features and eyes, he almost appeared to be of Anglo decent. "Has he renounced Christianity then, and embraced Islam?"

"Hakim," Salah al-Din said calmly, but sternly. "You will stand aside."

Hakim's eyes narrowed threateningly, contemptuously at first to Alhasan, then to me. But he did as he was ordered and took a step back and aside, becoming an observer to what was about to play out.

Salah al-Din then spoke directly to me. "Come here," he said with softness.

I glanced at Sir James out of the corner of my eye, a part of me seeking my commander's permission to obey the foreigner. I realized the absurdity of my glance immediately. Sir James' brow crinkled, silently saying, *don't be an idiot, lad! Go!*

Alhasan quickly came to me and pulling out a small knife, cut the bindings around my wrist and the long thong that connected Sir James to me. I stepped forward to the man in the high-backed chair. A feeling of utter respect for the Sultan suddenly washed over me, compelling me to avert my eyes to the ground out of respect as I approached, no doubt to the satisfaction of Commander Hakim. I stopped three feet before the chair, eyes still to the ground. An awkward moment of silence passed. I suddenly felt all eyes in the tent roving over me, assessing me, weighing and measuring me, quartering me through and through.

"Alhasan," Salah al-Din finally said. "Bring the instrument."

I felt Alhasan's presence depart. My heart began to race and my mind to reel. *What instrument?* I wondered. *Something of torture? Worse?* I managed to sneak another questioning glance at Sir James. To my amazement, he was smiling.

FIVE

I stood before the Sultan and his court for what seemed an eternity, though I'm sure now that it had been no more than a moment or two. I felt a bead of sweat trickle down the left side of my face. I dared to look in the face of Salah al-Din then. What I saw astonished me. He too, like Sir James, was smiling. It was not a malicious smile, quite the contrary. It was one of kindness, mercy and curiosity. "We shall see if the other night was the trickery of your devil or if Allah truly works through you and the spear that pierced the Prophet Jesu's side," he said.

Before my further confusion could be given voice, Alhasan came back into the room carrying a thin item that appeared to be over six feet in length. The thing was wrapped in what appeared to be some kind of shining white cloth—silk, I was told later. It could have been a thin pole, such were its length and shape. Or...a spear. My head, where the injury was, began to throb with pain. Images suddenly impinged themselves before my eyes. I swooned briefly. The images seemed in part to be from the other night. But other images were from an age in the long distant past, images or visions which contained people that I knew not, and scenes and things that were alien to me; crucifixions of persons unknown, a spear with a unique pattern of reddish stains on its blade, a battle between ancient armies. Yet, I sensed that I was connected to all of them. The distant past images suddenly rolled rapidly by my eyes to be replaced by images still in a distant past, but not as far back. In these images I saw a group of Druids and a Merlin, a Master Druid of old, in and around the Great Henge of Stone in my homeland. Specifically, they encircled the great center stone altar in the middle of the Henge and the figure, a man, lying on this center stone altar. The same spear from the previous images lay upon his body——I recognized the stains on its blade. This vision rolled by and was replaced by a recent scene, one from a previous night in the present time. In this vision I held the same spear before the Sultan and Alhasan. I was awash in a white glow.

The images abruptly disappeared and I came to myself once more, standing before the Sultan and his court, Alhasan now next to me, still holding the wrapped item and looking at me with awe. I was panting heavily and sweating as if I had just made the run of my life. Perhaps I had.

"You see, great Sultan? Masoud becomes as one with the spear and he has not yet touched it again!" exclaimed Alhasan.

"Hmm," was the Sultan's response. Then, "Unwrap the spear," he ordered.

Alhasan did so hastily, but reverently, as if the thing were a firebrand and a sacred artifact all at once. Perhaps it was. Alhasan finished the unwrapping and held it out to me, cradling it with both hands, the wrapping now draped over his palms, the thing, an ancient spear, resting on top of the wrapping so as not to actually touch his palms. He then bowed his head slightly toward me, indicating, I presumed, that I should take the spear.

Two things ran quickly and immediately through my mind: one; take the spear, which, though old, appeared to be intact and able, from its stained blade to its somewhat chipped and dented shaft, and level it at the Sultan's chest and demand our freedom. Or, two; do nothing—refuse to take the thing. The first thought would have been foolish at best, for when the others saw Alhasan offering up the weapon to me, the military personnel present stepped forward, unsheathing their scimitars and holding them at the ready in the process. The others, the robed figures, merely stood by, passively watching the proceedings but with obvious interest.

"Take care, Alhasan," hissed Hakim.

"You take care, Hakim!" Salah al-Din barked, sending the soldier a withering look. "Alhasan does my bidding. Do you?"

Hakim's features became soft for the briefest of instances; a humiliated child in the presence of an angry parent. "Great Sultan! How can you question me thusly? My loyalty knows no bounds!" he said, with bravado. But it rang as insincere, an act.

"Ah, but that requisitions the question, does it not, Hakim? Is your boundless loyalty to me? Or to yourself?" asked Sultan Salah al-Din. I was not the only one to have seen through Hakim's pretentious bravado. "Put your weapons away," he said to his men, "and step back, Hakim," the Sultan continued, forgiving Hakim a bit too easily, which seemed odd. He then turned his attention back to me. "Take the spear, Masoud."

It was a soft, but stern command, not a gentle request. Forgetting all about the two thoughts that had raced through my mind a moment ago, I turned to Alhasan, still holding out the ancient weapon for me to grasp. "What am I supposed to do with it?" I asked to no one in particular.

"Listen to it, you see, let it *speak* to you" Alhasan said softly.

I reached out a hand and let my fingers wrap gently around the old wood. I then lifted it and held it before my eyes, examining the Blade. The stains were there, stains from antiquity, by the look of them. The shaft was chipped here and there, as I said, but overall was whole and hale. I then *listened*, as Alhasan had instructed. I listened for what seemed like quite a few minutes. Nothing. I heard nothing. I shook my head.

"Do you *feel It?*" Alhasan asked. "Do you feel a presence from it? *His* presence, the Power's presence?"

I felt nothing and shook my head once more. *A* piece of wood and metal, this was. Yes, it was very old, perhaps, but still just wood and metal.

"Well?" asked Salah al-Din of Alhasan, his tone now laced with impatience.

"Sire, your Greatness, we all saw what took place that night, the glowing presence, the Power that came from the spear, through Masoud and into his crusader friend, healing him!" Alhasan's voice was becoming high-pitched, excited.

"A magicians trick, I say," said a voice from beside Hakim. The figure was in black from head to toe; black robe and turban whose tail wrapped around his head and covered the lower half of his face. I did not know why I hadn't noticed this one until now. There were other figures behind him whom I now saw as well, all cloaked as he was but in the shadows of the tent. I could not make out any of the features of the men behind the one who had spoken, except one; one of them had a pair of yellow-gold eyes that peered out intently from an otherwise cloth-wrapped face. "A magician's trick," the first man said again. He was an imposing figure, the one who had spoken; at least a head-and-a-half taller than I——some six-feet, five-inches in height by my reckoning. One of his eyes was black as coal, the other as white as snow, its pupil opaque. I could not tell if the opaque eye was blind or not. But one thing I could tell was what I was sensing when this one spoke; a darkness to his countenance to match the darkness of his robe. I shivered in spite of myself.

"No, I don't agree," dared Alhasan. He then turned back to Salah al-Din. "We all saw what happened that night. The prisoners were seated on the ground, lined up on the dirt, hands and feet bound. Masoud was as if in a waking sleep from his head wound, but still held the hand of his friend, his fellow-invader, who leaned against him and who we all saw was dead. Then, Great Sultan, it happened. The cart carrying the rood and the Spear of Longinus, the same spear that pierced the Prophet's side and contains the Power of Allah, came careening out of control, its horse gone mad with fright, and crashed, you see, the long rosewood box splintering into a-thousand pieces and laying the Spear of Longinus out for all to see. Then, slowly, Masoud gets to his feet and with the strength of ten men breaks the thongs that bind his feet and hands. He walks to the spear and picks it up. It glows at his touch, giving us all pause," Alhasan said, now telling the story with theatrical intensity, clearly living it in his mind as any good bard will in the regaling of a dramatic yarn.

"Yes, yes. Again, I say a magician's trick," said the dark-robed, opaque-eyed man.

"Except for the next part of the story, my good Master Rashin. The raising of the dead is no magician's trick. Only Allah the Merciful can do that, and that he did through the Great Spear of Longinus and Masoud!"

I was stunned by what Alhasan was saying. I remembered nothing of it. I tried. I stood there shaking my head, willing myself to remember. Nothing. I remembered nothing of that night. But something else impinged itself on my mind; not a memory, but a reasoning. "Alhasan. You said, that...that I...I can scarcely say it...that I, with the aid of this spear," I said, indicating the thing in my hand, "brought someone back from the dead?"

"It was Allah, God working through the spear and you, you see," he replied.

"Was it the friend on the ground next to me?" I asked, my words brimming with hope.

"The same. Your friend..."

"Henry?!"

"I've heard enough of this," said the opaque-eyed Rashin. "Sultan, Salah al-Din, by your leave, I will tend to other matters."

The Sultan, clearly disappointed and none-too-pleased with my performance, or lack thereof, simply nodded his ascent to Rashin. The dark one shot a contemptuously daggered look at Alhasan and I, then let out a low, menacing cackle and left the room. Again, I shivered at the man's countenance.

Hakim stepped forward then. "Shall I dispose of the prisoners, Sultan?" he said in a strange, offhanded manner.

"No," Salah al-Din stated flatly.

"But..." Hakim began, foolishly.

"I said, no!" Salah al-Din said as he grabbed a thin short object next to his chair, a riding crop by the look of it, and suddenly lashed out with it, striking Hakim on the face which left a welting red line in its wake. "Your insolence will be your undoing. You may go and attend to your business as well."

To his credit, Hakim showed no emotion and looked at neither Alhasan nor I. He simply left.

"Leave. All of you may go. Alhasan, you and Masoud and his commander will stay," the Sultan said. Perhaps I should have been afraid, but he had not said it unkindly, but rather in such a manner that indicated he simply wanted to speak with us alone.

The others all filed out, save for two very large men. They went to the entrance of the room and turned back, standing at attention, on guard.

Sultan Salah al-Din turned his attention back to the three of us, then specifically to me. "Yes, Masoud. We all saw what happened that night, your interaction with the Great Spear of Longinus, if that be what it truly is. Our...mystics... sought to use it against your crusaders. I never believed it to have any powers whatsoever. It was simply a useful tool to play against the minds of your kind." He paused briefly before continuing. "Still. That night when you raised your friend-in-arms from the dead, I too thought this was truly a power-laced weapon. Briefly. But the power came not from the Spear, but from you, Masoud and..."

"And, from Allah Himself through the spear!" interjected Alhasan.

"Indeed, from Allah, Alhasan. Which perplexes me, Masoud. Why would Allah, praise be His name," Salah al Din said, looking up as he uttered the praise, then looking back to me, boring his intense gaze into my tired eyes, into my very soul, "why would He choose to wield His power through a Christian crusader, a butcher of my people?"

Despite my fear over the situation, angered welled within me. "I am no butcher, Sultan," I said.

The Sultan's eyes narrowed. He was clearly insulted by the way I addressed him. To him, I was not just the enemy and a butcher of his people, but the very definition of an infidel to a Muslim. "You will take care, Masoud."

"I mean no offense, Great One," I began again, forcing myself to civility and respectfulness. "But the more I see of your people, the less I see a difference between us." Something happened then. I still held the Spear of Longinus in my hand. To my amazement, I began to feel warmth coming from the thing, from where I held it. I almost dropped it, but something forced me to hang on. "You call God, Allah, Praise be His name," I was shocked by what I heard myself saying, but could not help but let the words come out. "But there is only One God by any name. You know this to be so or you'd not've allowed me to live to this point."

A dead silence filled the air around us. It did not feel ominous, this silence——as if the Sultan were about to burst with outrage——but I did not expect Sultan Salah al-Din to hold with what I had just proclaimed. The warmth from the Spear vanished. I looked sidelong for an instant at my commander, Sir Jonathan James. Again, he was smiling, and this time even broader than the last time I had glanced at him. I did not understand why he was smiling.

The Sultan looked at Sir James, as well. "Commander, you are of the...Templars are you not?"

"Aye," said Sir James, meeting Salah al-Din's gaze with equality.

"Your...student, a neophyte in your order, perhaps?" he said nodding at me.

I shook my head, both in silent answer to the question and disbelief at the question itself.

"Soon to be, me thinks," my commander answered, whose smile became even larger.

"Presuming you both live to see that day," the Sultan pointed out.

The shouts from outside the tent came suddenly; voices in chaos, frantic with the fear and panic. The Sultan stood at once, and addressed the guards that remained. "Find out what is happening," he ordered.

One of them turned to leave, to carry out the order, but was knocked down by Hakim as the latter ran back into the main area of the tent. "They attack! The crusaders come again with smoking weapons!" he declared angrily.

"With what?" I asked lamely.

The explosion that immediately followed my words knocked us all to the ground. My ears rang for an instant as I was showered with dirt and debris. I lay motionless for a time, unsure of whether I lived or not.

SIX

Day light streamed in through the torn ceiling of the tent. Dust and smoke choked my lungs, loud voices and the din of nearby battle filled my ears. I lived still. Orders were being shouted from all around. I looked up and saw not only the gaping hole in the ceiling but one whole side of tent gone, blown out no doubt by the explosion. It was the side of the tent that had been behind the Sultan's chair. Indeed, not just a wall, but the rooms which had been on the other side of it had been leveled. I could see several bodies among the expanse of the tent's cloth, the ruins of the tent's rooms.

An explosion? I wondered. I had heard that our army was able to create a fireball made of wood, dung, oil and other elements that contained the magic of a lightning strike when fire was held to it. But I had never seen it used. I could smell burning cloth, wood and skin. Putrid was this last unmistakable smell. I coughed and rose to my feet to see Salah al-Din running toward the outer reaches of what had been the tent's parameter, shouting orders as he went. A rough hand grabbed my arm, pulling me to one side.

"This way, Masoud, quickly," said Alhasan as he pulled my arm and lead me——still holding the spear——away. I looked to Sir James who was just rising to his feet, coughing and sputtering from the debris filled air. His hands were still tied. I reached out with the blade of the spear and cut through the leather thongs that bound his wrists. To my surprise, the blade still held a sharp edge and sliced through the leather with the ease of a knife through lard.

"Masoud, no!" exclaimed Alhasan.

"Masoud, yes!" I retorted.

"Let us be gone from here," said Sir James, by way of an order more than a suggestion.

"You cannot escape, you see?!" said Alhasan, panic lacing his voice. I interpreted his tone to reflect what will happen to *him* if he let us flee more than an attempt to imply the impossibility of us being able to flee.

Muslim soldiers began gathering at the opened side of the tent. "Back the way we came in, lad," said Sir James. We did just that, heading back through the long entry tunnel which had come through the explosion unscathed, and out in to a smoke-filled, chaotic morning. To my surprise, Alhasan was right behind us. "Wait! Masoud, please!" he cried.

The smoke was thinning and what I saw was not what I expected to see. No crusaders. Only Muslims. Hakim had said the crusaders were attacking. I saw none. What I had taken to be the sound of nearby battle from within the tent was actually naught but the Muslims converging on the scene of the explosion, yelling all the while, their scimitars at the ready.

We heard it then; a screeching sound to still the blood. From across the sky it came, shrieking as if it were a demon just released from the shit-stenched bowels of hell itself. "Cover! Now!" ordered Sir James, looking to the sky.

Following his gaze my eyes beheld a frightening sight; an arrow the length of a man, its shaft nearly as thick as one, was descending right toward us, trailing a smoke tail and screeching its death yell. "Bleeding Christ," I muttered at the sight.

"Aye. Its shaft is mostly hollow, filled with the fire-stuff, launched from a big crossbow," remarked Sir James. "Not very reliable, tend to explode at the bow, they do. Used for long range assaults on occasion." He grabbed my arm and pulled me away. "Run!"

Fire-stuff? came the absurd and inappropriate-for-the-moment question in my head as my legs began to carry me away. There was nowhere to hide, no shelter to seek. Why the Sultan had placed his tent so out in the open now baffled me. No matter. We simply ran.

The impact of this apparent second arrow or missile knocked us through the air. I landed atop my commander, bounced off his body and crashed hard to the ground, then tumbled some fifteen feet before coming to a stop. A split second later something or someone slammed into me; Alhasan. We had not been struck by the missile itself, but rather, we had felt the sweeping effect of its initial impact some twenty yards away from our present position. All was black with smoke and unearthed dirt from the point of impact. My ears rang with near deafness from the sound of the massive explosion. I coughed and sputtered from smoke and debris in my mouth. I pushed an unconscious Alhasan off of me. "Alhasan?" I said, shaking him slightly by the shoulders.

He groaned and opened his eyes, coughed. "Powerful weapons. We have the 'fire-stuff' too, you see," he said smiling, "though, we've not used it in such as a large arrow."

The surroundings began to clear. More voices in chaos could be heard gathering at the point of impact. It became clear that not all the voices were expressing chaos. Some were voicing anger and outrage. I looked around the immediate area, searching for my commander. I spotted Sir James some fifteen feet away. He was clutching his injured side again and being helped to his feet by someone dressed in the under tunic of a crusader. I recognized the man aiding Sir James at once. It was Henry! "Bleedin' Christ!" I said again.

My friend heard me and nearly dropped our commander in his rush to greet me. We embraced as long-lost brothers. He looked at me and then at the spear I held in my hand. "That...thing. And, you. You healed me, brought me back to life!"

"So I've heard," I said in exasperation. "But I don't remember a damned thing of it! Where were you? Why did they not keep you with us?"

"I don't know," he replied.

"Time enough for that later, lads. We need to move, now! Take advantage of the attack and get out of here," said Sir James, already moving off in the direction from which the last missile had come, its entrails of smoke still visible in the air, though rapidly dissipating.

"No, Masoud!" pleaded Alhasan, now on his feet and joining us. "You must stay!"

We ran for our lives. The entrails of the large missile arrow were all but gone, yet it had pointed us in the right direction, away from the Sultan's tent and the encampment proper, and toward our own people and our freedom from captivity. We ran and ran and saw no sign of pursuers. Hope crested in my chest as we ran up a rise in the desert. I knew what we would see on the other side, even though they may still be a ways off: we would see our army and the lovers of the Christ, the noble crusaders of God. In that moment I had all but forgotten my change of heart toward the Muslims; that they were in reality no different than us, that they were not the evil infidel they had been portrayed to be by the stagy and corrupted Church. All that had been set aside for the moment as I raced up the rise. But what greeted us was not our Holy army.

Commander James, though clearly in pain as he ran up the rise, was the first to make its crest. He froze in his tracks. Henry and I nearly crashed into him as we made it to the crest as well. Alhasan, still with us, stopped along side of me. We all panted with fatigue. "You see?" said Alhasan, pointing to the other side of the rise. There before us, sitting on horseback were Hakim and the dark-robed, opaque-eyed man, Rashin. They were flanked by a century of Muslim soldiers. The soldiers stood calmly, quietly, all facing us. Their demeanor reflected that of Hakim and Rashin. They were completely ignoring the din of noise going on behind us at the points of impact. It was as if they were there waiting solely for us. My heart sank. But I was also shocked to see Hakim. *He was just in the tent! How could he have beaten us here?* I wondered. I then noticed Rashin looking intently at the spear in my hand, his opaque eye moistening and squinting lustfully at the thing. It was then that I was struck with a most extraordinary sensation; I knew this man. *Impossible!* I berated myself. *I could not possibly know this man. Perhaps he was a Muslim or a Sufi Mystic and Magician I've heard our priests rail against, and thus he has me in some kind of spell to make me think I know him so that he could get to the spear and...*my mind was rambling. I caught it and stopped it, but still the feeling persisted; I knew this Rashin.

"I think not. You dogs will not escape this day," bellowed Hakim, from atop a black steed.

Rashin sat tall on his brilliantly white and tremendously large stallion. He said nothing, but continued to eye the spear and me.

Still the feeling of familiarity persisted. For the moment, I pushed it aside, being pressed by the more urgent matter and threat of reentering the state of captivity.

"The spear," called Rashin, "I want the spear."

"But, my lord, it does nothing, as was just demonstrated, you see," answered Alhasan.

"Then Masoud will have no opposition in giving it to me," Rashin countered.

The spear grew warm in my hand, vibrating as well. I looked at the thing and I was suddenly thrust back a thousand years in my mind's eye. I saw a darkly cloaked figure with paste-white skin. I was in another body, looking upon this individual and a company of ancient pagan, Druid priests of the *Old Ways*, as my mother would say, flanking him. A fire, the fires of the Wickerman, burned near them. *Wickermen*: the ancient Celtic method of dispensing with an enemy via placing him in a giant wooden cage in the shape of a man and setting it alight with fire. The flames purged the enemy of evil and released his soul to cross over to the Otherworld. At least, such was the belief. But the practice had been outlawed. Yet, here I was, watching the ritual burning of a Wickerman through the eyes of... of...Longinus. I looked at my hand, Longinus' hand. The spear, the same spear I now held in my hand as Masoud, was there and vibrated. I felt Longinus concentrating, placing his attention on the elements. The rains fell then, smothering the fires of the Wickermen, putting them out. The dark cloaked one was infuriated. "Draco," my Masoud-self whispered. The *vision* vanished and I was on the rise again, staring at Rashin, comprehending to a degree, but nothing more. I felt one other thing from this Rashin; though he was obviously strong of will, he did not seem as powerful as he had in that ancient lifetime as Draco.

"What did you call him, Masoud?" asked Alhasan.

"Draco," Sir James answered for me. "It means 'dragon' in the Old Tongue. Apt name for him lad."

Sir James clearly misunderstood my reference. But I said nothing to correct him, to make him understand. How could I when I did not understand it myself?

"Allah help us!" exclaimed Alhasan, eyes growing wide as he looked at the spear in my hand. "It speaks to you again."

The spear pulsated a bright red. I almost dropped it, believing that it was about to be too hot to hold. But it became no hotter than the warmth I had felt from it earlier.

A murmur arose from those in Hakim's ranks. It was the murmur of fear, bordering on outright terror. They were all, to a man, staring at the spear, watching its seemingly supernatural display. I held it aloft, not quite sure why I was doing it, nor knowing what I was going to do. But my display and apparent command of the spear of Longinus was enough to cause the soldiers who were with Hakim and Rashin to cower, sending most of them to their knees in a posture of supplication.

"On your feet, all of you, or I will have you flogged right here!" Rashin bellowed.

The moment dragged on. I had no idea what to do. "Go on, lad," urged Sir James.

"I hate to say this, commander," I began in a whisper through tight lips, "but I don't know what I'm doing, it's just for show, my raising the spear,"

"No, no! You know what to do, you did it to bring back your friend, you see," said Alhasan. "Think, concentrate."

"On what?!" I asked nervously.

The men in the opposing battle group before us began to murmur again, but this time it was the murmur of confusion tempered with anger; they were beginning to realize they had been duped, that my gesture was empty, that I was a fake. Though the spear still pulsated, the other men rose to their feet, a cry of anger and vengeance escaping their mouths.

The intuitive realization of the spear's glowing pulsation, its meaning, then came to me like a fresh breeze, quickly but gently enfolding my being and washing me in the truth of its caress: it was a warning. I started to back away.

"Liam, what are you doing?" asked Sir James.

"Yes, Masoud, do not flee, especially in the direction we have just come," echoed Alhasan.

"It's a warning, the spear's glowing, it's a warning that we must leave here, now!" I turned and ran back in the direction we had come.

I felt the others follow more than saw them. There was no time to turn and see, to make sure. A spilt second later, we heard a howl in the air and a third missile hit not more than a few feet in front of where we had previously stood. It had apparently landed right in front of Hakim and Rashin's men. We were all knocked down by the blast. The smoke cleared after a moment and I could see Hakim and Rashin lying on the ground not far behind us. They had obviously spurred their horses into following us and thus missed the brunt of the explosion. Their men had not been so fortunate; bodies and body-parts lay everywhere. Moaning and crying of the wounded and near dead filled the air. Rashin, as if possessed by a demon, suddenly sprang to his feet as if he had only been taking a nap. He roused Hakim who was much slower to stand, but stood nonetheless.

I felt the spear——which no longer glowed——in my hand. It was tugging, almost pulling me to the left, away from the large tent we had been in just a short time ago, and back toward the hospital tent we had initially come from. "This way," I stated flatly, no longer feeling the doubt that plagued me a moment before.

"That way leads..." Alhasan began.

"I know where it leads. The spear, it's pulling me that way. That's all I know," I replied.

"So be it," said Sir James.

I ran, the others followed. We were completely ignored by the dying, the injured and the chaotic as we made our way to...I knew not, but my intuitive sense to follow this spear's lead had taken over my being. I, we, had little other option at the moment.

We made it to the hospital tent, which was still standing, and went beyond it. We all stopped in our tracks, confronted again by a platoon of Muslim soldiers, scimitars at the ready. They seemed to be as surprised at the sight of prisoners on the loose as they were by the aerial attack.

"Stop them!" Hakim yelled from behind us. He and Rashin were on foot with naught but a small contingent of soldiers. "Do not let them escape!"

The lead Muslim soldier in front of us stepped forward to carry out the order. He was dropped to the ground, dead before he could complete the first step; an arrow sticking out the side of his head. I looked in the direction from whence the arrow came and was greeting by a blessed sight: a host of crusaders swarming on the Muslim encampment. I looked back at Hakim and Rashin. They were gone.

"Praise be, eh, lad?" smiled Commander, Sir James.

"I must...I must..." cried Alhasan backing away.

"Stay with me, Alhasan. I will see to it that no one harms you! If you leave they will kill you to be certain!" I said to him. "There's no choice in it, 'you see'," I said to him, using his own favorite phrase, hoping he would not see it as a mocking of his English, but as a sincere form of adulation. "Please, my friend, allow me to help you as you have helped me."

Fear was on his face, but trust filled his eyes. "As you wish, Masoud. As you wish," he said.

SEVEN

The soldiers of Christ overran Salah al-Din's camp, but had no follow-through. Their arrogance was such that the initial success of the catapulted exploding arrows lulled them into a false sense of superiority; that they would simply be able to walk into the Muslim camp and be in command. As such, the ignorant fools, much to the consternation of their commanders, lost discipline and began looting and pilfering what they could.

"Agh! La! La!" screamed a woman nearby, a harem bride by the look of her richly appointed attire. No mere camp whore was this. Three men, crusaders, had her pinned to the ground. A forth, a sergeant no less as indicated by his particular tunic, was ripping her gown and undoing his belt and tunic all at once.

"You there! Sergeant! Cease! Secure the edges of..." barked a nearby commander. He was cut off in mid sentence, however, by an arrow through the neck. The sergeant and his fellow soldiers, having given the commander barely a glance to begin with, now proceeded unabated with the rape.

Someone had a hold of my arm and was pulling me in the opposite direction. "Come, you, away from here!" said a voice with the accent of a Franc.

I turned expecting to see my commander, Sir James, holding my arm and perhaps Henry nearby. Instead I was staring into the face of another man who wore commander's insignia, but who had the toothless grin of a commoner, not a noble; obviously, a commander by circumstance, not by birth. It was he who held me by the arm. "Where is Sir James and Henry?" I demanded.

"Who?" asked the toothless commander in his Franc accent.

"*My* commander and my friend," I said. "The men who were just with me."

"Most likely on their way to the general's tent for debriefing, as should be you. Come, S'il vous plait," said the toothless commander. It was then he saw Alhasan. "Take that one prisoner!" he yelled, addressing any crusader within ear-shot to capture Alhasan. Most were in the process of looting, raping or killing the remaining remnants of Muslim soldiers, but two heeded the order and stepped toward my friend.

"No! He's...with me," I said, stepping in front of Alhasan. The crusaders stopped in front of me.

The toothless commander looked me over and his mouth broke into a lecher-ous grin. "Aye. Not enough of the lovelies in this hostile land, mon ami? Keep your...servant then. Does not matter."

"Agh! La! Laaaaa!" the woman screamed now between sobs. She was putting up an intense struggle, frustrating the sergeant's efforts at making penetration. He raised a bare hand across his shoulder and backhanded the woman's face. Blood began to seep from the woman's mouth.

I stepped toward them, the toothless commander grabbing my arm tighter. "Plan to join 'em?"

The spear began to vibrate in my hand, then to glow as before. The toothless commander's eyes grew wide with fear as he saw it and he let my arm go. The two other crusaders in front of me stepped back with awe in their eyes. I then turned and ran toward the four men attempting to rape the woman. "Release her! Re-lease her now!" I yelled at the men. They ignored me. Though I had never before used the spear, or any spear, as a weapon, I suddenly found myself wielding the one in my hand as if I had been born with it attached to my limbs. It was an ex-tension of me. The butt of it found its mark in the temple of the raping sergeant. It sent him sprawling to the ground unconscious, his small, exposed, erect penis flopping and deflating as he landed. The other soldiers who had been holding the woman down now became enraged. They stood as one, releasing the woman, who scurried off like a cat which had just escaped a pack of dogs.

"You are dead," stated one of the men flatly, staring straight at me.

"I doubt that," I replied defiantly, arrogantly. What happened next was a blur, both to the eye and to my mind. Alhasan later told me that I had closed my eyes in that moment, *Attuning with the divine spear!* as he put it, and used it to thwart the men, whirring and whirling the thing as a windmill, striking each man precisely on the side of the head above the ear with the butt end of the spear, never the blade, thus mercifully incapacitating the men, but doing them no lasting damage. All I remember is that a moment later, I came back to myself, holding the spear at rest while four men lay at my feet. Feeling eyes upon me, I looked to my left and saw the woman I had rescued. Her eyes were incredible; beautiful lavender colored eyes stared at me from behind a pile of baskets and large broken ceramic. Terror was still in those eyes, but she managed a nod of her head toward me which I interpreted as a *thank you*. It was then I noticed a cloaked and turbaned figure near her, crouching behind a partially destroyed supply wagon. His eyes—which was about all I could see of the man's face—were a stark gold in color and focused intently on me, as if watching, observing my every move. I recognized the man as one of the men who had been in the Sultan's tent; one of those who had stood silently behind Rashin in the shadows then, watching my every move just as he was now. A shiver ran up my spine as I returned the man's stare. And, another feeling of familiarity washed over me. I had known this man before as well, but could not presently place his past identity in the forefront of my mind. The only thing that did come to mind about him was that he had been some kind of Christian priest in that past existence.

"Ah, Masoud! You show again your connection to the spear and the power therein, you see?" said Alhasan gleefully.

I looked from the gold-eyed man to Alhasan, then to the toothless commander, who stared at me dumbfounded. He looked at the men I had just dispensed with. "That will not sit well with the general," he said.

"If he's any kind of general, if he's got any kind of honor, he will not condone such behavior from the crusaders of Christ," I replied.

"'Honor'? 'crusaders of Christ'? You speak as one of *them*." he stated.

"One of them?" I replied, annoyed at this wretch's insolents and confused by his words.

"Knights of the Temple. You talk like them. If you are, I meant no offense, I just..."

Sir James suddenly appeared from behind the man, placing a hand on the toothless Franc commander's shoulder. Henry appeared just behind Sir James. "He is not. Yet. But take care, my friend, how you would address him. You don't know to whom you speak."

"Yes, sir," said the toothless commander. "But you should be at the general's tent by now. All of you," he said looking to me.

"I simply came back when I saw the commotion," replied Sir James.

I looked back to where the woman was. She was still there, staring at me. I then looked to where the cloaked man with the gold eyes had been a moment before. He was gone.

Shouts came from the other end of the camp, from the direction we had come.

"Your men, commander..." began Sir James

"Commander Laffite," said the toothless Franc commander with a false mantle of authority.

"Your men lack discipline. They care more about looting and causing mayhem than they do about gaining and securing this camp," said Sir James. "I suggest you tell your men to fall back before it's too late."

"You are not in command here. I will..."

Three Muslim soldiers descended on a pair of crusaders some forty feet from our position, cleaving the arms off both men with their scimitars. Both crusaders stood in stunned silence as their life's blood spouted from their shoulder stumps.

"Salah al-Din will retake *his* camp, by leave of your incompetence," said Sir James.

Laffite hesitated for but an instant more before taking Sir James' advice. "Replier! En arriére!" yelled Laffite. "Fall back!"

The crusaders had indeed become enamored and thus distracted with the lust of a would-be conqueror. Salah al-Din and his army raided their own camp with merciless brutality, taking back what was theirs and disemboweling any crusader who was stupid enough not to immediately follow Laffite's orders. Lafitte, Sir James, Henry, Alhasan and I were fortunate enough to make it out. Alive.

ﻟﺠ   ﻟﺠ   ﻟﺠ

Night comes slowly to the desert, especially when a near full moon rises at the same time the day's sun relinquishes its command of the sky. Such was the way of it this evening. The crusaders, including Sir James, Alhasan, Henry and myself, made it back to an English encampment in tattered rags and fatigued bodies, fortunate not to have been pursued by Salah al-Din and his men. For now. At the crusader encampment we had been given quarters, a change of tunic and wash basins with which to cleanse the past days from our being. We were summoned to the general in short order. A golden hue washed the land as we walked with our escort across the camp to the general's tent. The sky looked as though God himself had sprayed it with his breath of the most high, so golden it was. But there was something ominous, foreboding about it too; as if a portent were being conveyed of sorrows yet to come. I could not put my finger on it, but I felt it at the core of my soul. The spear too, which I had not let out of my sight since arriving in the camp, seemed to sense something, for it was in a constant state of mild vibration in my hand.

We were ushered into the general's tent, which was large on the outside, but not nearly so as the Sultan's. The inside was also large, but filled with all things practical for the work of a commander who sent men at arms to death or glory. I laughed to myself at the thought of our generals having such an ornate, even audacious, of a dwelling on the field of battle as the Sultan's was. But, then again, Salah al-Din was a king. Perhaps our own king–generals, King Richard's for example, had similar richly appointed dwellings in the field as the Sultan's. I had never been in a king's tent, let alone a general's. This general, General Blackthorn, was no king. He was a large man in his sixty-fifth year by all accounts and was also known as a Templar Knight. He stood before us now in the middle of his simple general's field command tent, large though it was. His eyes were dark and intense; full of authority and questions. His beard was grey as was his shoulder-length, grease-filled hair. The smell of lilac flowers filled the air and I realized it was coming from the general himself. The man seemed attached to cleanliness. Most men I knew, myself included, washed periodically, yet bathed only once in a moon's cycle, if then. I came to find later that General Blackthorn, a haughty member of the English nobility, bathed twice daily if at all possible before becoming a Templar Knight. But once a Templar he had to adhere to their code; not to bath and always remain dressed for combat. Apparently, he insisted on using oils from the lilac flower, thereby giving him a fresh aroma at least, if not a truly clean one. The scent was quite contradictory to his appearance; that of a hardened soldier and leader of men. Just above his grey beard, on the cheek below his left eye ran a scar. It traveled down from his lower left eyelid and curved around the cheek to his left ear which was missing its lobe, no doubt from the same event that caused the scar itself. He looked to me to be in the bloom of late forties rather than mid-sixties. But then again, I had always been a poor judge of another's age.

Several crusader commanders were in the tent with us, including the Franc commander, Laffite, who stood off to one side.

"You there," Blackthorn said in a deep voice by way of addressing me, "you are the one who brings the Spear back to us, back to its rightful home, yes? It is an honor, my son, to meet you. I am Sir Horatio Blackthorn, commander of the host of crusaders and liberators of Jerusalem."

"But I thought King Richard leads us," I said lamely.

"Aye, 'tis true. But the king sees fit to consort with our Franc friends," replied the general, looking at Laffite, "than to actually be here with us. I lead in his stead and by His Majesty's grace, along with a couple of other generals who are en route to us," He looked directly at the spear. "Bring it to me," he ordered.

I was taken aback by the command. I suddenly never wanted to let anyone else touch the instrument I held. Still... "I...by your leave, sir, I must warn you that it may not...that is, it may become..."

"Oh, come lad. Do you disobey a direct order?"

I looked to Sir James and Henry, neither of whom looked to offer me any help.

"My son," Sir Blackthorn began in a gentler tone, "I have heard of all the feats you have performed with it; the restoring of your friend here to life, how it glowed in warning to you, leading you away from certain death; how it became an instrument of defense and magic in your hands, thwarting evil from our midst."

I could only guess that his last reference was to the combat I had entered into, which resulted in the saving of the Arab woman who was being raped. "There was no magic to it, Sire," I said.

"Oh? Its glowing is not magic? Would you say it's not of God, our father then?" asked Sir Blackthorn.

"I do not know of such things, Sire."

"But it does communicate with you, does it not? What does it say, lad? What does it say?! Does it tell you when our Lord Christ will come again? Soon, I hope!" The general was becoming excited, like a schoolboy wanting a secret to be revealed. He waited a moment for my response. But when I offered none his smile grew large, stretching the scar on his face such that it appeared he had two smiles. He threw back his head and laughed a belly laugh as I have never heard. I was confused by it and that confusion must have shown on my face. The general stepped forward and clasped his large, strong hand on my shoulder, sending a shooting pain throughout my upper body. "I jest with you, lad." He leaned in close, his lilac scent nearly overwhelming my senses as he whispered into my ear. "We all know the Good Christ's second coming will be in the mind and hearts of all men, that we will come to see the Christ beholden in each other as ourselves. We all know that's the Lord's true *Second Coming*, do we not, soldier?" He stepped back then and stared into my eyes, looking questioningly as to how I would respond to his query. I had never heard anyone say such of the Christ's next coming; that it would be in our minds, our hearts, through us, as us. This man spoke like no Christian I had ever known.

Yet, what he said sparked a realization within my own mind and heart. "I know naught of these things, Sire," I said again. "I am but a humble man from poor origins. But, what I have seen in this land has led me to question everything I was ever taught on the side of our Lord Christ. These people in this land worship God as we worship Him."

A snicker came from the direction of Laffite or someone standing near him.

"Silence!" the general bellowed. "Go on, my son," he said to me.

"I don't know, Sire. As I said, I know naught of these things," I replied.

"You know more than you think. Much more. Does he not, Sir James?" Blackthorn said, turning to my commander.

"I would say so, your Grace," replied Sir James.

"You are right. He will make a splendid candidate," said General Blackthorn.

"Candidate?" I asked.

"We will speak of it later, my son. For now..." said the general, holding out his hand for the spear.

I slowly stretched out my hand and reluctantly released the spear into the general's palm.

"Aagh!!" the general screamed in agonized pain at the spear's touch. I was horrified. He abruptly stopped the scream and stared at me. In the next instant he burst into another belly laugh, the rest of the company in the tent joining him this time. "Again, I chide you, my son. Oh, you are too easy. Come. Let us dine whilst I examine the instrument that pierced our Lord's side. It is amazing that it's still in such good condition..." the general babbled as he looked at the spear oddly, I thought, almost lustfully. Food was brought in. We reclined on pillows and I had the most sumptuous food I had eaten in quite some time.

EIGHT

We finished our meal and retired to our quarters. I looked forward to a wonderful night's sleep; one that filled the mind and soul with heavenly peace, restored the heart to truth and faith, and replenished the body to full strength and vigor. But it was not to be. Every sound in the night, no matter how small, impinged itself upon my senses, keeping true rest and peaceful sleep at bay. It did not seem to be affecting my quarter-mates that way. Henry slept on a nearby pallet like the dead, snoring rhythmically, and Alhasan snuffled quietly next to me on his own sleeping pallet, oblivious to the nocturnal noises keeping me from slumber. I noticed at one point that Sir James was not in the tent with us. I was not surprised, however. He was a senior officer and an English noble, after all. He would have option to be housed elsewhere. Still, when I looked to the empty pallet that was near our quarter's entrance——our quarters being a simple four-man field tent——the commander's belongings, his dirty tunic and side-arm, were there.

"The soul floats nightly," whispered a heavily accented voice from just outside the tent. The accent was Arabic. I immediately grabbed the spear, which Sir Horatio Blackthorn had reluctantly, begrudgingly, I thought, given back to me at our meal's end, and brandished it at the ready. "The soul floats nightly," said the voice again.

I threw open the tent's flap which revealed a man dressed in black and brown. I had seen the attire before, but could not immediately place where, though I knew it to be Arabic. The man, whose face was obscured save for the slit in his headdress that allowed his eyes to peer out, jumped with a start. "Do not move," I commanded. I was about to sound an alarm, to yell at the top of my lungs that we had an Arab intruder in the camp, for that is surely what he was.

He then stopped me with a familiar voice, no longer a whisper. "Wait. Do not call out. I was informed that this was the quarters of the Temple Master," Hakim said. I was stunned to silence. "Give him this." He handed me a folded paper. I examined it. It had a strange seal on it: a pouncing lion made of Arabic letters. In addition to the lion, there were symbols on it which I had never seen before. It seemed to be an alphabet comprised of triangles and dots.

"I don't..." I began. But, when I looked back to Hakim, he was gone. I could only assume the folded parchment was meant for Sir James. Why was Hakim, who had seemed so ruthlessly antagonistic toward us, delivering a message for Sir James?! And, how did he get past our sentries?

"What troubles do you have?" Alhasan asked from inside our tent. I turned and saw my Arab friend sitting up on his pallet, groggily rubbing his eyes and yawning. "Is it urgent? I hope not, for I would greatly like to sleep a fortnight, you see."

"I do see, for I'd like to sleep a long sleep as well. There's no trouble...least I think not. This is most odd, though," I said, once again examining the strange markings on the sealed parchment in my hands.

"What is it?" Alhasan said, suddenly becoming excited. He leapt off his sleeping pallet and bounded up beside me to see what I held.

"Ahh, your Knights Templar. It is their code, the writing there," he stated.

"You mean these strange open triangles and dots?" I asked.

"Yes, yes! It is their language, their secret alphabet. It must be the name of whomever the missive is for, you see." he said.

"This reads, 'Sir James'?" I asked, doubtfully.

"No. They would not use the actual name, but the title or rank within the Order," Alhasan pointed out.

"The messenger said it was for the 'Temple Master'." I said.

"You see? And the messenger delivered it here. Your commander, Sir James is a worthy guess." Alhasan looked out the tent. "The Templar messenger has vanished into the night."

"But that's just it; I don't think it was a Templar messenger. It couldn't have been," I said. I turned over the missive and showed Alhasan the Lion emblem in Arabic letters.

His astonishment was palpable. "Masoud, who delivered this?"

"You won't believe it. It was Hakim." I said.

"Truly?"

"Truly."

"That explains much," said Alhasan cryptically.

"Do you know what the lion script says?"

"It is the emblem of the Ismaelian Knights, Masoud," said Alhasan gravely.

I thought for a moment. I had heard of that Order before, but always in the context of it being called by another name; one of an Order of unholy and near satanic men. "You mean, The Order of Assassins? They are cut-throats and degenerates, smokers of the hashish and opium, are they not?!" I asked, now completely dumbfounded.

"No, they are not, Masoud," Alhasan said defensively. "You have been listening to too much of your crusader ignorance. They are a noble Order of Knights which is akin to your Knights Templar Order. The Order of Ismaelian Knights or Assassins, as you call them, even work with your Knights Templar for the betterment of all and the perpetuation of the concept of the One God."

"I don't know anything about the Knights Templar, save that they protect Christians on pilgrimage. But you seem to know a lot about the Order of Assassins," I said haughtily.

"You will soon come to know much about them too, and your Templar Order. Look..." he said pointing to the spear in my hand. Its blade glowed a beautiful, soft green.

I held it up, looked at it closely. Somehow, its glow was soothing.

"What does it mean, Masoud?"

"I don't know, Alhasan." The soothing feeling I received from it quickly abated and was replaced by a feeling of frustration. Contrary to what I had just said to Alhasan, I suddenly felt as though I did in fact *know* all the answers regarding the spear and my connection to it, already knew in my soul all about the Knights Templar and everything to do with all things relating to the One that Alhasan had just spoken of...but I could not fully remember. I closed my eyes and willed the frustration to leave, willed the deep seated knowledge that I possessed to come forth. I laughed oddly at the thought of being in possession of such knowledge.

"Masoud?" asked Alhasan. "Are you not well?"

I did not answer him, but kept my eyes closed to let the soothing quality of the spear's glow wash over me again.

"Yes, Masoud, turn to it and to Allah, for the answer. All the answers you seek are there," Alhasan said, apparently understanding what it was that I was doing. His voice altered in its timbre to an audible gentleness which matched the visual softness coming from the spear.

"I...must lie down," I heard myself say. My eyes still closed, I next felt myself being gently guided toward my sleeping pallet. I lay down on the soft rushes, the spear by my side, and let the feeling of softness wash completely over me.

And then they began again; visions of things from many centuries past. But they were different from previous visions of the past: a forest; a sorceress; a Merlin by the name of Myrriddin———me. I saw a battle between good and evil, wherein the evil was thwarted but not destroyed, never destroyed. Balance to all, in all of ALL. Leaping ahead in the vision, in this same time frame, this same life, the visions showed our Britain's true founding king, Arturius himself; King Arthur, as he is known to us now, at least by legend. Many doubted a man, a king the likes of him ever actually existed. But I saw him now through my vision, through the eyes of my former self; Myrriddin. He, Arthur, was tall with green eyes and fair-skin like his mother, Igraines. Yes, Igraines had been her name; mother to this great king. His face was handsome like that of someone from the High country and his hair was light brown and shoulder length. Uther Pendragon had been his father. The thoughts, images and memories came flooding into my mind as if I were reliving the events in the present. Arthur turned to me, said something to me, "Bring it back, Merlin," he said, "'Tis up to you. You, who are the legacy, the bloodline, of him to whom it belonged, of the one who pierced our Lord's side. You gave it to the good bishop Rozinus all these years past, in good faith, I know. But it now resides with the Grail in the hands of blasphemers and infidels. Wrest it from them. Bring it back whether it takes this life or more."

"'This life or more,'" my Liam Arthur Mason self, my Masoud self said aloud. The vision faded.

"Masoud? Masoud?" Alhasan said.

I opened my eyes and looked at Alhasan. "I am well, my friend. I am well," I replied. I looked at the spear. It had ceased its glowing.

"What did it show you?"

"It?"

"The spear, Masoud. Surely it was showing you something. Your eyes moved beneath their lids as if you were watching something. Your lips moved as if speaking in a dream or being spoken to in a dream, you see," Alhasan said excitedly.

"You're quite observant," I said. "I don't know that the spear *showed* me anything. But I did have a vision; a vision of the past or *a* past."

A loud snort came from the other side of the tent. Henry stirred on his pallet. He rolled away from us, coughed violently, then rolled on his back, eyes still closed. I noticed, perhaps for the first time, that my friend looked thin, too thin, as if he had not eaten in days. I then noticed something else; a stick protruding from his clenched teeth. His jaw moved as Henry lightly chewed on the object even in his sleep.

"What is that?" I asked quietly. "He may choke." I sat up on the pallet intending to go to my friend Henry and take the stick from his mouth.

But Alhasan's hand stopped me. "No, Masoud. It is the only thing that enables him to sleep fully now, you see."

I was confused. How could chewing on a stick enable him to sleep? But then I remembered something that Sir James had said in the healing tent. "Is it...?"

"It is the opium, yes. It has become his best friend, I fear," said Alhasan.

"I had no idea," I replied sadly.

"He hides it well, or so he thinks."

Before I could think on how to help my friend, the tent flap opened and Sir

James entered. He stopped and looked oddly at me, as if he suddenly felt that he had interrupted something. He then looked at Henry and back to me, a look of understanding spread across his face. "You did not know," he stated, referring to my friend's addiction.

I shook my head.

"It eases his pain. When the time is right, we'll help wean him from the opiate's teat."

Though I nodded my understanding, disappointment and renewed concern for Henry's well being coursed through my being.

"What do you hold there?" asked Sir James regarding the folded parchment I held in my hand.

"It was delivered for you by...Hakim, of all people," I replied, handing him the sealed item.

Sir James examined it.

"From the Order of Assassins!" I volunteered.

"They are actually called the Order of the Ismaelian Knights," he gently corrected.

I glanced briefly at Alhasan, who looked just a little smug.

"The Order of Hashishim, too," I said. "They suck the hash pipes and kill. I heard that they murdered the Christian King of Jerusalem; Conrad of Montferrat? It is their method, murdering for their benefit."

"They do not murder," Alhasan said. "They also see what they do as intrinsic to preserving our way, the way of Islam, and our land and people, you see."

"Sometimes, Master Liam Mason——Masoud——one man's murderer is another man's savior," said Sir James.

I was stunned again. Not only had Sir James received a missive from the Order of Assassins or Hashishim or Ismaelian Knights or whatever they were called, but he was standing before me defending them. It was then that I noticed he was wearing a crisp, white outer tunic with a red cross upon it. I had seen him in something similar many times before and I knew it to be the attire of a commander within the crusader ranks. But this one was different, longer, down to his shins and the cross on it seemed to be sewn on from silk or satin. I now understood this tunic's underlying symbol; it was the tunic of a knight or commander within the Knights Templar. He was also wearing a brown garment underneath the white outer tunic; I remembered that the brown under tunic symbolized the simple priest that Sir James apparently was in addition to being a knight.

I looked at Alhasan. He was in black as he always was. For a fleeting moment, I considered the possibility that Alhasan was a servant in the Order of the Knights Templar——servants in the Order of Templar Knights always wore black. I immediately dismissed the thought as absurd. He was a servant, true, but a servant to Sultan Salah al-Din. But, then again, perhaps he was also a servant in the Order of Hashishim Knights that served his people.

I must have appeared confused, even fearful, for Alhasan softly touched my sleeve. "Masoud, our Order of Hashishim Knights was begun by Hasan-i-Sabah. Our faction of Muslims has always been persecuted by the Sunni faction, you see. The Order began to assert our rights to exist, to thrive and worship, by wiping out those who would seek to destroy us. The Sunnis now fear us!" concluded Alhasan.

"By 'us' do you mean the Order of Hashishim Knights, are you a part of them? Or, do you mean your faction, the..." I asked, concerned.

"Shiite," Alhasan replied.

"What is the difference?" I asked.

"Oh, Masoud, you do not know? Why, our Shiite Caliphs, which are the *only* true leaders of Islam, are direct descendants of the Great Prophet himself. The Sunnis' Caliphs are not. They are elected," Alhasan spat.

"There is much more to that and the establishment of your Order of Knights, Alhasan," said Sir James. "Perhaps another time would be more appropriate to..."

"Of course there is, but you are correct, commander. Masoud is not yet a Templar so one must curtail the specifics of the details until he is avowed, you see," answered Alhasan. "Another time, indeed."

"I only meant that right now we must tend to other matters," said Sir James as he opened the missive.

A thousand questions came into my mind. The questions ran from why people kept saying or implying that I am to be a Templar when it was not something that I had sought out at least yet, to questions that revealed my desire to have a deeper understanding of Alhasan's faith. I suddenly had immense guilt over being in this land and trying to kill his people when I had not the vaguest notion of their beliefs beyond that which our own religious leaders wanted us to believe.

"Well," stated Sir James as he looked up from the missive and directly to me. Do you wish to become a Templar Liam Arthur Mason, also known by the Muslim name of Masoud?"

I was taken aback at the question and my commander's grave tone in asking it. "I thought it was something that one was not asked, but sought out."

"And there was also a time when it was only for the nobles of our lands, which I believe you are, but that is beside the point. Time is of the essence now, lad, because of your apparent connection with the spear of Longinus which you hold there. We are asked to attend a joint session of the Knights Templar and your Order, Alhasan, to discuss the matter," he said, looking to my Arab friend. *So, then Alhasan was a Hashishim*, I thought. Sir James then addressed me once more. "Should you decide to seek the Templar entry, lad, I would be honored to sponsor you and to speak for you. And, tonight would be a good time to declare your wish to be a part of the Knights Templar, lad."

This was almost too much to take in; the Order of the Knights Hashishim *and* the Order of the Knights Templar holding a joint meeting?! I should make my voice heard tonight to become a Templar?! This was nearly too much. Nearly so.

Sir James seemed to read my mind. "I know. 'Tis a great deal to think about in quick manner. But search your heart, Liam, your soul," said Sir James in a calming voice. "I think you will come to realize it's where you belong in this life. Come. Come. We should just make it," he said as he headed out through the tent's flap. I looked lamely at Alhasan.

"After you, Master Masoud," he said. Spear still in my hand, I left the tent, Alhasan following me.

NINE

We strode a short distance across the camp toward a nearby church, Sir James leading the way, myself following and Alhasan behind me. Very few other soldiers and crusaders were about. The camp was quiet. I was still unsure of exactly where we were. Near Jerusalem, that much I knew. But I had not realized there was any church close by. Yet, when I looked closer at the imposing structure we were approaching, I questioned whether it was a church. Its dome was huge and high and contained on the top of it the crescent moon and star; the symbol of Islam.

"We go to a mosque?" I asked.

"A church, a temple, a mosque," replied Sir James quietly. "It has been all of those things. They all serve God, do they not?"

"But, the crescent and star atop the dome," I pointed out.

"It has served the Muslims of late, the Christians before that and the Jews before that. We, the Christians have reclaimed it. We have simply not yet put our Lord's cross back on top," Sir James said.

We crossed through its courtyard, went through the large portico and entered the massive main entrance. The ornately carved wooden doors had already been propped open, beckoning us in. The large entry area was dim, lit by a nine-candle chandelier hanging five feet above our heads. The entry area was rectangular, spreading out to our left and right. It was empty; not just devoid of people, but also empty of anything save a small bowl of water atop a chest-high pedestal before the sanctuary's entrance, some fourteen feet before us, across from the church's main entrance which we had just come through. I crossed the entry area and stood in the threshold of the sanctuary. I could see into the huge area of the main sanctuary. There was sparse candlelight and sconce-light within, so it was difficult to see very far. But what I could see took my breath way. It was immense. The interior height of the dome was astonishing. It was inlaid with gold and ornate carvings; Muslim over Christian and in some cases utilizing the Christian art that had been there for many a century. I stepped through the threshold and began to wander further into the sanctuary.

"No, lad. This way," said Sir James.

He and Alhasan were standing near a narrow door off of the entry area. I had not noticed the door before, apparently because its design and appearance was that of the wall of the entry area, thus blending in to the wall itself. It was now open, having been opened by Sir James, no doubt, and opened to a staircase that descended into the bowels of the place. I approached my companions as they turned and descended the stone steps, Sir James again leading the way.

The passage downward seemed to become narrower the further down we went. A dry, musty smell filled my nostrils. It was not unpleasant, however. The deeper we went the cooler it became. Finally, we came to the bottom of the steps. We stepped into a large, square room with several doors on the walls. Torches burned in sconces on the walls, illuminating the space and revealing a shadowy group of men near a pair of large wooden doors on a far wall. There were ten men that I could see. The dry musty odor suddenly mixed with the slight smell of smoke from the wall sconces. Another scent then joined the mix as well; the scent of lilac. At least one of the men present must be General Blackthorn. I looked closer at the men; they all had their faces obscured by cloth and they all seemed to be in ritual garb——six of them in white tunics with red crosses emblazoned on the chest. But four of them wore black robes, each with a red-crescent moon and star on the chest. The Knights of Hashishim were indeed with the Knights of Templar. One more man came out of the shadows; another Hashishim. I turned and looked at my friend Alhasan and was astonished to see that he had donned a black outer tunic which also displayed the crescent moon and star symbol.

"Wait here, both of you," Sir James ordered. He left us and approached the group of men. After a few moments of private consultation with one of them, Blackthorn, I presumed by his stature, Sir James returned to us. The wooden doors near the men slowly opened and the eleven men filed in to the room beyond. The doors slowly closed, leaving the three of us alone in what I was beginning to feel was some kind of ante-chamber. Sir James turned to me. "Well, lad. The time has come. Do you wish to become a part of the Order?"

I thought for a moment before answering, the weight of the question bearing down upon me. "It is now or not?" I asked, not quite knowing why.

"No. There may come another time, but not one such as this. We are at war and I do not know how much longer the alliance between our two Orders," he said nodding to Alhasan, indicating the symbol on his chest, "will be able to meet like this. For you, because of your connection with the Great Spear, it is important that both Orders are represented at your initiation."

Initiation? I thought this was strictly a petitioning? I wondered. I closed my eyes for a moment and sought clarity. Two things welled up inside of me. One was a feeling of fearfulness; that things seemed to be happening too fast. But the other was a feeling of...*You are coming home,* whispered a voice. The voice startled me, but it had echoed the other feeling I had. I looked at both of my companions and could tell by the expressions that neither one had heard the voice. I looked at the spear in my hand and realized that the voice seemed to have come from it. I suddenly felt as though I was indeed coming home. That sensation completely subdued the feeling of fearfulness. I felt a deep, inner connection to what was apparently about to happen this night. Though I no longer felt any weight associated with the question Sir James had just asked me, there was one other question that came to the forefront of my mind. "Why?" I asked.

"Why what?" he asked.

"I am connected with the 'Great Spear', as you called it," I began, "that I know. But why must I join the Knights Templar? And why should the Knights of Hashishim be present?"

"Both of our Orders of Knights go farther back in time than just their recent history would reveal, lad. Both Orders are offshoots of ancient organizations and schools of the Mysteries that predate Christendom or even the Druids of old. We are descendants of the groups that were thriving during the time of the Pharaohs of Egypt. We were also at the time of Christ. Search your soul. You will come to know that you yourself have been a large part of all these, as well as a great adept on your own. I sense it in you, even though I do not know the specifics of your soul's journey, save for your connection with the spear you hold. The initiation here this night is the linchpin that binds you to your past and your future. It is a necessary step on your path of reconnection. You have sensed it up to this point and have had fleeting manifestations of it, but have not yet lived by it. You will, by your actions in becoming a part of the Order or Orders here tonight, be unleashing the power within to live again through you and the spear," Sir James finished.

What he said washed over me, bathing me with a confirmation of what I had been feeling and seeing in my mind's eye: the visions I had earlier in the evening, for example——my ancient self as Myrriddin in counsel with King Arthur. It made sense to me at the level of my soul, if not at the level of my thinking mind.

"Here, tonight, we are all of the same Order of Knights, we all stand for the One Truth," Sir James said.

"It is so, Masoud," added Alhasan.

"And tomorrow?" I asked.

"We live in the present, Masoud," answered Alhasan.

"Well said, my friend," said Sir James.

I wanted to think for another moment before giving an answer. But my soul answered for me. "So be it," I heard myself say. "In all haste, let us be on with it."

"So be it," said Sir James. We turned and faced the large wooden doors shoulder to shoulder, Alhasan on my left, Sir James on my right. We then approached the doors, step by step, as one. "Hold," said Sir James when we were two feet from the doors. The three of us stopped in unison. Sir James then stepped forward, raised a clenched fist and in dramatic and purposeful fashion struck one of the wooden doors once, twice, thrice. The sound reverberated off of the walls of the ante-chamber. An eternity seemed to pass as the three of us stood before the doors. In truth, I am sure that no more than a few seconds had passed. And, then it happened.

I held the spear in my right hand, its butt resting on the ground next to my right foot. The blade's tip was higher than my head by some four or five inches. A vibration began; it started at the blade, specifically at the place of the ancient stains that still resided thereon. I looked at the stains on the blade. A soft, green glow then appeared on the spot of the discolorations.

The vibration and the glow descended the blade, then the shaft and went into my hand. My hand tingled slightly from the vibration, as if a small charge had come into my palm. Then, my hand also began to glow the soft green. Yet, while the soft glow stopped at my hand, the tingling sensation continued through my arm and into my body, coursing through my entire being. My breathing became deep. Something profound had entered my being, my very soul. I searched it for meaning and found it to be a sensation, an awareness of my connectedness with and to the past, present and future; to everything and every person that has ever existed or ever will exist and that our connectedness is due to the fact that we are all made of the same thing——the same *soul substance*——the same Mind that is God's Mind, whether one calls himself a Christian, a Muslim, a Jew, a Druid of old or an adherent to any other *religion.*

Religions are of men, said a voice in my head. *We are all simply individualized expressions of this God-Mind, the One Mind,* the voice continued.

The emotion that accompanied this sudden insight, this gift of an ultimate understanding nearly overwhelmed me. My breathing began to quicken.

All knowledge, all answers are within. The voice seemed to come from the spear and deep within the core of my soul at once. *It has always been in your soul, but is re-learned or revealed to your small, human mind over and over in part through several life-times,* the voice continued.

Why? I asked in my mind. *If this is so, why must it be that way? Why can I not simply and easily remember my past experiences, my past lifetimes? Why can't any of us?* The concept of reincarnation was not at all foreign to me. As I have alluded to, my mother was a *good Christian* woman, but still held with some of the Old Ways of our Celtic ancestors. The notion that our souls lived many *lifetimes* in different human bodies was one of them. But the question remained: if we revisited this earth in different human forms, why do we not immediately remember our previous lessons learned? Why must they remain there, in our being, but hidden from our mind?

A gentle hand touched my shoulder and I became aware of the fact that my eyes had been closed and my breathing had become shallow and rapid. I opened my eyes and forced myself to breathe deeply and normally, my inner dialogue suddenly silent. Sir James stood before me, his arm extended, hand on my shoulder. "That's the way, lad. Breathe steady and true. You left us for a moment. A deep trance is what you entered. The spear glowed and you were gone—in spirit, at least," he said. I glanced at the spear. It appeared normal, the glow was gone. "I *know* you are ready for this night," added Sir James.

"Yes! Truly," said Alhasan with awe.

At eye level, a small panel on the wooden door slid open, prompting Sir James to turn back around to face it. The opening was in the shape of a small triangle; about six inches from bottom corners to apex and six inches across the base. All we could see through the opening was darkness. Suddenly, a pair of eyes, a piercing ice-blue in color, appeared in the triangular opening. The eyes peered at all three of us in turn, remaining on Sir James. "Who seeks entry into the inner sanctum?" asked the shrill, squeaky voice in perfect English behind the eyes. *Who was this person?* I wondered briefly. But I quickly released the thought, dismissing it as irrelevant. I was still in the fog of the *trance,* as Sir James had called it, and I wanted to linger there. Indeed, something told me that I needed to remain in that profound state of mind for what was to come.

"The noble Keeper and Guardian of the Great Spear; one who has guarded said Spear through the centuries," intoned Sir James, assuming his role as the Temple Master. "One who has guarded it even back to his original ownership of it, back to the time of the second-to-last Great Prophet, my Lord Jesus the Christ. And one who has served our Orders in its various incarnations over the past thousand-plus years. He has always served with honor and humility through every one of his lives."

The eyes in the triangle shifted to me. "Is this true? Are you and have you always been the Guardian of the Great Spear?"

I hesitated. My little, all too human self wanted to say, *I am not at all sure!*

But fortunately, still being in the mists of a trance, I spoke from the depths of my spirit, my soul. "I am the Guardian of the Great Spear," I heard myself say.

"And having been among our ranks, one of the Brethren in lives past, do you now wish to renew your vows in this life, thus reaffirming your devotion to the Order of Knights of the Great Brotherhood; Keepers of the Great Mystery of Mysteries, and protectors of the faiths and faithful?" the voice behind the eyes asked.

I was surprised by the words, but felt in my soul they rang true, even as the Temple Master had said; I had been in the Brotherhood for many a life, of course! "I do!" I intoned with all sincerity.

"And who will vouch for and speak on behalf of the candidate?"

"I, the Temple Master and High Knight of the Order," answered Sir James, the Temple Master. "The office of Knighthood is also to be bestowed upon the candidate——the Guardian of the Great Spear——at my behest."

I saw the eyes in the triangle widen at this. Indeed, I felt my own eyes grow wide with surprise at the *behest*. A knighthood? I had not dared to even think of it.

"His Guardian's status and soul's journey through the centuries speaks to this, as does his deeds in this life," added the Temple Master, Sir James. "They exemplify the pinnacle of all that is True and Good and Honorable about our Order, so say I!"

There was a brief pause. The eyes in the triangle looked askance for an instant, as if the person behind the eyes was listening to someone else near him. The piercing blue eyes then came back to me. "So be it! Enter the inner sanctum and prepare for initiation once again into the Mystery of Mysteries, into the Order of Knights of the Great Brotherhood," proclaimed the voice behind the eyes. The panel slid shut, closing the triangular opening. With the creaking of ancient hinges, the two large doors before us began to open inward, inviting us to enter the dim interior of the sacred, inner sanctum. The Temple Master led the way, followed by myself; the Guardian of the Great Spear, and then Alhasan; the devout Servant of the Brotherhood.

TEN

We took three steps into the room and halted; the Temple Master on my right, Alhasan the Hashishim servant, on my left, the Great Spear in my right hand, the shaft's butt resting on the ground. A haze filled the room, this sanctum. It was a long, rectangular room. The interior was dim with candle-light and the scant light from three torches in the wall. But it was enough light to see all. On the far wall from where I stood at the sanctum's threshold there was a wall mural made to resemble an open-air end of a temple——ancient Egyptian, by the look of it—— thus giving the painted impression that this far wall was open to the outside. A rising sun was cresting the painted horizon: the east. The far wall was made to represent the east, I was sure of it. I had entered the sanctum from the west end. A cowl-hooded, looming figure in a Templar robe stood before the eastern wall. Again, judging by the man's stature, I recognized the figure to be General Sir Horatio Blackthorn. Between Blackthorn and I, which was some thirty-five feet I estimated, were two objects resting in the center of the sanctum. The one closest to Blackthorn was a chest high pedestal, an altar, with three lit candles thereon. Direct and centered between the altar and I, was a wooden rectangular box on the floor. It was approximately three feet wide, six-and-a-half feet long and two-and-a-half feet deep. It was positioned lengthwise to the shape of the sanctum itself. The thought struck me that this box very much resembled a coffin. I nearly laughed at the thought. But the laugh never came forth because the realization hit me that it resembled a coffin because it was a coffin; a simple wooden sarcophagus. I felt panic well-up in my being, but squelched it before it could take hold.

I noticed then that flanking the walls on my left and right—the northern and southern walls respectively—were pews running lengthwise along the walls. In these pews, four to a side, were the other men I had seen a few moments ago outside in the ante-chamber. Interestingly, every other man was a Templar or a Hashishim Knight. It was not the case that one side contained Templar Knights and the other Hashishim Knights, as for whatever reason I expected. All were of One Order of Knights in this place, on this night.

"I am the Master Knight of Initiation," intoned the figure of Blackthorn. "In this life, you have been among your brethren but ignorant of our great work, blind to the Great Mystery of Mysteries to which we adhere and practice. You have lived the life of our brethren in other of your soul's existences, but seek now to shed the veil of ignorance in this life, to die to an old, outworn small self, and awaken to the Grand real Self of your being, to connect to and with your True nature and learn the Mysteries of our Order once again. Candidate, is this not so?" asked the Master Knight of Initiation.

It was then I noticed that there was an edge to his voice which I found disturbing, *almost a resentfulness*, I thought, trying to place it. *But that would be absurd*, I told myself, dismissing the perceived edge in his voice as theatrics for the initiation. "It is so," I replied, bringing my focus back to the moment.

"Your deeds in this life and your exemplary behavior as the Guardian of the Great Spear in your previous lives is known to us," continued the Master Knight of Initiation. Because of this and your desire to enter into our midst once again, we gladly confer upon you this night the office to which you aspire. You will now repeat the oath of our Order. Obedience, Trust and Honor, Chasteness and Secrecy will be tantamount to the oath. Repeat after me: It is not for my will, but for the will of God and the betterment of all that I serve the Order——"

"'It is not for my will, but for will of God and the betterment...'" I heard myself saying, as I began to fade into the depths of my soul. The trance had come upon me again. I heard the Master Knight of Initiation continue to administer the sacred oath and my voice repeat what was said. Deeper and deeper into the trance I went.

Several minutes went by. I heard myself repeat the phrase; "I Am in God, And in God I Am. So it is. Amen."

"It is time for you to die to this world of darkness if you are to be born into the world of Light," intoned the Master Knight of Initiation. I felt hands lightly grasp my upper left arm and my upper right arms simultaneously. My eyes opened as slits and I saw that I was being gently guided, spear still in hand, to the coffin. We circled it several times as the Master Knight of Initiation continued the incantation, "Die to this world that ye may be reborn into the world of Light. Die to this world that ye may be reborn into the world of Light. Die to this world that ye may be reborn into the world of Light! So be it!"

As if floating, I was then guided to a lying down position in the wooden sarcophagus. I kept the spear with me, lying it on top of me, resting it lengthwise along the right side of my body from just below my right foot to the top of my right shoulder and beyond; the shaft's bottom at my foot, the blade near my right ear. Through my trance-haze, I could see the silhouettes of the men standing above the coffin; they were those who had just guided me in. They then placed a sheer, white cloth——a shroud——over the top of my sarcophagus. Once their duty was complete, the figures disappeared from my sight, presumably to retake their seats in the pews.

"Your body," intoned the Master Knight of Initiation, "is of the earth and to the earth it will return. Contemplate your True nature, the nature of your Soul and be reborn to it."

My mind went deeper into my soul. And all went black. I died to this world then, at least for a time.

My mind, my spirit drifted. I could smell the smoke from candles in the sanctum. The smell of incense also drifted to my nostrils, something I had not noticed before. And, the faint sent of lilac wafted to my nose as well. But then another smell abruptly took their place; the foul smell of rotting earth and mud mingled with the fetid stench of loosed bowels and spilled blood. My mind reeled at the odoriferous reek. All thought of being in a coffin in a secluded underground sanctum left me. A scene came bright before my eyes; a Roman crucifixion played out in front of me. Three men on crosses before me hung in utter agony, their blood draining from wounds——wounds, by the look of them, inflicted by sinister implements of torture——and spilling on the ground at the base of their crosses, mixing with their own loose excrement which had dripped down the perpendicular post of the wooden cross and to the ground below.

One of the crucified men, the most brutalized and battered of the three looked directly at me, though *I* didn't seem to have any form in this...vision. But his eyes chilled me to the bone. He looked nothing like the depictions I had seen in the artwork of the twelfth century and before. He was much darker of skin and His eyes, though blood-red in the whites, were dark brown in the iris. Yet my soul recognized Him instantly. *My Lord!* my mind whispered.

A centurion approached my Lord Jesus then. I willed my perspective within the vision to move so that I may look at the Roman, as I could not see his face from the angle I was viewing from. With the speed of thought I was in front of him, the cross with Jesus upon it now between the Centurion and myself. I looked into the Roman's face and saw one very much resembling my own—— Liam Arthur Mason. With no hesitation, the centurion reached out with his spear and stabbed the crucified Christ. *No!!* my spirit yelled. But even as it did, the scene abruptly changed.

I was now an ethereal observer in a King's court; the court of King Arthur or King Arturius, as he would have been known then. I knew it was the King Arturius by the attire he wore——a deep burgundy felt tunic emblazoned on the chest with his family's emblem; the Pendragon. He stood near a large, but plain chair, a throne that befits a king for and by the people. Nearby was a huge table, oblong, yet near round. There were four people in this room; a young, Franc and Nordic-looking, blonde-haired man, a knight of the realm no doubt, judging by his silver tunic——also emblazoned with the Pendragon——and his stature; an old woman dressed in fine silk and bright yellow cloth who was undoubtedly a beautiful lass in her day; and a white-bearded, cowl-hooded old man robed in the way of the ancient High Druids——a purple robe with ancient symbols on it, symbols that if memory served me were called runes. He leaned on a large, ornately carved walking staff. But my memory again told me that it was no walking staff he leaned on but a Druid's staff or a Wizard's staff. My memory suddenly also served me for another purpose; the recognition of the old woman and old man.

Her face was known to me, to my soul, my spirit. *Igraines*, my mind said. And, the old man too; I knew him, felt it. Again, as with the centurion, I willed my perspective to a different position within the vision so that I may see closely the face of this old one. The vision quickly shifted and I was now in front of the man as he spoke. I looked into his wrinkled face and knew him instantly——*Merlin, Myrriddin*, was the thought in my mind. He stopped in mid sentence and seemed to look right at me much as the Christ had done on the cross in the previous vision. It was then that I looked into his eyes and saw my own soul. His face did not resemble mine as Liam Arthur Mason, but I knew him to be me in this former life; it was in his eyes——his soul, my soul, looked at me through those eyes.

"Well, Merlin," said the King. "What say you? 'Tis time we retrieve what is rightfully ours, I say. Do you not agree?"

The aged wizard looked on his King, the ethereal presence of his future self, me, all but forgotten for the moment. Anger flashed in his voice and his eyes. "Do you seek a war, Arturius? For that is what you will have. These items are naught but material things."

"Powerful material things," answered King Arturius.

"False power, I assure you," answered Merlin.

"You wielded the spear's power yourself all those years ago, or have you become so long in tooth that ye forget, my friend?" quipped Arthur. "I have asked you before to retrieve the spear and the other things. Yet you've ignored my bidding."

"Have you learned nothing I taught you? The spear, the grail——if it is even a *thing* at all——the rood; none of them hold any real power save what we give them," the aged wizard replied.

"If they hold power which is bestowed upon them, then that is power truly, is it not? 'Tis the power of faith, of politic. Either or, it is still power." Arturius went silent as Myrriddin stewed, clearly not happy about what the king was leading up to. Arturius stepped up to Merlin and lay a hand gently on the wizard's shoulder. "If one withholds something I desire, and I am angered by it, then the thing itself contains power over me, for it is of my desire to possess it."

"Only in your mind does it hold power," said Merlin. "But these...artifacts of the Christians——of which I alone possessed the spear of Longinus for many a year——contain naught but the power of death and destruction if you pursue the course of action you are proposing."

"You said yourself that your visions revealed wars over these things."

"Many, many years hence, Arturius. But your actions here may be the catalyst that sets all that in motion," Merlin replied gravely.

The king returned to his chair, plopping in it with what seemed to be exaggerated exasperation. "The Holy Region is being overtaken by certain nomadic... infidels," he said. "It is said that they have obtained our most sacred relics, and..."

"'*Our* most sacred relics'? Have you completely abandoned your Old Ways, Arturius?" Merlin asked.

"No, Merlin, I have not,"

"Then you know," began Merlin as he approached the king's throne, "that one teaching of our Old Ways beseeches us to be unattached to things and the conditions we find, for all is transitory; of the One, and thus not ours to begin with. Why do you think we Druids keep our temples in the open, in the forests of our Mother, Dana? Why do you think we keep no written records?"

"I always thought you kept no written records because you guarded your secrets with all jealousy!" joked Arturius, clearly attempting to lighten the mood.

"Pray you be not serious, Arturius. You know us too well for that notion."

"And as to your temples being only the forests? What are the Henges that we see dotting our land?! Wood or stone, are they not temples; permanent structures built by the hands of your kind!?!" said Arturius, voice now raised, humor abated.

"No. Those are demarcations of power centers; places where the Mother's power, the power of the One is focused and harnessed or used for good. You know that, Arturius," said Myrriddin.

"Ah. So *things* can hold otherworldly power, eh, Merlin?" countered the King.

"The power in this case is not of the Otherworld, Arturius."

"But, all power is, 'the Power of the One', right, Merlin? That's what you always tell me."

"And that is true, but you play with my words," said Merlin.

"Will you both cease this?!" said Igraines. I had forgotten that she was present. Apparently, so had Arturius and Merlin, for they both jumped with a start.

"Forgive us, my lady. You must be tired from your journey," said Arturius, leaving his chair and going to his mother. He gently took her hand and then turned to the other man in the room, whom I also had lost mind of. "Lancelott, please see to my mother's comfort,"

"Certainly, my Lord," answered Lancelott, who had the brow of an eagle; furrowed and eternally serious. His grey eyes pierced one to the soul. A striking fellow he was indeed. He took the lady Igraines' hand from Arturius' and began to lead her away.

"My sister?" inquired Arturius, causing the queen to stop and look at him quizzically. "Morgaines; is she to join us too?" asked the King with an odd, lecherous excitement that I found unsettling.

Igraines' expression was masked, but I could tell that beneath it there was sadness. It was no doubt a reaction to Arturius' question. "Yes, Arturius. She will be joining us tonight."

"Good. That is good," said Arturius.

Igraines and Lancelott left us then, Merlin, my former self, thoughtfully watching her leave. For a brief instant I felt his/my feelings for her well-up in my being; loving emotions that had truly spanned centuries. They were there for only an instant, though, before being suppressed back to the netherworld of my soul's experiential library.

"Come, Merlin. Let us retire to my chamber to discuss this further. We have already established an Order of Knights to grapple with this. Let us not waste the Knights of Jesu. Let us instead make all haste in deploying them for their divine purpose." said Arturius contritely.

Merlin did not immediately respond, only stared after Igraines.

"Merlin, Myrriddin, I beg thee, come."

Finally, the wizard turned to his king. "All military endeavors profess to be of divine purpose. Ridiculous. How human, solely human."

"I beg thee, Merlin; come," Arturius stated again. He turned to leave and Merlin followed. I willed myself to follow too, but a mist enshrouded me, preventing me. Then, all went white.

ELEVEN

A moment later, the mist cleared. I looked up and saw a thin white cloth draped over something that I was otherwise enclosed in. There was semi-darkness beyond the cloth. I was back in the coffin at my initiation. I could not tell how long I had been in the coffin, or on the sojourn of my soul. All was quiet in the chamber, the sanctuary, as a meditative silence hung in the air. I closed my eyes again, concentrating on the visions of Myrriddin, or Merlin once again in the hopes of being able to resume my observations there. Nothing. Then, suddenly...

"Myrriddin! You're here! I thought not to see you again," said the sweet voice of Igraines. I opened my eyes to see a lovely face; a much younger Igraines. Obviously, my soul had journeyed further back in its history than it had the last time. She was beautiful. We stood in a large chamber room, in front of a large, fireless hearth. She stared right at me. I, Masoud, was not only an observer in this vision, but was in fact looking out through the eyes of my former self, Myrriddin or Merlin. She stood before me, Igraines did, with a small female-child of about four years clinging to her leg. And, in spite of the long flowing light blue gown Igraines wore, it was evident she was very pregnant. She looked down at the little girl clinging to her. "Well don't be rude, child. Say hello to Master Myrriddin, Morgaines," Igraines said.

The child Morgaines looked as if she were angry with me for some inexplicable transgression. But I quickly realized her apparent grave expression was actually one of seriousness whilst performing a mental exercise. She was assessing me. At last, her small mouth curved up slightly at the ends, no doubt the result of her conclusion that I posed no imminent threat. "Are you the great warlock I've heard tell of?" she asked none too timidly.

I smiled. She had the brashness of her mother, to be certain. "Some call me wizard, child. None call me warlock. That title bespeaks of ill intent, does it not? I seek only the good in and for all," I replied.

"I've told you, Morgaines," Igraines interjected, "Myrriddin is a High Druid."

"But King Uther says the Druids don't live anymore, that those like Master Myrriddin are but wizards and warlocks using magic," Morgaines said as a matter of fact.

"Aye and Uther Pendragon forgets much, not the least of which has been the service which Master Myrriddin has given to him and this land, 'magic' or no," replied Igraines, a bitter tone seeping into her voice.

I kept my eyes on the child Morgaines. "'Magic,'" I began with mock seriousness, "is but a term the ignorant use to describe what is simply the use of natural laws or *The* Law. And I serve Uther and the land by extension. In truth, I serve only the One."

"He has been saying that for as long as I've known him," said Igraines to Morgaines a little too sardonically.

We stood in silence for a moment, a sudden awkwardness weighing down upon us. "Morgaines, go play while I visit with Myrriddin for a spell," Igraines finally said.

"Yes, mother." Morgaines left her mother's side, skipping to the other side of the chamber.

"Well, Myrriddin. It has been four years at least, since our eyes last met. Since just prior to Morgaines entered into the world," Igraines said.

"'Tis true."

"You helped Uther and the Bishop Rozinus rid us of the Saxons and then you disappeared to that cave of yours, or so I was told," she said, with a poorly concealed sour edge. "Though I know Uther has seen you since. Tell me, Myrriddin; did he ask something of you? Did he ask you to give him a...what did you used to call it...a *glamour*, a spell of some kind?"

I sensed that my Myrriddin self knew exactly what she was talking about, but I, Masoud was at a loss. She pressed on.

"I carry his child, Uther's. I think you know that," she blurted out. She paused for a moment, clearly trying to decide whether to go on. By the look of her, she had a story that needed to be told and I was the pertinent audience for whom it was meant. "My husband Lot came home from battle one night, a new fresh scar on his left cheek. His handsome face had always been flawless so I noticed the scar instantly, even though he seemed to be hiding it. I should have seen something amiss immediately: he was trying to hide his face that night, I know that now. He kept in shadow and used a cowl covering. I assumed it was because he was embarrassed by the new scar or because he didn't want to be seen by servants as having come home from war even for the night." Igraines fell silent for a moment, obviously reliving the events of the night in question, smiling in spite of herself. "Lot was more amorous that night than I've ever seen him. He insisted we couple right then and there, couldn't even wait for the bed chamber. He threw me down with the passion of a demon in lust and impaled me right there in the entry hall. He eventually near dragged me to the bed chamber where he thrust into me again, over and over and over, dumping his seed in me at least five times that night. I awoke near dawn, my weeping servant shaking my shoulder. 'What is it?' I asked her. 'Oh, terrible, terrible news!' she said. 'Your husband is dead, Master Lot is dead! Killed in battle yesterday!' she screamed. 'No,' I said, 'he's right here.' I turned to the other side of the bed. The bed was empty. 'His corpse is at the gate, my lady. They travelled through the night to bring his body home, they did,' said my servant," Igraines recounted.

Though Igraines did not weep openly, tears came to her eyes at the telling of her tale. She turned from me then and went to a chair near an open window. She sat heavily in the seat and stared out at the pasture below and the horses passively grazing there. The peaceful sounds of birds' songs wafted to our ears from the trees beyond. I crossed to her and simply stood patiently near the chair, waiting for her in her own time to continue.

"There was a cart at the gate," she went on, "and several men on horseback surrounding it. I paid no heed to them but went straight to the cart. Something was in the cart, under a blanket of animal skin. I threw back the skin and there he was; Lot of Orkney, my husband. Shock and numbness filled me." Igraines hand went to her swollen belly, caressing the life beneath. *"Had I slept with his ghost?* I wondered. But that was ridiculous and I knew it. Then I looked at his body, his face. He was dirty and bloody from head to toe and his tunic and mantle torn and rent. But his face was still unblemished; there was not a scar on his face, no fresh scar on the left side of his face! As if to seek an answer, I looked at the men on horseback. One of them was Uther," she said looking up at me accusingly. "And *he* had the scar on his face! The same scar I'd seen the previous night! He had appeared to me as Lot, even wearing his clothes! I felt completely betrayed and despoiled. *Why would he do that?*! I thought. And then it struck me; he had made many advances toward me which I had spurned. He had glammed himself as Lot that night to rape me," she said.

"No," I heard my Myrriddin self say. "Lust, yes, but not the other."

Igraines laughed. "Do you say that to appease your guilt, Myrriddin?"

I made no reply. Her words hit close. A long silence ensued. I nearly turned to leave, knowing not what further to say. But then Igraines spoke again.

"Uther said that you are to take the child when he's born, to rear him," she said through a veil of soft tears. "It is a boy, I know it. He is a bastard, but is the taking of him necessary?"

"Yes. It was my doing. All of it," I, Myrriddin confessed, turning back to Igraines. "You now carry the future hope of the land and people. I saw it, saw you carrying this male-child, our hope, long before this pregnancy. When Uther was insistent on having you I knew the fulfillment of my vision was at hand. I'm sorry, Igraines, but the needs of the people, the future...they are more important than the needs..."

"...Of one woman? How convenient, Myrriddin. Uther is king and will reign for a long time. His other son, Ramey, is heir and will follow his father to the throne."

"Uther will die in battle and so will Ramey," I said in an urgent whisper, leaning in to Igraines. "I have seen it in the scrying bowl as well, just as I saw his seed, his future son, whom you now carry, as king of this realm," I said, falling silent for a moment, allowing my words to wash through Igraines. "Uther does not know that I have seen his death and that of Ramey's, and he must never be told. I say it again; the son you carry is the future king."

She sat in shocked silence for a time. "The future is up to us, I've heard you say such," said Igraines after a time. "So why not tell Uther of what you've seen that he may avoid it, chart a different future?"

"Because for him or Ramey to live will mean the destruction of all of Britain," I replied.

"Which you have seen as well, I suppose," offered Igraines without sarcasm.

I simply nodded.

She fell contemplative for a time, looking at her swollen belly, at the unborn child, the uncrowned future within. "The people, the council, will not accept him as Uther's heir to the throne," she finally said.

"That is why I must rear him; to prepare him for his rightful place; that he may prove to the others his worth," I explained. "Uther thinks I take him to cleanse his conscience of that night and the bastard he left behind. Let him think what he will."

"So that is why you have come back; to take my child?"

"You are not yet due. And I will not receive him until he is well weaned from the teat. I am presently here to reclaim two items of great import which I foolishly entrusted to Uther and Bishop Rozinus respectively.

"The sword and that spear? Why? You've always tried to convince others that they are naught but metal and wood," Igraines said. "You gave the spear to Rozinus and the sword to Uther."

"Because I believed they knew their worth. They have chosen to revere the items as holding powers beyond this realm. This has corrupted them and their followers. Bishop Rozinus pledged to give the spear to his Church. He broke that pledge, instead keeping it for himself in a vain attempt to wield power over others," I said more contemptuously than intended.

"So only the righteous may possess them; namely, you?" she said sarcastically. "And besides, they do hold power, I've seen you use them, especially that spear."

"The *power* to which you refer is in each and every one of us. It is from the One, from the Source of all. I am able to use the spear in particular as an extension of myself to channel this power, that is all," I explained.

"Me thinks there's more to it, but I'll leave it there." She still had a hand on her belly. Suddenly, her other hand flew to her side. "Ah! He kicks. Feel, Myrriddin!" she said with gleeful surprise.

She removed her hand from her side so that I could place mine there. I did. The future king kicked my palm forcefully. "He is strong. Like his mother," I said.

I pulled my hand away from her side but she grabbed it, clutching it between both of hers. Igraines looked at me, tears once again brimming her eyes. But this time, I could see they were tears of joy mixed with the fear of the unknown. "I have always loved you Myrriddin, always. In our previous lives to now. I have always trusted you. I trust you now in all that you say. You will rear my son, our future king and I am glad of it."

"Fear not, woman." I said.

"Forgive my emotion, it's all just..."

"Overwhelming?" I offered.

"Yes. Well perhaps. Everything affects me now. I am quite pregnant, you know," she said smiling.

I laughed. But my laughter was cut short by a loud explosion. The whole building shook. "By the One, what was that?" I said.

"What was what?" asked Igraines calmly. She still sat in the chair as if nothing had happened. Indeed, nothing was amiss in the chamber; we were where we had been for the past few moments and Morgaine still played at the other end of the room, the beautiful birds' songs still wafted to our senses from outside. Then I realized what was happening.

Igraines began to fade from sight. "Igraines!" I yelled. The whole room went dark.

"Igraines!" I cried again. I had the sudden realization that I was being dragged upright down a corridor, my feet, barely touching the dirt ground, yet bumping objects as we went. I came back to the present and opened my eyes.

"Quiet now, Sir Masoud!" said Alhasan. He was under one of my armpits, Commander James under my other, my dangling arms around both men's necks as we moved rapidly along, both men trying their best not to drag my feet as we went.

TWELVE

We were travelling down a dimly lit, tall but narrow, musty, dirt corridor, the walls little more than shored up earth, with a few small, lit torches in them. The explosion hit again, sending a fair amount of dirt and dust tumbling from the walls, but not collapsing them.

"What is happening?" I asked, coming fully back to my present self; Liam Arthur Mason.

"We're under attack," Alhasan answered. "We finished the initiation, at least. Then, it hit; the first explosion."

"We finished the initiation?" I asked.

"Do you not remember?" began Alhasan. "We lifted you from the coffin, you recited after the Master of Initiation and accepted the sword as a Knight Templar, though I am not surprised if you do not remember. You were in trance the whole time, even though you spoke the recitations!"

I suddenly panicked. "The Spear of Longinus! Where is my Spear?!"

"It's here, on my back, Sir Mason," replied Sir James with mirth in his voice.

I looked back over my shoulder to his back and saw the great spear sticking blade up, rising well above his head. There was something else there too; a sword hilt. "Is that...?"

"Your knight's sword, yes," he said. "We should halt."

We stopped and the men put me down. We listened for a moment. Silence. It was then that I noticed I was in the tunic or mantel of a Templar Knight. The pristine white tunic with Red Cross emblazoned on front and back had obviously been place over my head and tied at my waist at some point during the initiation, though I did not remember it happening.

"It seems to have stopped for now," said Sir James. "You passed out at the end of your initiation, as soon as you held the King's Sword that was bestowed upon you. You said, 'at last' as you caressed it, and dropped."

"I don't remember. May I see it?"

Sir James reached behind him and loosened the straps that held the things on his back. First he handed me the Spear. It felt good to feel its weight in my hand. Then he handed me a sword; the most beautiful thing I had ever seen. I took it by the hilt and became light-headed at the feel and sight of it. I knew this instrument, had held it before in the distant past I was sure. I was sure in the same manner I had been with the spear. The thing was nearly the length of a small man. Forged from a metal I had never seen——at least in this life——and engraved with ancient runes up and down its magnificent blade. I was awestruck.

"Much debate went into bestowing this upon you," said Sir James. "But in the end, it was determined that he who was the keeper of the Great Spear was to be the keeper of the King's Sword as well. It is said that this sword was the one given to the legendary King Arthur by his wizard, Merlin the Magician. "Some call it Excalibur."

I looked directly into Sir James' eyes, my attention to the sword broken by something my commander had said. "Merlin's name was Myrriddin and he was a High Master Druid, not a mere magician," I said rather too defensively.

"What?" asked Sir James, his brow crinkling with confusion.

I almost laughed. "Nothing. 'Tis not important," I said. "If it had belonged to the past great King of Britain, should it not now belong to our present king, King Richard?"

Sir James' face contorted in obvious disapproval of the thought. "That pig is a pawn of the Franc. He deserves naught," Sir James stated. "The King's Sword has been in our Order's possession since one of our incarnations as the Knights of Jesu, founded by our King Arthur...and Merlin. Today, some call that Order the Knights of the Round Table, although I don't think there was really a round table. Just a story, that."

"No, there was one. But it was more...oval, almost round, shall we say," I said, recalling my vision from earlier and thus correcting Sir James. He looked at me quizzically. "Perhaps you're right; just a story."

"In any event," continued Sir James, "it is more appropriate that the sword stay within the most inner circle our Order of Templar Knights today, of which King Richard is not a part. He is not even aware of its existence, this inner circle. It was furthermore deemed appropriate, as I said, that the keeper of the Spear be also the First Knight of Excalibur. Do you not agree? It feels right in your hands, does it not?"

"It does indeed," I said. Suddenly, the building shook with yet another explosion. "Where are we?"

"We went down, deeper into the church's bowels, when the first explosion hit," said Alhasan.

"And the others?"

"Scattered," replied Sir James. "As I said, you passed out at the conclusion of the initiation. We had picked you up and were starting to file out when it hit. The others scattered to the outside, I think. I thought that too vulnerable, so I took us down here."

I looked around at our bleak surroundings and saw things on the ground in the dim light, the things that my feet had been bumping into: skulls and bones——human skulls and human skeletons. Some of the latter still had rotted clothing clinging to their morbid frames. "What in God's name is this place!?" I said.

"The Pit is what it's called," answered Sir James. "Certain prisoners were cast down here...forever."

"And this is where you thought to have us escape?" I said more forcefully than I had intended.

"Take care with your tone, Sir Mason. Your status has been exceptionally elevated, but I am still your commanding officer," said Commander Sir James authoritatively.

"Yes, sir. But can we please leave now, before we become the new residents?" I asked.

"Aye, you're right. I did not intend for us to come down this far to begin with; simply wanted to keep you safe until you came back to your senses. Can ye walk on your own now?" he asked me.

"Yes," I replied. "Lead the way, sir."

With that, Sir James headed back the way we had come, followed by Alhasan. With the Spear of Longinus in one hand and the great sword of Arthur in the other, I headed out with them.

ﻟﺪ   ﻟﺪ   ﻟﺪ

A chaotic din of voices in panic assaulted our ears, becoming louder and louder the farther up the steps we went. The way up and out of the bowels of the church where Sir James had thought to take us——me——for protection seemed to go on forever. As we approached the main level of the church from within, the chaotic din of voices from without became more pronounced as screams to curdle the blood; human screams of agony.

We poured out of the church, Sir James in the lead. He suddenly stopped on the church's large portico, causing Alhasan and I to nearly slam into him. We peered out into the church's courtyard. Many soldiers and crusaders were running about, apparently trying to avoid the explosions and subsequent flying debris, or racing for their arms, as some of them came running back to the courtyard, side arms of swords in hand. Others lay on the ground, bodies or limbs torn asunder by the hurled exploding instruments of destruction. It was these poor, retched souls from which the agonized screams emanated. The area was no longer dark with night, but dim with a cloud of choking smoke from the explosions. A breeze parted the vile cloud for an instant and I could see the orange of a birthing new day peek through.

"They timed their attack precisely," noted Sir James. "Dawn: assembling of the troops here in front of the church."

"Dawn? It seemed only moments ago we entered into the sanctum of initiation," said Alhasan with genuine surprise.

"Alhasan! I thought you said your people don't have exploding missiles!" I said.

"We do not. We use the fireballs, you see!" he replied.

"But..." I began. Before I could finish my sentence we were violently knocked from our feet as one of the hurled balls of fire hit the church's dome, exploding and sending hot particles raining down upon us. It was all we could do to scramble out of the way and under a sturdier portion of the portico's roof. Where we had stood only an instant before was suddenly crushed by a huge, fiery section of flaming church dome. It was the size of a large pig and smashed the entire portico where we had been standing. Something else too; a black, slick liquid accompanied the fire and explosion, falling on part of the portico. Debris and oil came down in the courtyard, the oil splashing on the hapless victims writhing on the ground, inflicting further agony, but withholding the mercy of death.

"Oil. They're using hot oil in their fireballs as well," yelled Sir James over the ever increasing loudness of the din.

A feeling suddenly arose within me that was completely unexpected, one that only days before would not have entered my mind. But something had shifted at the core of my being these past days, culminating in the initiation and the visions, the realizations, of the profound *past* of my soul. Passionate anger rose within me at the absurdity of our plight in the moment and at our overall plight in this part of the world, and by extension the sheer stupidity of war in general. It was made all the more poignant by the fact that only hours ago, there had been many of us from so-called opposite sides of this conflict working in harmony and like-thought to install someone, me, into an Order of like-minded, gallant purveyors of *Truth*. And now this?! But stupidly, I directed my anger at Alhasan. "Where are your people from earlier tonight, your Hashishim Knights?! I don't see them," I said. Indeed, none of them were around; only Christian soldiers and crusaders, running to arms, to put out fires, to help the wounded. "Had they run off to give the order to attack?!"

"That's enough, Liam!" ordered Sir James.

"And where is Commander Blackthorn?!" I yelled. "Why did he not see this coming?"

"My good Knight Mason! That is enough, I say!" barked Sir James. "I tell you, you will not insubordinate yourself. You will..."

He stopped in mid sentence, staring at me with a mixture of awe, respect and even a little fear. Or rather, he stared at the weapons I held—one in each hand: the Great Spear of Longinus and the King's Sword of Arthur. They both now glowed with an angry red, and the glow began to pulsate in a steady rhythmic manner after my own seething emotion and my accompanying pattern of breath of the same. Gaining the rein of my anger, I stepped off of the portico, or what was left of it, and out into the middle of courtyard, gently stepping over the wounded and dying.

Stopping in the center of it all, I looked toward the heavens and raised the weapons over my head, the Great Spear in my right, the King's Sword in my left. I had no idea what I was going to do, but let my controlled anger, and more importantly my soul——my Merlin self, so to speak——be my guide. My eyes closed. "By the One Source of all there is and all that is...by the One Source which courses through me and all; I bid you come through me now! End this night of destruction and death, and sow the seeds of peace and life here and now. So Be It!!" I intoned. "By the One Source..." I began again, repeating the incantation, for that is what it was, over and over and over again. With each saying of it, I felt my mind fusing more and more with the words, and more importantly, with the thoughts and passion behind the words. Thus, in that instance, I truly came to know the reality of the power of the One Source. This Power began to course through my being. I, Liam Arthur Mason—Masoud knew not from where these words and thoughts, passion and Power came from. But my soul knew. I simply got out of the way and let it be so. And what happened was astonishing.

I felt the power well up through the earth, up through the ground beneath my feet, enter into the lower portion of my body and vibrate its way up my legs and through my chest as if a fiery, shaking snake was rapidly winding its way up and through my whole body. It suddenly went into my limbs, raging through my arms and bursting forth from the spear and sword. Light, as if from a lightning charge, bolted from the weapons in my hands and into the air, disappearing into the smoke and dawn beyond. Then the winds came; howling winds that carried with them a strong, lovely, sweet smell; it smelled like candy. I felt the effects of this scent instantly. It soothed the mind, the senses, and thus the body. The winds raged, instantly overwhelming the fires as the breath blows out a candle flame. The smoke in the area swirled rapidly on the wind and dispersed, leaving the area altogether. We then saw two more fireballs hurling through the sky in the distance, heading directly toward us. Two more bolts shot from the instruments I held, one from each. The explosion was bright even in the dawn sky as each fireball was destroyed in midflight by the bolts from the Spear and Sword, thus preventing both fireballs from ever reaching their targets.

The bolts from the Spear of Longinus and the Sword of Arthur suddenly ceased. A moment later the winds suddenly abated. And then the truly marvelous occurred. We watched as one by one, the injured stopped their cries and began to rise. Some, whose limbs had been torn from the explosions showed visible signs of weakness in the previously injured limbs, but were nonetheless healed; limbs had been put back together and in some, even reattached or re-grown in an instant. It seemed impossible, but the evidence was before us. Unfortunately, the dead did not rise, which I thought strange. Supposedly, I had brought Henry back from the dead. Why not these men?

I lowered my arms, putting the weapons, the instruments, to rest at my side. I sensed Alhasan and Sir James rush to my side. The three of us stood in observation of the *miracle* unfolding in the courtyard.

"Allah be praised!" exclaimed Alhasan. "I told you Masoud. I told you that Allah works through you and the spear! Just as that night with your friend. It was the same, you see! Or nearly so."

"Aye, Sir 'Masoud'," said Sir James mockingly, but kindly. "Dear Jesus. Unbelievable. Truly. But why did the dead not rise as your friend had? You brought Henry back that night," asked Sir James.

Alhasan turned to Sir James. "Why, these souls have already willingly departed. 'Enry's had not on the night in question or at least not completely, you see," he answered, as if it were the most obvious thing in the world. "Is that not so Master Masoud?"

"Indeed," was all I said. It sounded perfectly reasonable.

"Still, your power with the spear and sword is amazing," said Sir James.

"'Not I, but the Father within doeth the work.' Wouldn't that be more accurate, Sir James?" I asked.

"Or the magician in you," he replied.

"The Father, the Magician, the Merlin; by any name it's the same thing: the great Source of All working through me as me, or you."

THIRTEEN

It took nearly the whole day, but we gathered the dead and created a mass burial site for our dead brother-soldiers and crusaders. Interestingly, it was those who had felt the direct effects of the healing at dawn that insisted, almost as one, on gathering our dead comrades from the church's square and from elsewhere where they had fallen, and bringing them to the burial site. The Christian rites were said by priests and the dirt shoveled into the great hole in the earth. Finally, by late afternoon, with The King's Sword in a make-shift scabbard on my back and the Spear in my right hand, I made my way back to our dwelling amid the stares and murmurs of those of my fellow crusaders and soldiers I passed along the way. Word had spread quickly about my use of the Spear of Longinus and the Sword of Arthur. Most who looked upon me as I walked to my tent did so with awe or fear etched upon their face. Some, however, looked at me with a mixture of contempt and disbelief. It was as if they were saying, I believe not the story being told of this one! Or, who is this would-be knight? One thing was certain: my life had just been irrevocable changed within a handful of hours.

As I approached the tent's opening I became excited to share all that had happened with Henry. I darted into the dwelling only to find it empty. Henry was nowhere to be seen. Although, why should I think he was still in here after all these hours. It was late afternoon, after all. A horrific thought suddenly occurred to me: *Perhaps he had been injured in the attack!* I turned to run out of the tent and back to the church's square, but I was stopped, jarred as I ran into someone just inside of the tent's threshold, knocking him flat on the ground. The collision knocked the breath out of my own body for a brief instant. Alhasan lay sprawled at my feet. "What the devil, man? Are you my shadow? Am I not to have a moment's peace?!" I said much too harshly. My harshness was a vain attempt at covering my own startled embarrassment at having been so easily snuck up on. Besides, this was after all Alhasan's tent too.

"Ah, Masoud. Shadow, no. But I must be your aid, your servant always now. There are those who would seek to exploit you and I must remain at your side to help fend them away," he explained. "It is my...how you say; calling, you see. It is my place in the Order of the Hashishim Knights."

"Ah. And how do you know this is your calling?" I asked, mirth and suspicion warring within me.

"As you *know* your place as the Keeper of the Spear of Longinus and the Sword of your Great King, so too do I know my place is by your side, my Lord Masoud," he said, picking himself up off of the ground, the floor of our tent and bowing deeply before me and holding his bow.

He held the position, clearly waiting for me to release him from his bow and thus acknowledging his official position as my *servant*. "Or, perhaps it was ordered as your calling by your Order of Knights, or better yet, by Salah al-Din himself, as more a mission of espionage than servitude, eh?" I said.

Alhasan slowly unbowed himself, standing upright and staring straight into my eyes with genuine hurt and insult. "You aggrieve me, sire, truly. What have I done to earn your wrath so?" he asked.

I smiled and put my hands up, palms outward toward him in a gesture of surrender and apology. "Alhasan, I pray you forgive me. The events of these past many hours have been enlightening and tumultuous, inspiring and confusing all at once. I simply have trouble understanding why you choose to stay with me when your people and my people war so. It's simply confusing. Your people attack us when we had just held vigil together in a joint initiation. Why would they do that?"

"Those that attacked are not those who were with us in the sanctuary. Remember; they too were caught in the attack. They are working within a system that has taken on a life of its own; that has become a beast in its own right. It is the same with every war, is it not? There comes a time when the enemies cannot stop the beast they created because the beast has come into a life of its own, you see. Such is the way of this war too," Alhasan pontificated. "Yet, as in past conflicts between our peoples, there are those bodies in the beast who will aid in its ultimate destruction to preserve the overall Truth of being. The beast is thus slain from within. You are now important to that process, Masoud, you see. And I serve to slay the beast with you."

"What you say is more riddle than anything else, my friend. But my heart feels the truth of what you say," I said. "So be it, then. But just give me a little solitude now and again, will you?"

"As you wish."

"Right now," I said, looking around at the empty tent, "I would very much like to find Henry. You have not seen him, have you?" I asked. Alhasan's expression suddenly changed to a somberness that distressed me. "You *have* seen him. What is it? Is he...is he dead?" I asked, bracing myself for the answer.

Alhasan shook his head. "His body lives, barely. But his soul is slowly being pushed out, I fear."

"I don't understand," I said.

"It would be most simpler to show you," said Alhasan. "I would venture that he is where he is most days at this time; where he's gone daily since...since the night you brought him back from the side of the dead. But, be warned: you will not like what you see."

"Lead on," I said. Alhasan nodded turned and walked away from the tent. I followed him.

ﺟ   ﺟ   ﺟ

We walked for nearly half-an-hour. The sun was now beginning to set and I had the latent thought that this day had been the oddest of my life. Yet, it was not over. We left the outskirts of the encampment, traversing the rugged area on the western-most side and leaving the perimeter guards there, soldiers from the ordinary rank and file——that which I had been a part of on just the previous day——agape at the sight of the Sword and Spear I carried, as well as the tunic that I wore. "See to it that you say nothing of my whereabouts," I said.

"Aye," one of them managed to say. "What of him?" he asked, eyeing Alhasan suspiciously.

"He is with me. That's all you need know," I replied.

"Yes, sir. There's naught out there but the latrines and the den, sir, you know," said the guard.

I ignored the comment. The latrines I knew of. But the *den* I knew not of. We moved on, Alhasan and I.

The stench of the latrines was soon upon us and we moved down an embankment and into the bed of a stream which had a good and steady flow of ankle deep water running through it. To our left some thirty feet away and up on the other side of the embankment were the mounds of a freshly dug area: the trench for the latrines no doubt. "Are they daft?" I asked rhetorically. "Who gave orders to dig the latrines so close to a water source?"

"I doubt those who dug it were properly supervised, My Lord Masoud," answered Alhasan.

"Would you stop that, Alhasan!" I said. "Stop calling me Sir, Master, Lord. Just Mason, or Masoud! Much has happened this past day, but not that much! And where in hell are you taking us, anyway?"

"'Where in hell,' indeed!" he said cryptically. There were rocks whose tops protruded through the surface of the water, giving stepping stones of a sort to the other side of the stream. The embankment of the other side was approximately ten feet away. Alhasan easily hopped from rock to rock across the stream and up the five-foot embankment of the opposite side. He stopped at the top of the other side of the embankment and pointed to something off in the distance. "There is our destination," he said.

I reached the top of the embankment and stood next to him. Before us was an olive grove whose trees reached some twenty feet in the air with branches full of their offering. At the other end of the grove was a hillside. In fact, the grove actually butted up against this hillside. In the hillside was an opening, a dim light emanating from within. It was the opening in the hillside to which Alhasan pointed. A steady stream of smoke also came out of the opening. "A cave?" I asked. "Henry is in there?"

"Come," Alhasan said gravely, walking through the olive grove. I followed.

It was dim in the grove because of its canopy of branches, and it was still warm from the day. But the air within carried a staleness to it that seemed foreign to the immediate area. I then realized it was the staleness of a smoky residue. I stopped briefly at one of the trees. Its trunk appeared a little darker than would a normal olive tree trunk. I ran a finger down part of the trunk and came away with a black residue of smoke on my finger tip for the effort. Yet, in spite of this same dark coating on many of the trees, they still bore the harvest of their olives. However, the fullness of the branches I thought I saw a moment ago was not because of the healthy fullness of the offering of these trees, but because of a droopiness of the branches' leaves. I looked ahead at the cave's opening and the smoke coming out, which did not seem to be a terrible amount at the moment. But I realized that this was the source of the trees' smoky layer and the reason why the branches were drooping. *There must always be a steady stream of smoke coming from this cave,* I thought. But it just did not seem possible that enough smoke could come from the cave to coat the trees even over an extended time. Then I noticed the ground at my feet. I was standing in the remnants of a now dead and cold campfire. Surveying the area I saw dozens and dozens of old, ashen camp fire spots dotting the area within the grove. It was as if at any given time, this grove was used for a camp. No wonder the trees had this residue on them. The trees' leaves were choking from the smoke being layered on them from all the fires that had been here. They could not breathe. The notion suddenly struck me as ridiculous; *trees don't breathe!* But the spear's voice suddenly and unexpectedly asserted itself. *They are living beings made from the same substance as you. Never forget that,* it said. I looked at the spear. It was normal; neither glowing nor shaking.

"Masoud. Come," said Alhasan. He was standing at the opening, the entrance to the cave. I made my way through the rest of the grove and joined him.

He ducked through the five-foot by five-foot opening and disappeared into the dimness beyond. I ducked and entered as well.

My eyes stung from the haze that hung in the dank air. It took a moment for my vision to adjust. The cave was big on the inside. It extended far back, some sixty feet. Its ceiling seemed to rise to a peek at about thirty feet. The cave itself splayed out in a fan shape from the entrance to be approximately eighty feet wide at its widest point deep within. About twenty-five feet in was a central fire. Several sleeping pallets lined the walls and piles of rushes were strewn about the dirt floor near the central fire. Men lay on most of the piles of rushes, reclined in sleep or apparent stupor or both. Three of the forms on the pallets near one wall appeared to be wrapped from head to toe in rags. The stench of sickness hung in the air and seemed to be coming from the direction of these wrapped men. I dared not think what illness had them.

Also near the fire were what appeared to be clay jars, the kind the locals used for carting water and grain; each stood two-feet tall. There were five or six of them. But these jars had been altered for a use other than the carrying of liquid or grains. Several hoses, each made from what appeared to be tightly woven straw, protruded from each jar near the bottom, spaced equally apart around the base of the jar. The top of the jar housed a metal bowl. Smoke trailed up from most of these bowls. There were about thirty people lying or sitting about. In addition to those on the rushes, there were those on the pallets along the other wall. Some, with eyes closed, were ranting mindlessly in sleep, or in some fixated dream-state, in a place in mind or spirit that seemed more a place of torment than pleasure, judging by the tone some had; it was fearful, as if they were small children living out some demon infested tale of woe. Still others who were on the rushes near the fire and the jars, were sucking on the end of a hose extending from a given jar, drawing in the smoke of the opium——for that was obviously what they were doing——draining their soul with every inhalation. I looked closer at the men before me. To my utter surprise, not all were soldiers of Christ as I had presumed. Several of them, judging by the appearance and clothing were actually members of the Islamic army under Salah al-Din!

All are One. In richness, in poverty, all are One, said the voice of the Spear. *You are the richness. You are the poverty.* "I understand. 'I am *that,* I am'," I heard myself say aloud.

"Liammm?" said the slurring, but familiar voice of my friend, Henry. "Is that truly you?"

I moved toward the sound of his voice. There, on one of the piles of rushes near the fire was my dear friend. I removed the heavy sword from my back and placed it on the ground along with the spear. I sat next to my friend; Henry on my right, the weapons on my left. I was silent for a moment, looking at the others who sat near us on the rushes. They were oblivious to my presence. I looked then to Alhasan. He remained respectfully away, staying near the entrance. I turned my full attention back to my friend. Henry looked even worse than on the previous night, or perhaps I was truly just noticing his appearance in its entirety. Even in the dim firelight of this smoky place I could see that his skin had a yellowish tint to it. His thinness was sickly. "You look horrible, Henry," I said.

He laughed a drunken laugh as he placed the hose end he was holding into his mouth. He inhaled deeply, drawing the opium smoke into his lungs. He rolled his eyes and tilted his head to one side with the pleasure of it just the way an infant does when drawing the life-nurturing flow from his mother's teat.

"Why?" I asked, stupidly.

He did not answer right away. But instead, held his breath, and hence the opiate smoke, inside his lungs. Finally, he released the smoke from its prison. Little of the stuff escaped from his mouth, giving me pause that much stayed in his body. He closed his eyes and smiled the grin of one who was not entirely in this world...and loved that he was not. "'Why,' you ask?" he finally said, keeping his eyes shut. I...went home when I died," he said, with surprising lucidity.

"Home? I don't understand," I said.

He laughed for a long time. Finally, he drew another inhalation on the hose, holding this one in only half as long as the previous one. He opened his eyes and looked at me. Though his eye lids drooped like the branches of the olive trees outside, it was Henry who stared at me and not some half-witted, drug-controlled person I did not recognize. He was somewhat detached, but it was him. Yet, it was clear by his next bit of rambling that he was connected to a deeper part of himself because of his state of mind. He regarded my Templar tunic. "I see you be one of them now, eh? Matter 'o time, was all, is that not right, Myrriddin my friend," he said to me. "Or Longi...Long-i-nus, or whatever name you be using this time. You remember me? I was hanged with you, right next to you, on the cross over all those centuries ago, I was," he stated. He then began to laugh as another thought, another *memory* apparently entered his now inebriated mind. "They hanged you on the cross upside down, do ye remember? Pissed 'em off you did!" Henry laughed uncontrollably, until a coughing fit nearly had him vomiting.

Though I was surprised at his *memory*, I did not show it. "You're a Christian. Since when did you start believing that you've been here before?" I said.

He made no reply.

"Come," I said as I took hold of his arm.

"No!" he said vehemently as he jerked his arm from my grasp. "I am fine here. More than fine here. I remember things with this," he said, holding up the hose.

"You don't need that to remember things," I said. But my words felt empty, and thus sounded empty even to my own ears.

"What do you know of it?" Henry replied. He then looked at the weapons at my side, the Spear in particular. "They hanged us for that thing, all those centuries past. And, here it is againnn. And againnn and againnn and againnnn will it keep showing up in our lives," he said as a statement of fact. "But you...you think it's destiny, I suppose. Well, I want off," Henry said raising his voice to a near yell, "ye 'ear me?! I want off this ship!"

"Shut yer yap, ye shit-hole!" said a voice from a pallet deeper within the cave.

Henry laughed again. He leaned in to my ear then, as one about to reveal a great secret to me alone. "I haven't shit in near a week!" he whispered. He sat upright with a laugh. "'ave ya heard of such?!" he said in a normal, matter of fact tone. "I feel like I gotta, but..."

"Let me take you back to the tent," I offered.

He did not answer me, but became silent for a time, staring into the fire in front of us. A tear brimmed one of his eyes. "I was home for a time, Liam. I was," he said in a lament-filled voice. "It was so beautiful. Then I was yanked back to here. By you and that...spear of yours. Why? Why didn't you let me go?" He began to weep, sobbing as a babe in the arms. I tried to think of something to say. But there was nothing to say. I put my hand on the spear thinking perhaps it could help. It had helped work wonders earlier. But I knew that was futile. Henry's condition was of the mind; one that was a conscious choice on his part, and as such only he could change it. At last I did what he probably needed most from me in that moment. I simply put my arms around him and held him as the friend I loved.

We stayed in the embrace for a few moments, tenderness and bitterness warring within me; tenderness for my friend, bitterness at my inability to help him. I looked over towards the entrance. Alhasan stood just inside the entrance. But there was someone else now there as well. The other man was silhouetted in the entrance itself by the light spilling in from outside. But I could see his gold eyes staring at me from beneath his turban. I turned my attention away from the gold-eyed man and back to my friend, and gently laid him down on the ground. He was already asleep. I then jumped to my feet, determined to speak with this gold-eyed man. I took one step toward the entrance and froze. He was gone. The gold-eyed man had vanished. Again. I ran up to Alhasan. "Where'd he go?!" I asked. I poked my head out of the cave for a brief moment. There was no one about.

"Who?" asked Alhasan.

"The man, the Arab with the gold eyes. He was standing just there," I said indicating the cave's entrance.

"There has been no one here but me. No one else has come in. I would have known it, you see," he replied vainly.

"I know what I saw, Alhasan," I said. "This man was also in Salah al-Din's tent. He stood behind Rashin, dressed as him but had stark gold-eyes. You must know of whom I speak, as you know the men who attend the Sultan and his hangers-on."

"I do, I do, Masoud. But...Masoud, there is no one in attendance of the Sultan or Rashin who appears as you say, no one with eyes of gold, you see," replied Alhasan.

I was dumbfounded.

"Come, Master Masoud. You are tried and tired from the day's event," he said nodding back toward my now sleeping friend Henry. He then turned and left the cave.

There was naught to do but follow him.

FOURTEEN

I left Henry at the den that day concerned about my friend and mystified by the stranger with the gold-eyes. I could no more force Henry to come back with me than I could force him to let go of the opium. It was his friend, or at least that was his perception for the time being. I cursed myself for not having seen his plight before. He had not been in the healing tent while I had been there. And, I did not see him until that day in Salah al-Din's tent. It was with heavy heart that I entered our tent, Alhasan at my side, and spent the rest of that evening and night in a state of self-loathing, guilt and moodiness over my friend. I finally fell into a restless sleep. But it was sleep nonetheless and I remained in it for a time. Until the visitor came, that is.

It was near dawn when I heard the scratching at the tent's flap. My first thought was that an animal was digging for something just near the tent. Alhasan and I exchanged a glance. He had clearly heard it too. But it became obvious that the scratching sound was in a purposeful, rhythmic manner; three scratches and moment of silence, followed by three more scratches. Over and over, the sound came. It was no animal making this noise.

Finally, I got off my sleeping pallet. I glanced over at what had been Henry's sleeping pallet. It was still empty, which disappointed me. So, too, was Sir James', though that did not surprise me at all. I grabbed the Spear of Longinus and slunk stealthily to the tent's flap. "Identify yourself," I said in a harsh whisper without opening the flap, spear at the ready.

"Sultan Salah al-Din wishes a word, Sir Masoud," said the squeaky voice in a hushed whisper. I recognized the voice at once: it was the same voice that had greeted us at the sanctuary's door through the small, triangular shaped window or opening on the door just before entry for my initiation ritual.

Slowly, I pushed aside the tent's flap just enough to peer out at the visitor. He was alone and covered from head to toe in the black of the Knights Hashishim. As at the sanctuary's threshold, only his stark blue eyes were presently visible, this time through a slit in the cloth around his head and face. "You. I thought you to be one of us," I said, genuinely surprised.

"Ah. My English is quite good, is it not?" he replied, with pride.

"Yes. That and you're bright colored eyes led me to an incorrect conclusion," I said.

"Yes. The eyes. Franc mother, truth be told," our visitor stated flatly. "I say again; the Sultan wishes a word," he insisted.

"The last time I was in the presence of your Sultan I was a prisoner. And you expect me to now just walk into his camp and his tent to bid a fond and warm salutation?" I asked, sarcasm dripping from my words.

"Your life's position has been quite lifted, he is aware. He is also aware of the fact that you performed a great feat with the aid of the spear and the sword," my uninvited caller said.

"That does not answer my query," I replied.

"He wishes to ask you something, something of great import, something that could bend the way of this conflict," he said. There was an unspoken meaning to his words which I saw reflected in his eyes, I could see it, sense it. I sensed too that this meaning was of a profundity that needed to be heeded. My skin tingled at the realization and the spear gave a subtle vibration in my hand. My guest seemed not to notice, or pretended not to. "Your passage and safety is guaranteed, you have Salah al-Din's solemn oath on the matter."

I thought for a moment. It could be utter suicide, walking into the camp of the *enemy*. But then again, was I forgetting all I had experienced the past couple of days since the initiation?

"The Sultan's word is gold, Masoud," said Alhasan from behind me.

"Is that so?" I asked rhetorically, not looking back at him but instead keeping my eyes on our visitor.

"It is," replied Alhasan. "We must go to him if he wills it."

I now allowed the tent's flap to fall back into place, rudely falling in the face of our visitor, the messenger, and turned to Alhasan. "'We?' And what of you? You served the Sultan. Will he not want you back if you accompany me?"

"If it be the will of Allah."

"Or Salah al-Din's,"

He considered for a moment before answering. "I serve you. If Sultan Salah al-Din has invited you with guarantees of safety then that extends to your property as well... which includes the Spear, the Sword and me," concluded Alhasan. "But, as I say..."

"I know, I know; 'if it be Allah's will,'" I said. I turned back to the tent's flap and opened it. My caller, Salah al-Din's messenger waited patiently. "Very well, but give me a minute."

"As you wish," he said with a bow. He then stepped backward some ten feet and waited in the shadows.

I closed the flap again and began to gather my tunic. Alhasan just stood there watching me. "Well, come on," I said.

"I am presently ready, Masoud," he said.

Indeed, he was already dressed in his black servant garb of the Knights of Hashishim, something I had not noticed until that moment. "I see. One might think you half expected the messenger, Alhasan," I pointed out.

"I did, by 'half', as you say," he replied.

I stopped putting on my tunic, my head barely through the neck hole of the thing. "Then do you know what this meeting is really about?" I asked.

"No."

"Do you know this messenger outside? An acquaintance? A friend, perhaps?" I asked.

"Yes," was all he said.

I was unsure whether to be annoyed or amused at Alhasan's quick and crisp responses to my questions. I choose the latter and resumed dressing. "Just thought I would ask," I said. I placed the sword on my back and picked up the spear once again, then exited the tent into the waning night.

The messenger guided us stealthily through our camp, moving tent to tent, shadow to shadow, avoiding any of my people who were still about, which were very few. I thought it unnecessary. "We needn't move so through my own camp," I pointed out.

"And where would you say that you are going with myself and Alhasan here, especially dressed as we are?" he was quick to point out.

"Then you should've dressed differently. Besides, where I may go does not concern them," I said, knowing full well that it was a false statement.

"I had no time to 'dress differently'. And, your officers would state otherwise," he said.

Regardless, we were outside of the camp in quick order. The moon was half full and waxing, providing enough light in this desert land for us to see where we were going. We journeyed for not more than half-a-mile, before coming to a rise, a small hill, which we surmounted with ease. Before us was the encampment in which I had been imprisoned only a short time ago, now rebuilt from the attack perpetrated by the crusader army. My heart began to race. The dawn was still an hour or so away. I felt a sudden desire to be back in my own camp by then. Despite the messenger's assurances, I did not want to be seen in Salah al-Din's camp in daylight. We paused briefly at the crest of the hill and looked upon the Muslim camp. Some cooking fires were scattered about. As there had been in my camp at the present hour, there was a quiet lull to this camp as well; the quiet before the dawn.

"Come, Sir Masoud," said the messenger. "This shant take long."

We descended the other side of the hill and entered the camp of my former imprisonment.

Indeed, there were very few Muslim soldiers up and about. But there were a handful. Those who saw the three of us looked away, paying no heed, at least, at first. No doubt they simply thought that two of their comrades were bringing in a crusader prisoner. The attire of Alhasan and the messenger of Salah al-Din, and my crusader/Templar tunic spoke to that. But then, upon seeing that I held weapons, they stopped whatever they were doing and stared, some even stepping toward us. Those who did this were assertively waved off by the messenger. We moved through the camp, across it and to the other side. On the outskirts of the camp stood the grand tent of the Sultan, Salah al-Din.

The guards at the entry tunnel to Salah al-Din's tent eyed me as I approached with my two companions but showed no surprise at my appearance. No doubt they were expecting me. They simply stepped aside, allowing the messenger, Al-hasan and me to pass. We walked into the tent's stuffy entry tunnel and came out the other side on the interior of the tent and into the main chamber where Salah al-Din held council.

The space looked the same as the first time I had been there, the tent's walls and ceiling having since been impeccably and imperceptibly sewn back together after the violent explosions that had torn them apart. Salah al-Din was in the same high-backed chair. Some of the same soldiers and court appendages that were in attendance the last time were there again. Among them: Hakim, the commander that Salah al-Din had slapped with a riding crop, who then turned up at our tent dressed as a Hashishim Knight, and the dark-robed, opaque-eyed man, Rashin too. He stared at me, Rashin did. I felt that his discolored eye saw me better than his normal eye; it felt as if he were probing my very soul with it. The sensation of knowing this man returned to me. Only now it was more pronounced and more definite than it had been the day on the hillcrest. A name came to me unbidden, then another, and I spoke them both aloud without thinking; "Draco. Creconius Mab," I heard myself saying aloud to Rashin, yet not to him. A wide grin appeared on the man's face as if he knew exactly what, or who, I was talking about. And indeed, perhaps he was completely aware of the names I had just spoken as being those he had been identified with in two previous existences.

"Rashin," said Salah al-Din.

I looked at the Sultan with what must have appeared to him as an expression of confusion.

"His name is Rashin and he is, how shall I say," Salah al-Din began, looking at the opaque-eyed man with humorous contempt, "my court soothsayer..."

"I beg the Sultan's indulgence at my interruption, but I do not use that archaic term, great Sultan. I am of the extreme Sufi..."

"Yes, yes," said Salah al-Din irritably. "You are a great mystic and are able to see the future. That is one of the definitions of a soothsayer, but I use the term more in jest than anything else, you should know that," he said with finality. He then turned his attention back to me. "I thank you for coming, Masoud. It shows courage on your part. Congratulations are appropriate as well. You have risen yourself to a grand height and proven beyond doubt that you are the Keeper of the Spear of Longinus," he stated flatly. I could not tell if he was being sincere or sarcastic. He paused, then. The silence in the tent dragged on for more than a few moments. In fact, it hung in the air for so long that I began to become aware of sounds outside the tent; the sounds of a military camp beginning to come to life in anticipation of the campaign's new day. "We will speak in private, you and I," Salah al-Din said at last as he stood and stepped toward me.

"Great Sultan!" Hakim said. "I must insist that we be present at this... undertaking."

"No," was the Sultan's terse response.

"Salah al-Din," began Rashin as he stepped forward, brazenly stopping between myself and the Sultan, effectively blocking Salah al-Din's path in getting to me.

The Sultan's face flooded with controlled rage.

But Rashin did not back down. In fact, though his back was to me, I could hear that his voice was filled with authority; the kind of frightening authority that comes from the depths of the soul or from the depths of a soulless beast, depending on one's perspective. "I am the one who controls the item we have and the power that it contains. Do not forget, my Sultan," Rashin said.

I peered around the form of Rashin to look at Salah al-Din, to gauge his reaction. The Sultan's eyes appeared as though they were going to pop from his head, so anger-filled he was. He took a deep, visible breath before he spoke. "You have yet to prove that to my complete satisfaction, Rashin. You will wait here in this chamber while I speak to Masoud. Alone. Move aside."

A tense moment ensued as Rashin appeared determined to defy his Master's orders. But, after a moment, the opaque-eyed man deferred to his superior and stepped aside. Rashin then turned his gaze upon me, or rather, on the spear in my hand and then the sword on my back. His gaze at the sword was particularly intense and the look on his face was strange, even lustful; as if he were staring at the object of his most base, carnal desire, not unlike, oddly enough, Sir Blackthorn's gaze at the spear when first he beheld it.

"Come, Masoud," said Salah al-Din as he brushed past me. I turned and followed him out of the tent's main chamber, but I could not remove Rashin's licentious expression from my mind. I glanced back at Alhasan who had been standing this whole time near the entrance through which we had come. He simply inclined his head toward me. It was a gesture I interpreted to mean that I should obey the Sultan as he, Alhasan, is by staying put. Thus, I followed Salah al-Din.

FIFTEEN

The two of us walked out of the main room and through three other adjoining rooms or chambers which were nearly as large as the main receiving room we had just been in. We then proceeded down a hallway of sorts. The chambers and hallway served as reminders of just how large this tent structure truly was. Finally, the Sultan led me into a chamber that was small by comparison to the others. It was brightly lit by several hanging oil lamps and tall floor candles. Laughter seeped into this chamber through the tent wall and venting space at the bottom of the wall. The sound appeared to come from the room immediately next to the one we were in. The laughter was lilting, pleasant and feminine. Women. The next room contained women. *A harem?* I wondered, *a room to house the Sultan's wives and concubines?* Some tales I had heard in my travels claimed that Salah al-Din was married to over one-hundred women. Of course, they were just that: tales; tales that were meant to further paint the people of this land as infidels and fornicators in need of annihilation. Perhaps he was not married to one-hundred women, but a handful. By the sound of it, five or six women occupied the next room. Every tale has an element of truth, or so it is said. *What of it if these women are his wives in the pluralistic sense? How is that different then our forefathers of the Old Text taking more than one woman as wife, or even any 'Christian' married man taking a mistress?* I thought to myself.

There is none, said a voice from deep within my being. The spear vibrated in conjunction with the words, shaking slightly in my hand and emitting a low, subtle humming or rattling in harmony with its movement and the thoughts in my mind. *There is no judgment save by man, by woman. Rules are made by men, not God, not the One*, the voice continued. *The standard by which one conducts oneself is set by the consciousness within his own mind——which is part of the overall Mind of God——for his soul's learning, not by anything without.* The voice went silent, the spear became still.

"It speaks to you indeed," said Salah al-Din, eyeing the spear in my hand. Obviously, he had seen or heard the thing vibrating.

The laughter from the room next door died down and the sound was replaced by the soft, muffled voices of the women conversing among themselves in their native Arabic in what seemed to be casual conversation. I smiled at the sound. It was sweet and natural, even though I could not hear precisely what was being said, let alone understand too much of it even if I could.

"I bring you to this room because none of my men would dare follow me, us, here," Salah al-Din said, in a hushed whisper, obviously having taken note of my awareness of the women in the next room.

I looked into the Sultan's eyes. *Rashin would*, I thought, but did not speak it.

He then looked again at the Spear of Longinus in my hand, then to the King's Sword hilt rising above and behind my right shoulder. His hand then moved to his side, pushed the folds of his dark robe back and came to rest on the jewel encrusted hilt of his own weapon; a bare-bladed, gleaming scimitar fit for a king or a Sultan as the case may be. "I am a much more skilled fighter than you, Masoud," he began, "but no doubt you could kill me where I stand with those weapons of yours and the power that you wield through them," he said softly, the corners of his mouth tugging up into a grin.

"You know that is not why I am here," I replied. I am here at your request, though I cannot fathom what your desire to see me is regarding."

His grin faded and his features softened into a look of contemplation and thoughtfulness. He stroked his beard for a moment. "We are not that different, you and I. Our beliefs are not that far apart, that is to say," he declared. "Allah and Jesus' God is One God, the only God. They are the same. We Muslims have the same forefathers as you Christians and the Jews."

"But Jesus is not your Savior," I stated observationally.

"Is He truly *yours?*" he asked rhetorically. "Or do you *see* more, understand more now, Masoud? Muslims do not believe one is born in 'original sin', as Christians call it. So, there's no need for us to have the type of *Savior* you hold in Jesus. Besides, no one person——claimed to be a Son of God or not——can take away another's sins. Still, as I say, we are not that dissimilar, you and I." He turned then and stepped to a nearby table with two chairs near it. On the table sat a bronze, lit oil lamp and an ornately decorated, gold tea set. He lifted the pot by its single, angled, extended handle and poured the dark contents into two small gold sipping cups. "You English like tea, yes?" he asked as he turned back with the two cups holding out one of them for me. I had no time to respond, let alone tell him I take mine with cream. Hesitantly, I took the small cup he offered. I allowed Salah al-Din to sip from his cup first. I did this out of a sense of decorum, although the thought flashed into my mind that the Sultan might be insulted by this, thinking I was fearful of being poisoned.

But he said nothing. He held his cup to his lips and sipped the tea therein with a slurping noise that indicated his pleasure with the act and ritual of partaking in tea. I followed suit.

The liquid was dark and bitter. It was all I could do to keep my face impassive. I certainly did not wish to offend the Sultan, but his tea was horrid. The taste in my mouth was so foul that it was all I could do to swallow. A stinging tear watered my eye with swallowing the rank substance, giving away my distaste for the stuff.

Salah al-Din laughed heartily. "It does not quite meet with your English sensibilities?" he observed.

"I...uh, no, sire," I stammered, trying to speak through the fetid taste still in my mouth. *No one makes tea with the art of an Englishman*, I thought.

Salah al-Din fell silent for a time, savoring the tea from his cup and once again became contemplative. "As I was saying, we have many similarities," he said after a time, resuming his former line of conversation. "There is much within our Five Pillars that is quite similar to your Christian code."

"Five Pillars?" I asked, unsure of what he was talking about.

"To be truthful and to be sure, they are an oversimplification of a Muslim's practice of Islam, but they do serve to aid one in his practice and for the outsider to understand," he stated as a matter of fact as he moved back to the table and poured himself more tea. "They are the five basic tenets of practice that a Muslim must adhere to and live by: Declaring our faith or bearing witness daily, Salaat or daily prayer, fasting, charitable giving and service to others even if it is just in the form and of a simple smile," he said turning back to me and grinning, his eyes twinkling in friendship. "And of course, pilgrimage——in our case to Mecca," he continued. "As I said, these things oversimplify our belief or practice, but they are a good start and essential. And, surely you see by these that we have similarities, yes?"

"Yet, we war," I replied.

"Indeed we do, though it is not by our will," said Salah al-Din. "It is in our defense that we war."

"I could beg to differ. But, I've come to know that the whole of this war is pointless; the death, the destruction," I said. "It's foolish at best, especially knowing we serve the same God, the One God, call him what you will."

"Wise words, Masoud," replied Salah al-Din.

"Indeed," I said. A silence then fell between us for a time. I began to waver in my decision to be there. In fact, it seemed that we were skirting the issue of why I was there. "With respect, you did not summon me here to teach me the tenets of Islam or debate the merits of the war," I finally said, the slight edge of impatience slipping into my voice. "If you please."

"As you wish," he replied graciously. He drank from his cup of tea, throwing back the remainder of the second cup with vigor. He placed the cup back on the table and stepped up to me, his face turning gravely serious. He stopped so close to my face that I could feel his breath on my cheek and smell the bitter herbs from the tea thereon. "You have heard tell of the Rood, yes?" he asked in a hushed whisper that connoted a secretive agenda.

"The Rood. Do you speak of the wood from the very cross that the Christ was hanged on?" I asked.

"The very same," he answered, as he took a step back to a more respectable distance. Still keeping his voice in a hushed tone, he continued. "It is said that this Rood contains power much as your spear and sword."

I wanted to point out to him that I was coming to fully understand that these items contained no power in and of themselves. I refrained from doing so, however. "So it is said," I replied, wondering where this line of discussion was headed.

"We are in possession of the Rood," Salah al-Din declared.

I was not completely surprised by the Sultan's claim. They had initially possessed the Spear of Longinus before I came to have it. Rumor had also stated that they possessed the Rood. But questions did begin to enter my mind as to how they could have come by the Rood, and the Great Spear for that matter.

"We do not possess the entire cross, mind you. But we do have the cross section. It was apparently cut into pieces at one point..." Salah al-Din said.

At his last words, a sudden flash of heat wafted over my entire body. My head and face felt flush and I felt as if I would faint. An image impinged itself on my mind. I was looking out through the eyes of Centurion Longinus again, many centuries past. There were others with me/Longinus, a woman, an old man and a large red-haired Celt. I knew them all. Or, I had known them in that life: Irena, my love. Her name came to my mind. So, too, did the old man's and the Celt's; Jacobi and Dosameenor, respectively. But it was where we were and what we were doing that was the most interesting in this...vision. We were in the back of a covered wagon on top of the wagon's load; wood——the rood. We had a saw in hand and were cutting the Rood into sections, thirteen, to be exact...

"Masoud?" came the Sultan's voice, yanking me back to the present. The vision faded and I was once again before Salah al-Din in mind and body. "Masoud, are you ill?"

"No, no. It's just that...nothing. I am fine. Pray continue," I said.

"Yes, as you wish. We managed to fasten the pieces we have back together and it is definitely the cross section of the Rood. *His* blood, your Christ's blood stains the end pieces near where the nail holes remain even now. It is where His hands were...secured," the Sultan said, clearly trying to be respectfully delicate in his description.

"How do you know it is *the* Rood?" I asked. "How do you know that it is *His* blood? Perhaps it is a cross piece used in a crucifixion. But it could be anyone's blood, if that is indeed what it is."

"The same way we knew the spear you now carry was the one that pierced the Prophet Jesus' side; its powers were unleashed by one of our own," he continued. "No ordinary cross or spear would have performed thusly. Though, in the case of the Spear of Longinus, no one demonstrated its powers like you."

I pondered, mulled over, really, what the Sultan was saying and implying. "You say one of your own unleashed power from this Rood?"

"Indeed."

"Was it Rashin, by chance?" I asked, already knowing the answer.

"The very one. It was also he who was able to draw some of the spear's power out, though that display was not very impressive. However, what he did with the Rood was most fortuitous as to its potential use for us," Salah al-Din explained.

"Perhaps it's more that Rashin is a powerful individual. Or, perhaps he simply knows how to wield the Power of the One regardless of the instrument," I replied. I cringed from the very core of my being at the thought of Rashin wielding this power. I withdrew deep into my own thoughts. "The power of the One acts only by its own Law and may be executed for evil purposes. The power knows only to respond by the individual's intention," I said under my breath, deep in thought. But, apparently I did not say it far enough under my breath.

"One man's *evil* is another man's deliverance," replied Salah al-Din. "Or so I have observed. Given that, is there any true evil outside of what we rain down upon each other, what we ourselves create? And, if there is only the One Power, as you say, then there is no good or evil to It. It simply Is, is it not?"

"Yes, but do you really believe that?"

"Allah is all there is, and there is none greater. *That* is what I believe," he answered cryptically, smiling, smirking, as the words came out of his mouth.

"But your very words clarify my point: Rashin will use the Rood for the purpose of destroying us..."

"As you would use the power of the Spear and Sword to destroy *us!*" he retorted in a sudden burst of anger and impatience. "So you see, Masoud, in that sense, at least, we have a stalemate." His words hung in the air a time. "Masoud," he continued after a moment more calmly, "I believe we will eventually win this conflict and drive you all back to your homes, Allah willing. And I will accomplish this by intelligent use of my army and by superior battle strategies. I am merciful. I will hold none. Those who wish to stay may do so and even continue to worship as they see fit," the Sultan stated calmly, superciliously.

"How generous of you. But, you're a bit premature, are you not?" I asked, angered by his arrogance.

"I think not."

"Still, you would not be telling me about the Rood unless you feared the Spear and Sword and the Power..."

"The Power you wield through those instruments and the Power we wield through the Rood will destroy each side proportionally. And, then I would still win. Why succumb to all the unnecessary death only to have the same result in the end?"

"You don't know how it will end," I replied, lamely.

"Have it your way, Masoud. But do you not see my point; regardless of the final outcome, there will be mutual loss, and hence unnecessary destruction in the meantime, do you not agree?!" he said, his voice rising again with anger.

"I see your point," I finally conceded. The silence that followed lingered for a few moments. "I agree not to use the Power for such ends."

"As do I," he said, calmness once again pervading his voice.

A silence lingered in the air again. Silence all around, for it was then that I noticed the women's voices had gone silent in the next room. Disappointment seeped into my being. "May I return now to my encampment?" I asked after a time.

He walked over to me. "Yes, Masoud," he said and then placed his right hand on my shoulder. "I thank you for your wisdom in this. Your wisdom is rising. For that and other reasons you are showing the signs of becoming a great leader."

I stood in silence, not sure whether I should make a response to the compliment, but realizing it would be bad form not to. I inclined my head in a gesture of acknowledgement. He released my shoulder and stepped toward the doorway that we had come through. "If you will wait here, I will send Alhasan back for you. Please help yourself to some more tea," he said looking back at me with a wry smile.

I felt myself smiling as well. Salah al-Din turned and was nearly out the entrance of the small chamber. "You said, Sultan, that Rashin had not proven to you adequately that he could use the power of the Rood," I heard myself blurting out as the thought came in my head. "That is, you didn't actually mention the Rood back in your main receiving chamber, but it is what you were referring to when you spoke to him earlier was it not?"

Salah al-Din stopped in the entryway and turned back to face me. "Sometimes, Masoud, one must tell a subordinate that he is not meeting expectations in order to have him exceed them."

"That can work both ways, sire. Rashin is one to keep his own secrets. Me thinks that he could yield more power than he's showing you. He is probably keeping it hidden for his own nefarious purposes. I would bet on it," I said.

The Sultan smiled. "As a Muslim, I do not gamble. But if I did, I would bet so as well. You speak with such surety, as if you know him, Masoud."

I thought for moment as to how to answer. "I know the spirit of the man," I said vaguely. "He would love to possess this spear and sword I carry as well, I know that to be the truth."

"No doubt," he replied.

"Beware of him, sire, is all that I am conveying to you," I said.

"Thank you, Masoud. Alhasan will be with you shortly," he said. He then turned and left the chamber. I was left suddenly feeling quite alone; just myself, two weapons and bitter tea.

SIXTEEN

I remained in the small room or chamber for what seemed like an hour. I even tried some more of the tea which did not taste any better than it had the first time. Twice I went to the entry doorway of the chamber and looked out and down in both directions of the tent's hallway. There was no sign of anyone. The thought crossed my mind that perhaps I should just leave, not wait for Alhasan or anyone else. But then again, that would probably be among the more unintelligent things I could have done. A lone crusader with spear and sword would not exactly be tolerated walking through a Muslim military camp. Finally, I went over to one of the chairs near the tea table and sat, determined to simply wait for Alhasan. The room was quiet and the women's voices from the adjacent room were still silent. I wondered if they were there, perhaps sleeping, or if they had moved to another room altogether.

The silence dragged on. "I beg pardon," said a whispered voice, a whispered female voice, in English but with a heavy Arabic accent. The voice came from the other side of the tent wall, from within the room where the women had been. She was close to the wall, close to me by the sound of it, as the wall that the tea table rested near was the joining wall of the women's room.

Though it was but a whisper it startled me, so unexpected it was. *Is she speaking to me?* I wondered.

"Master Masoud?" she asked as if in answer to my thought.

I leaned toward the tent wall, toward the sound of her voice. "I am Masoud, yes. Or, rather that is what your people have chosen to call me," I said in a conspiratorial whisper. My words were met with silence. The quietude dragged to a point where I thought perhaps she had gone. "Are your still there?" I asked.

"Yes," she replied timidly. "I heard you speaking with the Sultan and recognized your voice."

Confusion crept into my mind. "You recognized my voice?" I asked.

"You...you came to my aid," she replied.

I was stunned by her answer. I could not fathom when I might have come to the aid of a woman in this campaign, much less to the aid of a Muslim woman. I was speechless.

"You do not remember," she stated with a tinge of disappointment.

"You must be mistaking me for another," I said.

"No," she insisted, her voice now becoming more assertive in tone. "I inquired as to your name after the...incident. And, as I said, I recognized your voice a few moments ago." She paused briefly before continuing. "Several of your own men were...how do you say in English...raping me, I believe is how it is said. You stopped them, killed one, maybe."

Of course. It came flooding back to my memory then. She was not mistaking me for another. We, Sir James and Henry and I, had still been in the Muslim camp, prisoners, when our soldiers and crusaders had attacked. During the course of that battle, a woman had been attacked by my own fellow crusaders. I had been appalled and intervened on the woman's behalf, fighting my own men. In the present moment, the woman's lavender eyes were all I remembered of her. "I remember what you speak of," I said.

"I am pleased that you remember and I thank you most sincerely for your bravery. You risked much in doing what you did," she said.

"The acts of those men were not befitting the honor and principles of our beliefs," I replied. "I could not let them get away with what they were doing to you."

"Much of your own behavior seems to be setting the example for all to see.

And follow," she said. "Even my Uncle respects you enough to speak to you privately, negotiate with you, that much is clear."

"Your Uncle?" I asked, surmising the answer, but surprised nonetheless.

"Sultan Salah al-Din, of course," she said nearly laughing. "Who did you think I was speaking of?"

"I thought...that is, I mean...I thought..."

"...That I was one of his wives?" She now laughed genuinely. It was a lilting, intoxicating sound. "You must have heard us, the women, in here when first you came in, yes?"

"Yes. That is true."

"I understand, then, how you might have thought what you thought," she replied.

A long pause of silence engulfed us then, as if we had run out of things to say. It had been a long time since I had been in the presence of a woman, any woman, let alone spoken to one. I wanted to see her face, look into those lavender eyes. I wanted to rent asunder the cloth and canvas wall of the tent that separated us. It was such a flimsy barrier really, but it might as well have been a wall of brick and iron, so separated were we by culture, by creed. I then noticed something on the wall, in the lamp's shadow. It was a closed flap near the edge of the table. The flap was square——approximately a foot-and-a-half square——and was held closed by a tie at its top. A window of sorts is what it appeared to be; a window to look into the adjacent room. Slowly, I reached out and pulled the tie loose. The flap, held secure at its bottom, flopped open, revealing the next room. A woman's face slowly appeared in the window's opening. I could see her clearly even in the lamp and candle light of the room. Though I had laid eyes on this woman once before, this was the first time I was actually seeing her, taking in her appearance. Her cheek bones were lovely and high and tapered down to her mouth——the corners of which rose slightly in a perpetual, warming smile——in perfect symmetry with the rest of her face. Although she wore a light-blue head wrap, black ringlets of her hair fell from beneath, resting on the medium-dark brown skin of her forehead. The eyes had an ever-so-slight almond shape to them and flowed gently to her slender, delicate nose, simply adding to the perfect proportion of her face. And, the shining lavender color of those eyes was stunning, as if the light of a-thousand light-purple stars twinkled therein; the priceless capstone on what was, in my opinion, the most perfect female face. She was beyond beautiful. I was instantly enamored. "What is your name?" I asked, near breathlessness.

"Najeeba. My name is Najeeba," she said shyly.

"Najeeba," I repeated, savoring the sound of it and the way it rolled off my tongue. "And what does it mean?"

"It means, 'Of Noble Birth,'" she declared.

"Apropos, given that you are the Sultan's niece," I said, suddenly becoming aware of the fact that I was grinning from ear to ear. I became self-conscious, even embarrassed by my own boyish giddiness. Yes, she was immensely beautiful, *but how could I be so taken by this creature in such short order?* I wondered. I stared deeper into her eyes, searching for...what, I was not sure.

"Many pardons, Sir Masoud! A thousand pardons for my delay!" Alhasan yelled as he came bounding into the room.

I jumped to my feet, toppling the chair I was sitting in. My thighs bumped the table violently as I stood, toppling the carafe of tea as well, spilling the dark contents onto the table, and nearly knocking over the lamp that was there too. I had been so startled that I found the King's Sword in my hand——I had obviously instinctively pulled it out with the sudden appearance of Alhasan, perceiving a possible threat in the moment——as well as the Great Spear in the other. "Damn you, Alhasan! Have you no manners?!"

"A thousand pardons, Sir Masoud! I was only just informed to retrieve you, you see! Please forgive me," he pleaded.

I looked over to the window. Najeeba's lovely face was gone. I leaned over the table and poked my head through the square opening in the tent wall. Peering into the next room I saw nothing but richly appointed throw cushions and lit candles. The room was devoid of anyone.

"Come, Sir Masoud. We must be off and away," said Alhasan.

"Very well," I said with unbridled disappointment.

SEVENTEEN

The day's sun was near gone as the mists enshrouded the land and the stones: the great monoliths of my people's bygone time. My soul knew these rock beasts as if they were of my own flesh, my life's blood, my very spirit, for they were. Many generations had passed since the carving and placing of these magnificent entities of the ages. They were alive, centerpieces in the vortex of natural and Infinite powers. I often came here when I was vexed or perplexed, when I was grappling with an issue of great import or of grand significance to the schemes and dreams of men. But I had come here many a time simply for the sake of my own spirit as well. Indeed, I had even been brought back from the dead once here during my life as a Roman Centurion, and had helped to shape and build the place many lifetimes before that. Now, I was in the light of a full moon, leaning with my backside against what remained of the center altar piece, the same place upon which I, the centurion, with the aid of the sacred spear, had been recalled from the Otherside.

A cowl covered the top my head and my eyes were cast down in contemplation. A gentle hand touched my face, stroking my left cheek lovingly. "Myrriddin," said Igraines.

I warmed instantly to her touch and her sweet voice. I brought my gaze upon her lovely face and looked into Igraines eyes, now turned the color of brilliant lavender.

"Myrriddin, my dearest," she said staring back at me.

I saw in those eyes Irena too, the persona of Igraines' soul I had known as Longinus. And the lavender color of her eyes now reflected yet another guise of Igraines soul; Najeeba. Such were the thoughts of my spirit in the present vision, dream, soul experience, whatever one wishes to call it.

"What vexes thee?" she asked soothingly.

"You have always known the ways of my spirit, have you not, my love," I stated.

"Always," she replied. "But it's not difficult to know something troubles you when you left the dinner so abruptly, almost angrily. Please, Myrriddin, what is it? Is it Arturius? His men?"

"Aye. 'Tis both, Igraines. They know not what they are about to spark. They follow an irrational order from the Church, to which they usually give only half attention, and are bent on beginning a legacy of death and persecution," I said.

"They are good and true men, Myrriddin. You judge them too harshly," reprimanded Igraines. "Besides, you have said that what they begin here will not come to fruition for many years."

"For many centuries will the pain of what they seek to do inflict itself upon the people of that which they call the Holy Land," I stated, rising in frustration and walking a few feet away before turning back to face her. "It will end with bitter divisions between people and their faiths for millennia to come. I have seen it."

"The men wish only to wrest the Holy relics from the Moors and make passage for Christian pilgrims to the region safe," she said.

"And would that be all it remained," I replied. "But it will not. Their desire for the *Holy relics* will turn into lust for power and the absurd assertion that the church's way is the only way to God and they will end in attempting to destroy the others' faith just as they've attempted to destroy our Old Ways."

"Arturius and his men will not do that! They have sworn an oath by your command and initiation to uphold all that is true and decent and honorable," she said defensively. "What you suggest is..."

"It is not Arturius' men that will perform what I speak of," I said. "But it will be part of the legacy they help to create. Many of those who come long after them will pervert the original purpose of the undertaking to come. Especially when the *Last Prophet* is come to earth near three centuries from now by the Christian calendar, I have seen this as well. He will inspire thousands to attempt the destruction of Christendom in part because of what is about to begin here."

"It cannot be so, Myrriddin. What kind of man, prophet or no, would do such a thing?!" she said.

I, Myrriddin, did not answer her, but instead walked to one of the nearby standing stones touching my palm to it. The warmth of the day's sun was still emanating from the thing. Images entered my mind, images of holy wars and crusaders and men that I, Masoud knew. And, I saw myself, my Masoud self holding the spear in the court of Salah al-Din. The image suddenly vanished and I was Myrriddin once again, yanking my hand away from the standing stone as if it were hot coal.

"What is it Myrriddin?" asked Igraines suddenly at my side. "I know you see things when you touch these stones. What was it?"

"It was a future self. In many centuries to come, I will be in the midst of all of which I speak," I, Myrriddin replied.

ﻟﺪ   ﻟﺪ   ﻟﺪ

I awoke to find a half-naked, dirt-streaked, very lucid Henry sitting on his sleeping pallet staring oddly at me. "You were speaking in your sleep. Kept me awake, ya bloody bastard. And, who on God's earth is Igraines?" he asked, a look of confusion creasing his brow. "I feel as though I know the name, but can't place it."

"It is a lengthy story, my friend. But, you're looking well, if not a bit dirty," I said, genuinely surprised to see him here in our tent shelter. It was then that I heard the noises of the camp outside. "What is the time?" I asked, noticing daylight coming in through the tent's seams.

"Late afternoon. You've been asleep all day," he said.

"All day?" I asked in wonderment, rhetorically. My thoughts turned to Najeeba and then to the dream or vision I had just awakened from. It was clear that my mind was seeing Najeeba and Igraines and Irena as one in the same. Or, perhaps my mind was correlating the women as a representation of my desire for a female companion. Yet, I knew better. It was much deeper than that. I felt it in my soul.

"Well I'm off," declared Henry as he stood and began dressing, throwing his filth encrusted outer tunic over his bare torso. The stench of his soiled clothing moving through the air of the cramped tent's interior wafted toward me. I nearly gagged from it.

"To where?" I asked, trying to avoid the urge to directly point out his lack of personal hygiene. "You haven't told me where you've been, how you've been. That is, the last time I saw you..."

"You should not have gone there, to the den, I mean," he interrupted.

"I was concerned, Henry. I wanted to help you."

"Hmph," was his cryptic reply.

"But you look well! Rested," I offered, trying to change the subject of the den, trying to stay focused on the positive.

"I occasionally get a good night's rest. Or day's rest, as it is sometimes," he replied. "Except when my bunkmate talks in his sleep."

He began to leave. "Where are you going?" I asked.

"Where do you suppose I'm going?!"

Disappointment crept into my being. "Back to the den," I stated, hoping he would deny it, even if the denial was false.

"Aye. My home away from home," he laughed sardonically.

"But what about your duties here? Surely, you've not leave to..."

"I do not need a 'by-your-leave' from you, Sir Liam Mason, or Sir Masoud, or whatever in the Devil's hell they're callin' you these days!" Henry said tersely, venomously. His sudden burst of anger was palpable and unexpected. "But, yes, I *have* been given leave by higher-ups to tend to my...ailments." He began to limp toward the tent's entrance. "You, on the other hand, are a grand knight now. I suggest you get off your arse and answer to the day before the day is done." With that he left, leaving me in contemplation as to how a bright glimmer of hope for my friend could so instantly turn into the anguished heaviness of defeat.

Henry was gone no more than five minutes when I decided to put him out of my mind for the present and move through the rest of the day. His banishment from my thoughts was not to be, however. My dear friend was stricken with the opiate crave and I, for all the *Power* of the One, was powerless to do anything to help him directly. But that was just the point; we all have this Power coursing through us, because It is us. And as such, we all have the choice, the free will to do with It as we will, for better or worse. This realization was sinking in more and more, day by day, as I continued on this strange odyssey which began with Henry's apparent trip back from the dead, the first time I came into contact with the Spear of Longinus. At least, it had been the first time coming into contact with it in this life. But then it struck me; what I could do for my friend in the present moment was to give him my thoughts and prayers of healing; to hold him in my mind as the perfect, whole being I knew him to be, regardless of the temporary, outward appearance. I had never thought along these lines before. Oh, I had prayed a beseeching prayer to God for whatever reason on many an occasion. I had always prayed the type of prayer that I was taught by the Church; a manner of prayer in which one speaks to God in a pleading fashion, hoping beyond hope that He may see fit to answer. Of course, He may not see fit to answer. Yet, I was coming to an inner realization that the power of a prayer is not exterior to the one praying, but in the intent and thought on the interior of his mind, and also manifested by the degree of feeling and conviction at the level of his heart, his soul. In other words, the Power of a prayer is to *Know*, unwaveringly, that the one who is *ill* is actually in a condition of appearances and not in a natural state of being. To *Know* this is to deny the condition its hold on any kind of reality. Thus, I decided to pray from right where I sat, to treat Henry in mind, to treat my friend and the condition he was presently caught up in, and have the *Knowingness* that the condition was not Henry, that Henry was but the jovial, healthy person I had known these many years. Taking a deep breath I simply let the words come of their own accord. "I know there is but One Power," I began, "One Source for all things, for any and all healing, and that this Source is All there is. Since this Source is all there is, I am an aspect of It, and the Power thereof flows effortlessly through me now and always, and through every other person on this earth because it is us, It is what we are. The Power of this Source is here now and always in the form of abundance and perfect health, and flows through me now and through Henry

Tobiason Andrews. He is perfect in health and perfect in mind. He has released the crutch of the opiate and is hale and whole. I see this now and know it to be so! I am grateful for this sight, for the knowledge and I let go of it knowing that it is done! So be it! In the name of the Christ, Amen!" I drifted in thought for a time, having induced through the prayer, a kind of trance state in myself. I then felt myself float out of my body, out of the tent and to a location not all that far away. I did not travel through time as with my other visions, but stayed present in time and found myself at the side of my friend, Henry as he continued his walk toward the den. He was alone, utterly alone, walking with his head cast down as if traversing the terrain in shame.

He stopped briefly and looked directly at me, or rather, where my form might be if my body had actually been there. He looked quizzically at me. "Liam?" he said, sensing my presence and suddenly spinning around, looking for me but not seeing me. He stopped then and simply looked straight forward in the direction he had been walking in. "You're quite the magician now are ye not?" he said to the air. "Either that or I'm goin' mad," he said under his breath.

"Know yourself, Henry. You are whole and hale," I said. Though he did not actually hear me, Henry closed his eyes and took a deep breath. He opened his eyes as he let the breath out and looked at the sky. A small flock of doves flew overhead. He watched the birds' flight and smiled, apparently savoring the moment and perchance life itself. Perhaps he had heard me after all. But the moment quickly passed and without saying another word, he walked on. It was a start, anyway.

I opened my eyes and found myself back in the tent. *That was interesting*, I thought to myself. I had been next to Henry in spirit just a moment ago. It had certainly been a present time journey of my spirit and not simply a travelling vision pulled up from the memory of my soul. I thought of the prayer I had spoken and laughed at myself for delivering the last part about the Christ. It had been a different kind of prayer than I'd ever spoken, but some habits fail to fall away. The thought then struck that I should save this prayer in my mind and recite it often for my friend, as often as needed.

The spear caught my eye and I looked at the thing standing upright——blade up and butt on the ground——against the tent's wall next to my sleeping pallet, the Great Sword of Arthur in its makeshift scabbard standing hilt-up next to it. Something grabbed my sense of intuition: a message was being conveyed to me. Now it was my turn to feel as though an unseen presence was with me attempting to tell me...what? But the presence was not in the form of a human spirit. The intuitive tingle, if you will, I was receiving was coming through the spear and sword. To my surprise, however, neither spear nor sword was aglow with warning or message as in the past. Yet, I suddenly and inexplicably knew I was needed elsewhere immediately. I threw on my tunic, grabbed the Great Spear and the King's Sword and left the tent.

EIGHTEEN

I followed my footsteps, not knowing exactly where I was going, only knowing that I must get there as soon as possible.

"Now! Get your asses into place!" yelled a commander with a Franc accent.

I looked in the direction of the voice and saw Christian soldiers scrambling to form up into ranks of ten, weapons at the ready, their commander, Laffite, barking orders and threats to make the soldiers fall into their proper lines of presentation. I made my way to them and stopped near Laffite and the men. Laffite looked at me and smiled, his gapped tooth grin exhibiting a strange mixture of contempt and respect.

"Ah...Sir Mason...forgive me, Sir Masoud," he said. "Come to join us, or are we now beneath your dignity?" he said.

I could not tell whether he was serious or being a jester. His tone was intense but not sarcastic and that grin stayed cemented on his face. I looked at the lines of men forming and knew the urgency I was feeling a moment ago had something to do with this. "What is happening, Lafitte?" I asked, choosing to ignore his taunt.

"We storm the citadel!" he proclaimed with a dramatic flair, slurring his words in the process.

"What citadel?" I asked.

"Jerusalem herself, sire!" he replied. It was then I noticed his bloodshot eyes and smelled the reek of inferior, self-made liquor on his breath. He was drunk.

"By whose order do you call the formations?" I demanded.

"Mine, Liam," said General Blackthorn from behind us. I turned and saw the general on a grand white horse trotting up to the formations. "Well, truth be told, King Richard himself has given it. Glad to see you here, lad. And your weapons," he added indicating the spear and sword I held.

Four other officers on horses of their own——one was Sir James, another was a lower ranking captain whom I had seen only in passing, and two others; lieutenants whom I had never seen before——accompanied the general, reined in their mounts next to Sir Blackthorn. The captain had an extra horse in tow. This mount was saddled, but rider-less. Presumably, it was for Lafitte. The captain and lieutenants stared at me and my weapons or instruments, as I preferred to call the Great Spear and the King's Sword.

Sir James grinned, apparently amused at the men's fascination with me. "Yes, gentlemen. It is he, Sir Liam Arthur Mason, also dubbed Sir Masoud, keeper of the Spear of Longinus and guardian of the King's Sword, the sword of King Arthur himself," exclaimed Sir James. "He has performed great feats of healing and miracles with these items, and will surely lead us to victory in our endeavor!"

I made to speak, to tell these officers that the commander exaggerates and that I am no leader of men; keeper and guardian of the Spear and Sword, perhaps, but not the leader that the commander professes me to be. I also wanted to tell them of my pact with Salah al-Din to not use the instruments in such manner. But I would not betray that agreement.

"Sire," began the captain holding the reins of the riderless horse. He was a fair-skinned, red-haired and red-bearded man who reminded me greatly of Henry. "Sire," he said again in a deep voice by way of addressing me, "your mount." He held out the reins of the horse, a magnificent beast of a deep brown and black, toward me. Apparently, the beast was not for Lafitte after all.

"Magnificent, is she not?!" exclaimed General Blackthorn with boyish excitement, nodding toward the horse. "I obtained her in Spain, I did. Please accept her as my gift to you. Her name is Macha."

My heart raced. I knew the name. Somehow, I knew the name. I approached the animal and looked into her eyes. Within those dark windows I saw and sensed an old friend and familiarity. It seemed as though her spirit was smiling at me. I was at a loss to explain it, but had learned not to question these things. *Just accept it as so,* I thought. And so I did, both the gift of an *old friend* and the gift from my superior officer. "Thank you, General, for such a lavish gift. I hardly feel worthy," I said.

"Nonsense! Can't have our Great Guardian and Knight without a mount," Blackthorn said.

"Come, Liam," said Sir James, "Mount. We must be off."

"We proceed to Jerusalem?" I asked.

"We do," he replied.

"But I thought our people were gaining much ground in her retaking?" I asked, confused. Part of the reason our particular regiment was stuck out in the open regions of this land was to keep Salah al-Din's men harassed, thus allowing the bulk of our crusader army to concentrate on obtaining the Holy City once again. Even Salah al-Din himself had come out from the City and camped to aide in fending us off.

"They, we, are, lad. But the campaign falters, they need our reinforcements," replied the general.

"Where is your Arab friend?" asked Sir James.

"Alhasan?"

"Aye."

I looked around as if I half expected Alhasan to appear on cue. Of course, he did not. "I know not," I said, "I have not seen him since early this morning."

"We need him as an interpreter. He is your servant now, is he not? I heard him speak as much," said Sir James.

"Yes, that is, he has said as much as you say."

"Take your leave and find him then rejoin us here. We march within the hour," ordered the general. "God willing, we join our men near the Holy City tonight under cover of darkness. We attack the enemy within by dawn. Go, lad."

With that, the red-haired captain tossed the reins of Macha to me. I mounted the fine horse and nodded my thanks to the captain. "Sir Blackthorn," I began, turning my attention back to the senior-most officer present. "Might I retrieve my friend Henry as well, sir? Will we not be needing all able-bodied men?"

But it was Sir James who answered in the general's stead. "Do not worry about Henry, Liam. The men at the den, at least ours, are being rounded up now, even as we speak."

That sounded more ominous than I wanted to admit. "You will do them no harm?" I asked.

"They will be fine, just find Alhasan," said Sir James, as he directed his horse toward the men still stumbling to assembly.

"'Tis more than I can say for the men of the enemy who also occupy that den of iniquity," said the general somewhat maliciously. "Mustn't let our plans be made known, eh, lad?"

These men, Sir James and Sir Blackthorn, seemed to be a contradiction. On the one hand they were Templar Knights who work with our Islamic brethren of the Hashishim Order for the betterment of all, or so they say. Yet, on the other hand, they were fierce warriors willing to spill that same blood in the name of Christianity. And, on the other side were the likes of Hakim who displayed this same apparent duality. *All in the proper context,* came the thought in my head, jarring me from my judgmental musings of the men. The thought seemed to come from deep within my own being, from the part of me I now knew to be eternal, where ultimate Truth and Knowledge are one and the same and completely accessible. Although I had only recently begun to truly pay attention to this aspect of myself, I was quickly coming to know and accept that it was just that; My Self—my True Self. The rapidity with which this understanding was impinging itself upon my mind I attributed to the various experiences, knowledge and information from my soul's past which had been coming to the forefront of my awareness these past few days with ever increasing speed.

"Off with ya, lad," said the general with urgency.

I said nothing more, but turned my attention to the horse beneath me. Macha felt sturdy and energetic as she pranced about for a moment. And, she felt perfectly natural beneath me. I spurred her gently forward and back to the tent in search of Alhasan.

The trip back was quick and revealed a camp in mid-disassembly; tents and shelters were coming down and being made ready for transport. Men were rapidly running here and there attending to the duties one has when breaking camp.

It was interesting how rapidly I had become accustomed to our community of tents. I nearly lost my way because so many of the temporary dwellings were already gone and thus my points of reference as to the exact location of my own dwelling were gone with them. That, and the fact that the tent I had been sleeping in only a short time ago was already collapsed. Alhasan stood from his labors in folding our shelter at my approach.

His eyes grew wide at the sight of Macha and I. "Ah, Master Masoud!" he exclaimed. "Truly befitting of one such as yourself! You appear as royalty, a Sultan in your own right!"

"Thank you, Alhasan. I had wondered where you had gotten to. Woke up not long ago and you were gone," I said as I dismounted and began helping my friend to finish with the folding of our tent.

At that moment two soldiers approached us with a supply wagon. "We'll take that for you, sir," said one of them, a child-faced lad.

I looked from the first to the second and saw the mirror image of the first: identical twins. They were tall, nearly six foot each. But their pink, hairless, child-like faces belied a youth of not more than twelve I surmised. "What in God's name are two doing here?!" I asked. "You can't be more than twelve the both of you. You should be home taking care of a farm or your parents, not out here in this..."

"Sir, our mother's dead by birthing a stilled baby sister and our father ran off," said the first in the cracking voice of a boy turning man, which merely served to confirm my guess at their age.

"Went mad, he did. Blamed us for mum's death and the baby's too for that," added the second, in the near same crackling voice, almost speaking over the first.

"Yes, called us 'devil's spawn,'" said the first on the heels of his brother's words, "said we were not his, never believed we were his."

"Yes, and hated our mother for a long time, claimed she had fornicated with half the village and we were the curse for it," said the second.

"But then when she became with child again he said he knew it was his, and he was happy for a time," the first continued.

"Until the birthing time when she didn't live nor the little one," the second lad said.

My head started to spin trying to keep up with the two.

The second suddenly turned to his brother. "I would have liked a sister," he said.

"I as well," replied the first.

"All right, boys. Enough. I'm truly sorry for your losses on all fronts. But to come here?" I asked. "What are your names?"

"My given name is Cain," replied the first.

"And mine is Lucifer," replied the second.

"Of course," I offered, sardonically, looking to Alhasan. My friend seemed more amused than anything else.

"But I prefer Canter," said the first.

"And I prefer Luscious," said the second.

"So be it, Canter and Luscious. Here's our tent for the wagon. I helped the boys load the now folded shelter onto their wagon. "Thank you," I said.

"Our pleasure, sir," replied Canter.

"Yes, our pleasure," echoed Luscious. "'Tis an honor to serve the likes of you!"

With one in the front of the wagon and the other in the back, they pulled and pushed the thing to the next grouping of dismantled tents.

"Come," I said to Alhasan after a moment. I mounted Macha again and held my hand out to Alhasan for him to grasp so that he could jump up behind me.

"I could not possibly, Masoud!" he said.

I could not tell if he was afraid or did not want to seem disrespectful by riding with me.

"We do not have time for this," I stated flatly. "The general wants your services as an interpreter for our new venture, so jump up here or have us both at the whip's end."

"Your general would not dare to treat you so!" he said, appalled.

"It's a jest, Alhasan! Now get your ass up here, that's an order!" I barked.

He did as I bade, taking my extended hand and leaping onto Macha's back with surprising agility. We trotted off to join the others.

NINETEEN

The organized chaos of a moving army is tempered only by its slowness. On the other hand, perhaps it only seemed chaotic to the individual soldier making his way as a pinpoint in a sea of men. Sitting on horseback as I was, however, gave me a completely new perspective. I could see over the heads of the sea of men and thus the entire army arrayed before me——or behind me, depending on which way I looked. I was travelling in the middle of the marching crusader army. Dust choked our nostrils and stung the eyes. Darkness was falling, but we were determined to travel on into the night in order to make our destination. Alhasan still rode behind on me on Macha which garnered stares of disapproval from some of the men. A few of the stares turned to whisperings, a handful of which I happened to overhear during the course of our journey; idle rumors and gossip mainly. One had Alhasan and I as lovers, claiming that was where my true power came from; an *unholy coupling*, as they said it. Still another said that I was a spy for Salah al-Din and Alhasan was actually my contact posing as my servant. Ignorant fools. None of these men would dare say these things to my face, of course. No matter. They would all have the challenge of their lives before long, so let them have their entertainment even if it was at my expense.

"Agh!!" Alhasan suddenly exclaimed from behind me.

"What is it?" I asked, alarmed.

"A pox upon me, Masoud! I have forgotten to give you something," he said.

A moment later his hand reached around me and held a folded parchment in front of my face. "What is this?" I asked, taking the item from his hand.

"A message."

I recognized the seal on it as being from the Sultan. "From Salah al-Din?" I asked, suddenly feeling a sense of foreboding.

"Nay. From another in his midst, you see," he said with a curious blend of mirth and disapproval.

I broke the seal, unfolded the parchment and began to read the delicate lines of broken English. My sense of foreboding was quickly replaced by joy as I read.

Sir Masoud, I beg forgiveness at the boldness of my person in putting words forth to you, and for my poor use of your written English language. Writing to a man of your faith or any man is not something I have dared do in past. I beg forgiveness also for taking leave of your person so swiftly this past time of our meeting. Alhasan has known me many years, since I was but child, and has great affection and respect for my person. I had no cause to vanish in his presence. I thank you again for rescuing of my person from direness and for opportunity of meeting with you. I wish only that our meeting had been extended. Perhaps in future it will, though I know not how that be possible. I saw in your face a fondness and recognition of my soul. I too felt this for your person and know it is truth. I again beg forgiveness for my boldness, but could not let these words go unspoken to your person. If you choose, Alhasan will carry any reply to me. I bid you a fond farewell until we stand before one another once more.

Najeeba al-Din

My whole body trembled with delight. I read the words again. Afterward, a feeling I had only felt once before in my life suddenly washed over my entire being. Love. Oh, I had experienced many forms of love before, but only once before like this. I could have stepped off Macha and walked on the air. *But,* the thought interrupted from the so-called thinking part of my mind, *you don't even know this woman!* "Bullocks!" I heard myself say out loud. *You have known this woman before and many a time,* said the voice of my spirit, my soul. That was the truth of it! As she said herself, I indeed had a fondness and recognition of her soul! "Najeeba," I said softly.

"Speak not her name, Masoud!" Alhasan whispered from behind me. "Grave danger if she is found out. You should destroy her words now that you have seen them, for her sake and for yours, you see."

"You...care for her, yes?" I asked over my shoulder.

"She is as a sister to me. I wish her happiness," he replied.

"But you don't approve of her writing this to me," I said.

"As I said, it is dangerous," he replied. "But I would do anything she asked of me."

"Anything? Are you sure?"

No reply was forthcoming from my riding partner. We rode on in silence, the darkness of night folding in around us. No moonlight was there to guide us. The lunar disc had not yet risen. There was scant light for our march but we trudged on. Then we saw it; a line of light off in the distance. We were traversing the crest of a hillside when the line of light on the horizon came into view. "Jerusalem," someone whispered in awe.

"The Holy City," said another.

"God's City!" said still another.

A murmur of excitement flowed through the men. Ironically, though we had all been in this region for some time, most of us in the company had never laid eyes on the city herself. She was, after all, the whole reason we had come on the crusade in the first place. I felt caught up in the men's excitement. Briefly. Over these past months I had undergone a drastic change in my reason for being here, culminating in the events of the past few days and weeks. There were other lights as well, small groupings of lights dotted the landscape before us just in front of the line of light. We proceeded on, cautiously marching down the hill's embankment in the near darkness and onward toward the Holy City. The line of light we were seeing in the distance now rose before us, growing clearer and more distinct. It was a line of torches and firelight atop the city's walls and battlements, daring anyone to challenge her sanctity and protected perimeter. The small dotted groupings of light on the land were campfires. They were campfires from the crusader army that had been here for weeks already, no doubt. Darkness had completely descended when we reached the land not far from the wall of the City.

"Sir Masoud," said Sir James trotting up alongside of Macha, myself and

Alhasan. I suddenly found it curious as to why he was calling me by my Muslim name and not my Christian one of Mason. "We're going to set a camp here and blend in with the army that's already here. I'm assigning you a century of men. Do not light anymore campfires. We don't want Salah al-Din to know how many more men are here," he finished.

"I, you're raising me in rank?" I asked.

"Aye," he replied. "Actually, Blackthorn suggested it, with my whole-hearted agreement, lad. Ye've proved your mettle," he said with a large grin on his face.

"What I've proved doesn't amount to the leadership of men," I said, a little too forcefully.

His grin turned to the smile of an understanding father as he nudged his mount even closer. "Be not afraid, Liam. You can do anything you choose. Anything that you put your mind to," Sir James said with all sincerity. "All of the One Mind, right? Whatever you put it to, It will respond in like form. Besides, I've more men than I have leaders for. Yours is the Crescent Century and will flock under the banner of the green Crescent moon three-hundred yards to the north of us," he said, pointing off to his right.

I sat in rather stunned silence for a moment.

"Well commander?" said Sir James by way of addressing me. I stared at him, a-thousand responses rolling through my head. "But, the men I am to command; they are to flock to a crescent banner——a crescent being a Muslim symbol——and follow a commander that is now commonly known by the name of Masoud——also Muslim. Do you not see a conflict there?"

"No," Sir James stated flatly.

"I..."

"Just make it work, sir Masoud. I know you can and will." With that he yanked his mount's reins, turning the beast's neck around, and galloped away.

"Your commander has strange humor," Alhasan observed. "Or, perhaps he has a grand plan in his mind."

"Strange humor, is more the like," I replied.

"Still, you possess the Great Spear and the King's Sword! All will bow down to you," he said.

"I don't want anyone to bow down to me. But we shall see how this plays out." I trotted Macha gently in the direction that Sir James had indicated, scratching my growing beard in thought. Of course, as a Templar I no longer shaved, as per one of the rules. Some of these rules, however, I would not adhere to in private; not bathing and remaining dressed at all times, for instance. Absurd. We trotted for a few moments, avoiding others in the somewhat crowded immediate area. In the dim light of the few surrounding campfires I could see a white flag fluttering in the night breeze. It was now but a few yards away from us. In the center of this white flag was a dark green crescent shape.

"I see the flag there, Masoud," Alhasan said, echoing my thoughts.

"Yes, Alhasan. I see it too."

"Your men await!" Alhasan said with excitement.

My men, I thought. My stomach suddenly lurched. I did not want to *lead* anyone. *And what if they don't wish to be lead by me?* I looked at the spear in my right hand, standing upright, its heel in the stirrup of my right foot and my nervous fear began to flow from me. It was slowly replaced by an inner confidence. *I am them, they are me. I lead myself by leading them. We are one body, one mind. One.*

"Sir Masoud!" Alhasan said loudly in my ear, breaking my transcendent musings and forcing me to rein Macha to a halt before I ran over some of the very men I was to command. The white flag with the green crescent presently waved not six feet before my face. A group of drop-jawed men stared at me, apparently shocked that I almost walked my mount right over them.

"Are ye daft?!" exclaimed one of them, an older, grey-haired, filth encrusted soldier whose regular army tunic, though carrying the markings of a sergeant, was soiled nearly beyond recognition. "Ye nearly ran us down," he continued in a Gaelic accented English, denoting his origin in the peasant-filled hills of my homeland.

"Whhhat matterrrr, Taliesin," said another soldier in slurred English, thick also with a Franc accent and flailing an arm with dramatic flamboyance. He held a large flask in the hand of the flailing arm and was a much younger man than the first one who had spoken. He was also obviously drunk. "Whattt matter, for we all die on the morrow in any event!" he continued in a louder voice, drawing many of the other soldiers in the immediate area to us. "Bet...better to die here and now than bleeeeeed to death in this place on the morrow," he stopped in mid sentence staring straight at me, squinting his eyes in the darkness to get a better look. "Bleeding Christ. You be him," he said in astonishment.

The first man, the one called Taliesin, walked forward, stopping within arm's reach of the spear shaft. He reached out to touch it, but thought better of it and pulled his hand back. He then looked behind me at Alhasan then at the King's Sword on my back. "You're right, lad," he said addressing his younger counterpart but not taking his eyes off of me.

I looked deeper into those eyes and yet another of my soul's images burst forth into my mind; two Roman legionnaires suddenly stood before me in my mind's eye; one older, one younger. They were from my life as the Centurion over a thousand years ago and I knew in that moment that I was familiar with this Taliesin's spirit as being the older of the Roman legionnaires. He had always been a loyal soul friend, as had the younger Roman soldier from that life, perhaps now in the body of the drunk young soldier before me. I smiled. "Taliesin, is it?"

"Aye, sir. That's what I be called," answered the man.

"You look in need of a bath and tunic change, Taliesin," I said.

"Ha! Aren't you Masoud, the Great Keeper of the Lance of Longinus and King Arthur's very sword!" exclaimed the younger man. "And that's your profound greeting to mon amie, Taliesin?!"

Taliesin turned suddenly and slapped his younger counterpart hard with the back of his hand, knocking the latter to the ground. "Had enough 'o you, I have! Shut yer yap, ya whiny shit or I'll dig yer grave here and now and fill it with ye! Show respect to your betters or by the Christ I'll do it!"

Bursts of laughter erupted from the men nearby. "Aye, and I'll help 'im!" said someone.

"I'm with you, Taliesin!" said another, eliciting even more laughter.

Taliesin turned back to me. "I apologize for his arrogance, my lord. He's been a pain in our arses for weeks, he 'as, whinin' and carryin' on about the end of our lives."

I did not address him right away but instead, looked to all the men who had gathered near the flag; nearly one-hundred by my reckoning. A century of men, is what Commander James had said was to be mine. I turned my head slightly and addressed Alhasan over my shoulder. "Slide off of Macha," I ordered quietly. He complied and was on the ground in an instant, standing near Taliesin. I then turned my attention to the gathered men, looking at many of them in turn as I spoke. "My name is Sir Liam Arthur Mason. And yes, I am also known by the Muslim name of Masoud. Whichever you choose to call me is your concern. I have come to be equally proud of both." I looked briefly at Alhasan as I said this last part, and he smiled with both surprise and pleasure. Turning my gaze back to the men, I continued. "I am indeed the guardian of the Great Spear of Longinus and the King's Sword. I am here as your commander by order of General and Templar Horatio Blackthorn and Commander Sir Jonathan James. We..." I froze in mid sentence. Some of the men gathered were men from my own company mixing in with the men like Taliesin who had been on this desert field waiting for weeks if not months. My eyes landed on one of them in particular from my company; Henry, looking weary but alive and awake. Relief washed over me at the sight of him. He was not only alive but with me. I could not have asked for anything more. "We will blend in together here and await orders," I continued after recovering from the surprise of seeing my friend. "The morning will be telling, but it will not be the doom of our forces as some have called for," I said, indicating the slapped soldier who was only now regaining his feet. "That I can assure you!" I said, thrusting the spear's blade tip into the air in a show of bravado.

"We are with you!" someone said.

"Aye!" said another. All of the men were now staring at the spear and murmuring softly in agreement and good cheer.

I brought the spear back to rest in the stirrup. The gesture had not been meant to imply I would use the now presumed magic weapon as the instrument of our salvation. But, that is clearly how the men perceived it. No matter. If it garnered their acceptance of me as their commander for now then so be it.

I swung my left leg over the top of Macha's neck in front of me, lifted the spear at the same time from the stirrup and dropped to the ground on Macha's right side, landing in front of Taliesin. Though I dismounted her on the *wrong* side, to her credit, Macha did not flinch. I smile at her and patted her neck, and then turned my attention to Taliesin. Our eyes met on level ground, our height being the same. "Thank you Taliesin for your aid in quelling an awkward situation," I said referring to the young drunk Franc crusader. "The men seem to look to you. I have need of you and them in the hours and days ahead. May I rely on you and your influence with them?"

"Your character comes before ye. They already know of you and respect you,"

"They may know of me and the things I have done but that's not the same as knowing the man," I said. I looked at the Crescent on the flag. "And, gathering under this symbol——that may garner resentment."

"Nay. I see it as mocking the heathens, sire! That symbol is a part of our Old Ways back home, if ye be knowin' what I mean, which is a great bit older than these upstarts' religion," Taliesin said with a wry grin.

"Master Taliesin," I said with amusement, "you sound like a Druid of the Ancient Ways."

"Aye. Been accused of worse, I 'ave," he replied.

The young man Taliesin had slapped now appeared standing behind him. It took a moment of looking at the lad's face in the semi-darkness, but his face took on a familiarity that I finally placed. "You!" I said, realization dawning on my mind. "You were in the field tent, the Muslim hospital tent with me and Commander James!"

"Oui, I was," he said.

"You were mad with fever, I believe, ranting about the devil coming for you," I said.

"I was mad with the opiate crave, being brought off of it, is what I mean," he replied.

My thoughts began reeling. Perhaps he could help Henry off of the smoke. The lad took another swill from his flask. Then again, this young Franc crusader appears to have replaced one craving for another. Yet, I could not accept his behavior now. I needed every man to have his wits about him. "I'll want you sobered by morning," I said.

Taliesin turned to the lad. "Ye've a count 'o ten with that thing," he said, indicating the flask. "If I see it after that, I break it."

The Franc youth turned to walk away. Taliesin grabbed him by the scruff of his neck. "Ye've not been given leave by your commanding officer, crusader François Drusee," he said.

The lad looked directly at me with defiant, bloodshot eyes. I waited for an instant for him to ask for leave. He did not.

But this was a tiny battle of wills not worth inflaming. "You may go, Francois," I said.

Taliesin released the lad who then scurried off in obvious embarrassment. After a moment, Taliesin looked to my Arab friend as if noticing him for the first time.

"This is Alhasan," I said. "He is my servant and assistant. He is to be completely trusted, do you understand, Taliesin?"

"Yes, sir. If ye be a trustin' 'im then that'd be good enough for me and the men."

"Good," I replied, relieved. Perhaps this command would not be as difficult as I'd feared. I looked at the night sky, now completely dark. "Beg yer pardon, sire, but don't ye Templars hold with Vespers at darkfall?"

"Most still do. But times have changed and I suppose I am not the typical Templar Knight Taliesin," I answered truthfully. "My prayers seem to come at various times, especially when I sleep, and are more trance-like meditations where I see...visions," I explained, not quite sure why I was telling this man these things. But then again, if the intuitive revelation from my soul regarding this Taliesin was correct, then I had trusted this man's spirit for over a millennium. No surprise then that I would share with him the fact that I had visions nearly daily of late.

"And these...visions; be they of this time or a past? Perhaps of Roman times?" he asked tentatively, expressing an obvious awareness of his own soul's journey through *time*.

"You, my dear Taliesin, are more than an ancient Druid of our Old Ways. You are a Seer, are you not?" I asked dryly.

"Humph," he voiced with disgust. He then leaned in closer to me and said in a whisper, "I been accused of such by the Church's men at the local parish. They think all us of the Hills be witches and wizards, warlocks and devils, beholdin' only to the Old Ways. I be Christian but I practice the Old Ways too. The Christ," he said, unconsciously crossing himself in the Church's prescribed manner, "performed miracles. But I say them that's witnessed it got it wrong. It weren't nothin' but the natural powers of Dana bein' wielded anew in front of ignorant folk. Our Druids and wizards been doing the same thing for thousands of years, don't ye know."

"You speak as a heretic, Taliesin," I said.

He looked at me oddly for a moment, clearly wondering if he had misjudged me.

I smiled. "Fear not. I understand what you say. And, yes; some of my visions had been of a Roman life, with you in it."

"Aye. I knew it. Good to know ye again, sir," he said.

"And you, Taliesin. But tell me; if you practice the Old Way ways of the Druids, how can you be a Christian at the same time?"

"The Christ's teachin's are for everyone, ain't they?" he replied as if I were daft. "And, as I see it, Jesus 'imself was the greatest of Druids; performin' the likes of raising the dead and what have ye. Much like ye, now. Ain't no miracle ye bringin' yer close friend back from the Otherside." Even in the darkness he must have seen the surprised look on my face. "Aye, we all heard 'bout that one. My point bein' that you, that spear and that sword just be pullin' on the same power that the Christ used."

"But, it's said that Jesus is, *the only begotten son of the Father*, implying that the Father's power only comes through Him," I countered, more as point of argument than anything else, for truth was that I agreed with what he was saying.

"Nay, sir. 'Tis originally this: Jesus is *a begotten son of the only Father*, or of the One, we might say in the Old Tongue!" exclaimed Taliesin. "Been told so by a village elder and that's how I see it. He also be one of the parish Fathers, this Elder. Studied here in the Holy land, he did, when a lad. That's the proper way of readin' the Holy words, he says. It also means that all of us can do what the Christ did. We're all Druids."

I was not sure whether Taliesin was a foolish man or a man of superior faculty. But was there really a difference? I have found that one man's fool is often another man's sage. I looked at Alhasan who was simply grinning ear to ear in apparent agreement with Taliesin's point of view.

"Well, Taliesin, I should like to continue this discussion with you. But for now, let's bed these men down for the night," I said.

"Aye, sir," he replied. He then turned and began barking soft orders for the men to settle in for the night.

"He is an old soul, you see," said Alhasan said, referring to Taliesin.

"Aye. He is that," I replied.

TWENTY

Darkness swirled about me. A mist enshrouded my surroundings. Voices. Voices in argument came to my ears. They sounded far off, as if in a distant land. I could discern that they were male, but could not decipher what it was they argued about. Willing myself closer to them, I found myself being catapulted through the mists at an alarming rate of speed; as if I were being shot from a giant crossbow.

The mists cleared. I looked out through the eyes of Myrriddin once again. Men surrounded me and shouted at one another and me in turn. We were in the castle room that had the huge, oblong table. The men were Arturius' men, regaled now in their ornate armor of *King Arthur's Knights Of The Round Table* lore, complete with the Pendragon emblem, Arturius' family crest, emblazoned on the front, and a Christian Red Crucifix on the back. Lancelott was chief among the ones arguing. His face contorted with rage, and his thick Franc accent made him difficult to understand. He seemed to be directing his anger at another knight in particular. "Mon Dieu, Sir Perceval! You dare question your king? You are a coward, I say! And unchristian!"

This garnered another round of even louder protest from the rest. Arturius stood next to Lancelott, silent, head hung as if in shame.

"You condemn me as unchristian when you fornicate with your king's wife?!"

countered Perceval, a young, exceedingly handsome and stoic knight. His mane of dark hair and obvious muscular frame gave him the air of one from Greek legend.

The entire room fell silent at Perceval's outburst. Arturius bristled at the accusation from Sir Perceval and stepped toward the tall knight. "You will hold thy tongue, good knight."

Perceval was silent for a moment, as was Arturius again. "'Tis true then, my king?" he finally ventured, obviously disappointed that his king was not denying it.

"I will put this to rest now," Arturius began with an edge in tone that demanded attention, respect and a finality on the subject. "God has chosen that my seed be devoid of life," he began, addressing the men. "My First Knight came to my wife's chamber at my behest to aid his king in giving this realm an heir," he said, glancing at me while saying this last part, thus clearly conveying that the idea was not solely his after all.

"'Tis sacrilege!" someone said.

"Silence!" my Myrriddin self bellowed. The man who spoke the last words withered under my gaze. "What your king has done was done to aid the kingdom and should be considered an act of ultimate honor and sacrifice."

"No, Myrriddin. I have sinned grievously against God and man," confessed Arturius, hanging his head once again in shame.

"No, you have not," I said angrily. "The only *sin* you have committed is listening to the pompous asses of the Church, who shower you with praise and then threaten your immortal soul if you do not comply with their arbitrary rules and whims. Once was the time when you heeded them not. Once was the time when you saw fit to adhere to our Old Ways. Once was the time when you would have seen that what you requested of your First Knight was for the betterment of an entire race and perfectly righteous for the assurance of the longevity of us all, not to say that it followed the natural and perfect law of Dana and the Universe. But now you have been poisoned by these alleged men of God, these pretentious Holy Men. The shit that comes out of my ass is holier than these men."

Arturius suddenly looked up at me. "Myrriddin, do not speak so. You damn yourself by your words," he said. "It is not too late for your soul's salvation."

"Do you not see, Arturius! My soul, your soul is in no need of being saved, except from these so-called men of God! The Christ's very nature is within your very being because it IS your very being!" I was yelling.

"We are all born tainted by original sin, Myrriddin," continued Arturius as if speaking to an ignorant child. "The Book says so."

"A misreading of a book that was written by other pompous *men of God!*" I said, nearly screaming in frustration.

"Arturius, my king, I believe your wizard is going mad," offered Perceval, who looked at me with a mixture of extreme caution and fear; as if I were suddenly a dangerous rodent that needed to be killed.

I drew a deep breath to relax my tension. "Typical. 'Tis not I who is mad. Where madness reigns, sanity is deemed madness," I countered calmly. "I speak naught but the Truth. You would do well to remember that, my good knight."

The men murmured amongst themselves for a moment.

"The more pressing issue at hand is the road to the Holy Land. We embark on the sunrise again to make the way safe and to retrieve our rightful artifacts," said Arturius, clearly, desperately attempting to change the subject of his condoning, even sponsoring, his wife's infidelity.

"Aye," said someone.

"Yes," said another. Others nodded their head in agreement. Most of the men seemed willing to let the king's transgression fall by the wayside for the time being.

But Perceval was not so easily quelled. "This is not finished, my king. I will not be part of this venture if there be one rule for the common man and another for the king. The highest among us must be held equally accountable for his folly and sins," he proclaimed self-righteously. "And you, wizard," he said turning his wrath upon me, "you are an abomination to the Christ and all he stands for. I say your days at court are few in number."

"You overstep yourself, Perceval!" said Arturius, rising and stepping toward the knight, drawing the magnificent King's Sword, the very one I presently possessed in my life as Masoud. The blade rang a high, pure note as it was drawn from its leather and iron scabbard. To the fearful protests of the men, the king leveled the point directly at Perceval's chest, which was but a mere four inches from the sword's sharp point. Perceval, a hardened, battle tested warrior, nonetheless stepped back in fear and shock at the audacity of his king. "Draw one more breath against Myrriddin and it will be your last," Arturius stated through clenched teeth.

Sir Perceval seemed to waiver for a moment, unsure of what to do. Finally, he gathered his pride, turned and stormed from the room. Several of the other knights followed in his wake.

The mists enshrouded me again and hid the room from my view. The remaining men's voices continued in debate, but became distant once more.

ڵ   ڵ   ڵ

The pallet was comfortable as I lay on my back. A thick layer of soft rushes were beneath me upon the top of the pallet, creating a softness that rivaled the supple skin of Najeeba. Her naked form lay atop of mine and I kissed her neck tenderly, allowing my tongue to linger there. Her skin had the sweet taste of the gods' nectar in the morning. Our body's fit flawlessly together, our parts made for each other. To slide into her was to slide into the perfection of being. Our nude bodies entwined now, her dark breasts squished against my chest as our gentle thrusts of passion, lust and love echoed the formation of the universe itself. Looking at her face I saw the continuation of our souls' respective journeys. But she was Najeeba in this life, my Najeeba, at least for this moment of ecstasy. Our passion, our thrusts became quicker, more urgent, until our bodies reached the threshold of their ultimate release. The seed of my body welled up from deep within my loins and I exploded into her with the force of creation itself, she at the same moment bursting as the receptive form of the Great Mother Earth. Panting with exhaustion, our bodies collapsed together, as we breathlessly professed our feelings.

"I love you, Najeeba," I said.

"And I you, Masoud. I have loved you forever," she replied. I smiled and closed my eyes to rest, satiated on every level of my person.

After a moment, I felt a nibbling on my ear. "Najeeba," I whispered. I opened my eyes in the light of a predawn and turned my eyes toward the source of the nibbling. A scorpion crawled near my face, near where my ear had been but a second before, its wicked claws open and no doubt feeling for its breaking-of-fast on my ear but a moment before. It was not a soft pallet filled to overflowing with plush rushes on which I lay, but a cloth on the cold desert floor. Disappointment flooded my mind. It was then I noticed the dampness of my trousers near my groin. A nocturnal release spoke to the seeming reality of my time with Najeeba on the other side of night's veil. *Dreams are but the realm of the soul,* I thought. I wondered if she had dreamt of me on the previous night too. Our souls were obviously connected. I was sure she had held me in her dreams last night as I had held her. If we could not be together in the outer realm, then we would be together on the inner realm. The mind and body knows no difference.

My mind then drifted to the meaning of the vision of Myrriddin and Arturius or Arthur. There was a link between Arthur's knights and The Knights Templar, or so my vision had implied. The Templar Order was initially created to protect pilgrims on their trek to the Holy Land. At least, that was what the commoner thought. It seems as though Arthur's knights had taken on that duty first. But, why was I reliving some of my soul's past? Perhaps there was information I needed to learn again from that time for use in the present, but it eluded my mind for the moment. No matter. I would trust that all would be revealed at the proper time.

"Sir," Taliesin whispered nearby. I looked to my left and saw the man squatting next to me, his filthy tunic now brushed as clean as he could get it. He obviously did not have another. "The men begin to stir. What orders have ye?"

Orders? I thought. I had no specific orders, but could not let the men know that. I looked over Taliesin's shoulder and saw the sun cresting the hills to the east which rose above and behind the city from our position. The light began to bathe Jerusalem and gently cascade down onto the desert floor where we were. From what I could tell, we were quartered outside the northwestern wall of the city. A hill loomed before my eyes. It lay between our present position and the outside of the city's northwestern wall, which itself was elevated to a slight degree above the desert floor. Both of these features had been imperceptible in the darkness of the night before. The hill itself had apparently been walled in at some point, judging by the multitude of broken stone blocks around its base. But no more. I looked closer at the hill, which seemed to rise only some fifteen feet off the desert floor. Though I had never been to this spot, something about this hill was beyond familiar. My heart began to pound inexplicably, my palms to sweat. *What was happening?* I wondered. Then I understood what it was. "This is where *He* was crucified," I heard myself say out loud.

"Sorry, sir?" asked Taliesin, obviously confused by my statement.

"The hill there; it's Golgotha, the Hill of Skulls. It's where the Christ was crucified," I said in wonder.

Taliesin rose to his feet and looked behind himself at the hill, then back to me. I rose to my feet, bed cloth wrapped around my waist, lest the night's emission be seen by any, and stood next to the sergeant.

"I don't know 'bout such things, sir, nor much care," Taliesin stated flatly. "Mean no offence, mind ye. Ye bein' a Templar and all, I suppose it means something to you. But I'm sick of this place and all its religious shite from both sides. Just wanna get home, sir."

"I understand completely and no offence taken. I admire your honesty and agree with you on all counts," I replied. I said nothing for a moment, assessing what exactly it was that I was feeling about the hill. Realization donned slowly upon my mind. "My interest in this hill is deeper than I can explain, Sergeant."

He smiled knowingly. "Aye. Been here previous 'ave ye?"

"No, I haven't," I replied. Just..."

"Just not in this body, eh, sir?"

I smiled at the man's accurate assumption. "Tell the men quietly to awaken, break their fast, and gather here before the hour is out. Orders are forthcoming," I said, making it up as I went along.

"Aye, sir," he said, spinning on his heels and walking quietly away to carry out his orders. I quickly changed my under tunic and breeches, preparing to meet the day and my past.

TWENTY-ONE

A light fog enshrouded the crest of the Hill of Skulls. I trudged up to where the top of it met the sky. Was this really the right place, the place the Christ was crucified all these centuries past? It was. I could feel it as if I had been there, for I had been there. As far as hills are, this place, Golgotha, was quite unimpressive. Puny in height by the standards of other hills——perhaps fifty feet at its crest——and not all that large in circumference, its one side butting up against the northwestern wall of the city. Still, it did not matter how large this place was. What mattered were the events that happened there. And, in my soul I knew those events all too well. The spear in my hand vibrated as if to confirm my insight. It too had been here with me as Longinus nearly twelve centuries before. My heart still pounding, I closed my eyes, fully expecting to see in my mind's eye the events of that day, a day that changed not only the path of a lowly centurion of Rome, but one that changed the course of the world as well. Yet, nothing came; no vision of Christ on his cross, no reliving of my stabbing his chest with the spear I now held. The feeling of the experience lingered in my spirit and mind, but I would not *see* the event played out again. *Why?* I wondered, somewhat disappointed. But then again, what did I expect to achieve by reliving the event, some sort of profound revelation or experience, maybe even redemption?

"Strange, is it not?" said the voice behind me.

I turned to see the figure of a man standing not more than six feet from where I stood. We were alone at the top of this Hill of Skulls. He stood with his back to the east, the rising sun, just above and behind him, silhouetting his body, his face, making it impossible to see his features, though I could discern that he was dressed as an Arab in a dark cloak and headdress. "Who are you?" I asked, annoyed at having my solitude invaded.

"Forgive me," he said, stepping to one side, allowing the light of the sun to play on his face. His gold eyes seemed to light up at the touch of the morning's rays.

"You!" I exclaimed. "You have been...I don't know, watching me?"

"In a manner of speaking, my son," he said, cryptically. "There are many who would be grateful for what I do."

"That presumes they *know* what you do. I do not," I replied.

Silently, he gazed skyward for a moment, apparently lost in his own thoughts. "It is strange, the perception of passing time. When one truly understands it, he comes to realize that there is really no passing of anything. It all exists here and now," he began, his handsome face contemplative. "Some of us remain here to aid others we have known for...well what you would call a very long time. Is that not so, Masoud? Or would you prefer to be called Longinus or Myrriddin?"

My head began to spin and I closed my eyes. Images flashed before my mind's eye. Not images and scenes of the crucifixion of so long ago in this place, but images of a different place and time; images, visions of Myrriddin flooded my mind in rapid succession. I was not in his body in these as I had been in other visions, but instead, I was looking from the outside in as an observer. Most of these images contained other people, but one person in particular; a Christian Priest who did not adhere to all the ways of his Christian brethren, but rather accepted the ways of the Old Religions as all being part of and expressions of the One God. The images stopped and before my mind's eye was the face of this priest from the past. I knew him well. Or had.

"Master Masoud!" yelled Alhasan.

"Sir!" yelled another.

The image of the priest and past snapped into oblivion. My eyes shot open and before me stood not the gold-eyed man, but Alhasan, the twin lads Canter and Luscious. They stood now where the Gold-Eyed one had stood moments before. My eyes darted all around the hill. There was no sign of the gold-eyed, Ancient Priest. None.

"Whom do you seek, sire?" Canter asked.

"Am I mad?" I asked rhetorically to myself.

Canter and Luscious exchanged a look of concern.

"Fear not, my boys. Your commander is quite well," Alhasan said confidently. "He now experiences things from the Otherside of the Veil; things that most of us cannot fathom, things that would drive most men mad, but not your commander, you see!"

The boys stared at me. "What are you all doing here?" I asked, gathering my wits.

"We came for you, sir," replied Alhasan, "before the others do. Commander James has come for you at the camp. The boys here have been given to you as servants."

"We asked for the duty sir," said Canter eagerly.

"Yes, yes, as soon as we heard of your promotion. Wanted to be a part of your crew," declared Luscious on the heels of his brother's words.

"'We must!' we said! 'He'll have us, he will!'" said Canter.

"Yes, yes! You will, sire, will you not? Please, sire?" asked Canter.

"Yes, please?!" echoed Luscious.

I laughed in spite of myself. These two were entertaining if nothing else. "Aye, lads. I'll have ye as my help as long as you stop chattering when I ask it!"

"Done!"

"Done!"

"Let's be off then." I said.

They turned and headed back down the hill toward the camp. I lingered just long enough to view the spot once again where the crucifixion had taken place. I then looked to where the gold eyed man had stood moments before. I was not mad. I knew that. And perhaps Alhasan had hit the mark; I was now in harmony with something much greater than myself, something that traversed *time* and caused me now to live from the place of my spirit more than I realized. More than I even cared to admit to myself. I headed back down the hill.

ﻟ   ﻟ   ﻟ

The commotion in the camp was frantic, yet quiet. The men gathered their meager belongings together with silent urgency. Each man knew that he must work in silence so as not to give too much away to the enemy regarding our numbers and intention, the latter still being somewhat of a mystery to more than one of us. Each man's face showed a tenseness that belied an uncertainty of the day's coming events. I still knew not what I would tell these men, my men, as to what the day's orders would be. But, fortunately, it became quite apparent that I would not have to. Commander Sir James and General Blackthorn, sitting high on their large mounts, were now in the middle of my men. The general and commander appeared to be waiting for someone, as they simply sat there, observing but not interacting with the men. It suddenly dawned on me that it was I for whom they waited.

"General. Commander," I said to one then the other in turn by way of greeting, shouldering my way through the busy men. Alhasan and the two lads were nearby, gathering my own belongings and placing them on Macha.

"Liam," began Sir James. "We assault the north-western wall within the hour. You will lead your men to the fissures in the cornerstones there," he said, pointing back up the hill to the somewhat crumbling corner of the distant wall. My heart jolted and a feeling that approached the sensation of what I took to be blasphemy——having never experienced a sense of blasphemy before, it was the only thing I could equate it to in the moment. The thought of marching my men up this sacred hill and over the actual site where *He* was killed, where my former self had stabbed *Him*, was near too much to bear. But I ignored the feeling, knowing full well the more pressing issue would be the sure loss of many numbers of my century.

"But...commander!" I stammered.

"I know. It will be difficult. Your men will take the brunt of an aerial assault from the tops of the walls, no doubt," he replied, "but it is necessary. And you are to remain at the back on your mount. Let the enemy see your weapons; the Sacred Spear and the King's Sword! Let it strike fear to their very core!"

"We cannot trudge over this holy ground! Do you not know where you are?!" said the none-too-quiet voice with a slight Franc accent from behind me. It was the companion of Taliesin from the previous evening, Francois Drusee, apparently sobered but heated, echoing my initial thoughts.

"Shut yer yap, Francois!" said Taliesin in more than a whispered hush, both men now appearing at my side.

"It is for this exact reason that we want you, Masoud," stated General Blackthorn, "to do this. The spear and its eternal owner have returned to claim the city, the hill, all of it! Roo-hah!"

I was dumbfounded on more than one level. Outwardly, it was a twisted, but good strategy; having me and the spear surge up the hill. But his reference to me being the *eternal owner* of it; was he seriously invoking my spirit as Longinus the Centurion? Or, was he being cruelly sardonic? I could not tell. His face was impassive. The scent of lilac wafted to my nostrils. It was mixed with the foul stench of body odor. It was obvious from whom both smells were emanating and in my mind accentuated the notion that Blackthorn was indeed being maliciously sarcastic. It was then too that I saw the glint in his eye; something I had not seen before, something he apparently kept well hidden from sight: a wickedness that lurked beneath the surface and seemed poised to burst forth at what I took to be the thought of the blood and death that was about to come. Bloodlust in the heat of skirmish was not a new concept to me. In battle, I had seen the glee play upon the faces of those in its grip as they slaughtered their fellow man in a moment of animalistic rage and frenzied, bloody destruction. I had heard that for some so-called seasoned warriors the mere smell of blood was enough to send them over the edge and into the gruesome bosom of the frenzy even years after their days of battle had ended. But what I saw now in the general's eye gave me more pause than witnessing a soldier momentarily caught up in the passion of blood-letting on a battlefield. What I saw in Blackthorn's eye was the darkness of an anticipatory joy in it, the near sexual gratification of potentially seeing another's grisly, bloody death. Yes, I received all that in the glint of the eye and knew it to be true. General Blackthorn, with his lilac smell poorly masking his real stench, suddenly took on a completely new persona to me.

"My good Masoud," he said to me smiling slightly, "are you in agreement with your man here?"

My face was obviously telling him of my dissent, but he was not clear on its meaning. My dissent was suddenly about his apparent dark character trait. I had never actually been with the general before or during a battle. My immediate commander, Sir James, could not have been more different in this context: calm, decisive, efficient in duty and the ways of battle and war. A born leader. Blackthorn, however, now seemed more to me the arrogant, aristocrat who simply had the title of general laid at his feet because of his station in life.

It matters not, Liam, Masoud, said the voice in my mind. *None have another's soul and path. Each chooses his own.*

I was confused by the voice's assertion. Was it talking about Blackthorn and his apparent penchant for a wickedness that I simply did not comprehend?

There is no wickedness in the eyes of the One. Law only and how it is applied. You have forgotten, remember...remember the Law of the One and that it is up to each as individual expressions as to how it is used, the voice said.

"The victims of wickedness may feel differently," I said.

There are no victims. Only participants.

"What are you mumbling there, Sir Masoud?!" demanded the general.

"Nothing, general," I replied.

"You will carry out your orders post-haste. Gather your men, inform them and execute your duty." He spun his mount and trotted away, nearly knocking over some of my soldiers as he left.

Anger splashed across Sir James' face as he watched the general leave us. My commander then dismounted and came up to me, looking back at the general then to me. "He gets this way before a battle," he said. "Like a different person. Dangerous to cross him when he's like this, Liam."

"Understood," I said.

TWENTY-TWO

An equine snort from behind me drew my attention around and away from Sir James. Macha stood behind me with Luscious holding her bridal and Alhasan standing on her other side. A firm hand clasped my shoulder and I turned my attention back to Sir James.

"Do as the general bade, Liam, but stay farther back," began my commander, "even farther back than Blackthorn says, so as not to be in harm's way of any arrows, yet still within the enemy's sight from the wall. They may see you and know who you are as well."

I bristled again on the inside at the thought of what that meant for the men now under my command. "And let my men perform the fatal charge on their own, while I rest comfortably out of range?! *You* would not do that and nor will I!" I replied, anger at the stupidity and pointlessness of this whole conflict rising within my mind once again.

"Liam. Masoud, take care. You border on insubordination," Sir James said with a wry smile of pride. I took that smile to mean he was hoping for that reply, but had to officially reiterate the general's commands. He mounted his horse and rode off in General Blackthorn's wake.

I spun on my heels and mounted Macha. I then turned her and trotted a few yards away, stopping in the middle of a large group of men gathering their meager belongings and weapons. "Those of the Green Crescent Banner gather to me now!" I called in a loud voice, no longer caring to hide us or our intent from the *enemy*. The men gathered quickly, Taliesin and Francois at their lead. Every one of the men had trepidation etched upon his face to one degree or another, caused by the anticipation of the impending orders, no doubt. They all stared at me now, waiting. I hesitated in conveying the orders. Guilt seeped into my being over the fact that I was about to send most of these men to their death. As if to seek help——or some kind of absolution——I looked at the spear in my hand. I then brought my attention to the weight of the King's Sword, still sheathed on my back, and then back again to the spear.

The help——or absolution; I knew not which to call it——came in the form of an epiphany, a sudden comprehension of a profound truth. The comprehension washed over me like a cascading waterfall. It was not something I had never heard before, but this was the time I understood it, felt it to my very soul's awareness. *There is nowhere that He is not——no place not contained in Him: God, The One, Allah, He is the same by whatever name one chooses to use.* Further comprehension flooded my soul. *All are <u>always</u> in and of The One and thus there is and can be no death, only Life; eternal existence in a myriad of forms and levels of being!*

"Masoud, sir?" said Taliesin, obviously concerned at my hesitation.

"He visions, you see," replied Alhasan now standing next to Macha.

"Ney. Not a vision, Alhasan," I said. "'Tis a voice I hear that speaks the truth of Truths to my mind." I then looked at the men, the soldiers before me. "Men!" I said in a loud voice for all to hear. "We make history this day! Here, on the very hill where the Lord was crucified," I continued, watching the men, some of whose faces showed astonishment at my confirmation of the significance, the sacredness of this particular hill, "yes, where *He* died to this world but did not perish; where *He* stepped willingly into *His* destiny with honor, demonstrating to us all on the third day that there is no thing as death, only life everlasting! We storm the wall at the top of this sacred hill to take back what is rightfully ours..."

"And kill the Muslim infidels!" someone shouted, garnering to my surprise—— and pleasure——only a few, half—hearted cheers of approval from the men.

"They are not infidels!" I countered. "Invaders, perhaps, but not infidels.

We all, Christian, Jew, Muslim, worship the One God by whatever name," I said, voice raised with authority, Macha dancing gently beneath me. "We take back the city that had been ours for a-thousand years and the Jews' for longer than time itself. We take it back now for our own, yes, but to also share it; that all may worship here as they wish and be part of Her sacredness." Yes, Salah al-Din said as much; that in his great mercifulness it is what he would do when he drove us away once and for all; that those who would stay may worship as they see fit. He was right. It was the way it must be. I felt sure the Sultan would not mind that I borrowed his merciful notion. Though I doubt my commanders would feel the same way. But none were within earshot of hearing me just then. Some of the men reacted with murmurs of confusion.

"Yes!" exclaimed Taliesin to the men, the crusaders and soldiers. "Our commander speaks the truth! We are merciful and tolerant, for all be one in the eyes of God!"

I cocked an eyebrow in surprise at my new friend. His use of the word *we* implied all of us present to be Christians which included himself. His statement seemed contrary to the attitude toward any of the Christian faith he had voiced on the previous night. But then, what I had just spoken of was not regarding any single human contrived religion, something Taliesin obviously understood.

"We are with you, Sir Masoud! Are we not, lads?!" Taliesin yelled to the men in a tone that dared any of them to defy him or me. It also revealed, at least to me, that whatever he was saying in the moment was being said to solidify the men's support.

"Aye," said some of the men, less than convincingly.

Taliesin jumped upon a nearby, small boulder, elevating himself some three feet off of the ground. He was now in clear sight of all of the men. "I say again," he began with intense fervor, "we are with you, Sir Masoud, are we not, Lads?!"

"Aye!!" rose the cry this time to an earsplitting battle-cry. "Aye!!"

"Lead us, Sir Masoud!" cried one crusader.

"Send the blessed Spear of Longinus before us! May its Christ powers protect us!" yelled another.

"And the King's Sword too!" said still another.

I let their excitement swell, their yells churning into the bloodlust of the righteous. When I judged the yells to be at its peak I gave the order. "Turn about and form ranks!" I commanded sternly. So new to my leadership role was I that I had a momentary doubt as to whether or not that was the right command. Yet, I had been a crusader long enough to know that the command was not that far off the mark. The men's response, however, alleviated any fear on my part. Almost as one they turned to face the Hill of Skulls, and the walls of Jerusalem beyond. They crisply formed up ten rows of ten, weapons——spears and swords mainly, some with bow and arrows——at the ready. It was then I noticed thousands of the other crusaders and soldiers across the increasingly sunlit field beginning to fall into formations of their own as if following our lead. "Forward!" I called to my century of men.

"Roo-hah! Roo-hah! Roo-hah!" Taliesin began chanting in a loud cadence, others picking up his call and cadence as we marched forward and up the hill.

I trotted Macha around the formation to take the lead in our march. Regardless of what Sir Blackthorn had said, I would not stop at a safe distance in leading my men to the wall. *I will trust in my protection*, I thought, grasping the spear tighter. A warmth suddenly seeped into the palm of my hand. It felt as if it were saying, *Indeed, do not fear.* A voice then spoke in my mind, the same voice as a moment ago. *Fear not*, it began in an echo of the message contained in the spear's warmth, *trust in Truth. Trust in the eternalness of yourself!* A shudder of new understanding went through my being. I felt my spirit relax and give in to these words, as well as to the words I had spoken only moments before.

The cheers and vocal cadence of the men continued to grow in intensity. I looked back at the men I was leading, into their faces. I now saw no trepidation, no fear there. Only the lines of hard determination were etched upon the features; determination to accomplish the mission of scaling these walls. It was then that I remembered something. I had forgotten to give a crucial order; the order calling for the assault ladders and bowmen. Obviously, we would need the ladders for the walls and bowmen to lay a cover barrage! *Fool!* I berated myself. Panic ran through my veins at the inept, incompleteness of my orders. But then I caught sight of Taliesin. He was trotting in front of twenty to twenty-five men, who were carrying the assault ladders, approximately twelve of them, two to three men to a ladder! I had not noticed the men missing from the formation, but apparently Taliesin had broken them away shortly after we began the march up the hill in order to carry the ladders. The men were now making their way up alongside of the main formation, looking to take the front where I was now. "Blessings upon you, Taliesin," I whispered to myself. "You know how to cover your commander's ass." I tugged on Macha's reins, turning her to meet the ladder-men and stop all my men at the hill's crest, which we were upon. "Halt!" I shouted, raising my free hand. Almost as one the men, the formation stopped. Though we were at the crest of the hill, the wall of Jerusalem was still a-hundred yards before us. "Those of you with bow, to me! Form a line here before me, shoulder to shoulder, facing the wall!" I ordered. The bowmen in my troop were not necessarily their own distinctive unit. Each of them was dressed in similar tunics and breeches and breastplates of leather as any of the other men in this group of soldiers. They also usually fought sword in hand alongside any of their comrades. Yet, as I learned in that moment, they could indeed become an elite unit unto themselves when called upon. Surprisingly, nearly a third of the men stepped forward in answer to my call, bows in hand, filled quivers on the back. I had not realized my century contained so many so many bowmen. They did as I bade, appearing before me in a crisp line of shoulder to shoulder men. I trotted Macha sideways, back and forth, inspecting the line. "As soon as the rest of us draw fire, you will shoot to cover our assault," I commanded. I had the feeling that I should say something more, but could not pinpoint what that something should be.

"May I, sir?" offered Taliesin who was now standing beside me and Macha.

I inclined my head in acquiescence, unsure of what he was going to say but intuitively trusting it to be the addendum needed to what I had just stated.

"Ready position!" Taliesin yelled to the bowmen in a tone that clearly conveyed his familiarity with this particular leadership role. All at once and in unison, the bowmen dropped to one knee, pulled an arrow from the quiver on their back and notched it to the bowstring. They then rested the armed but relaxed bow across the upright knee and awaited further instructions.

"Superb," I said in masked awe.

"Impressive!" exclaimed Alhasan, who suddenly appeared next to me panting breathlessly. He had no doubt endeavored to keep up with Macha and I as we ascended the hill.

"Impressive, indeed," I reiterated. "Thank you, Taliesin."

"You are most welcome, sir," he replied. "Hamish here is your man," he continued, indicating the bowman on the end closest to us, a large, cropped-haired, facially tattooed man. His tattoos were a mixture of ancient Celtic symbols; swirls and circles within circles denoting the eternality of existence, and those of Christianity; a small Celtic cross adorned his left cheek and a fish, the latter being in the middle of a Celtic swirl adorning his right cheek. "He has led this troop of arrow-men for some time, he has. "Trust 'im to give the order as to when and where to fire."

"After the leadership skills you just displayed, one would think..." I began.

"I go with you, sir," Taliesin proclaimed in no uncertain terms.

I stared at the man for a moment, admiring his character and forthrightness. "Indeed," I agreed. I then turned to Hamish. "The duty's yours, Hamish," I said to him.

"Thank you, commander," he said in a mousey, squeaky voice, which did not at all match the image of the man before me. I was stunned by it for a moment, but quickly recovered and looked to the ladder bearers.

"Ladders to the..." I started. But the words froze as my gaze fell upon the front man who had his left arm through the end rungs of what was obviously a heavy burden. Henry. I nearly leapt off of Macha, such was my desire to embrace my friend. But the decorum of my new found position of authority would not permit such a publicly blatant display of favoritism, nor would the urgency of our overall current situation. Henry looked pale and gaunt. Beads of sweat trickled down his trembling brow. His mouth moved as if involuntarily chewing on something that was clearly not there. Anger coursed through my whole body at what the worship of the opium had done to him. One might argue that the symptoms he displayed were due to the exertion of the march up the hill under the burden of a heavy assault ladder. Yet, none of the other men who had carried the ladders exhibited such symptoms or appearances. They were a bit winded, perhaps, but that was all. I knew better. There was no doubt in my mind that Henry's condition was the result of not having suckled on the opiate's teat this day or for perhaps many a day. I forced a smile to stretch my face and nodded in greeting to my friend. He managed an unreadable, feeble smile in return, but that was all. I would look after him later, presuming of course we made it through the next few hours alive. But it was my full intention on surviving the next few hours and well beyond. I turned my attention away from Henry and back to the matter at hand. "Those with shields to the ladder bearers!" I commanded. Most of the formation broke, shields in hand, and huddled close to those carrying ladders. The remainder scurried to be near those with the shields, not wanting to be left out of the semi-protective umbrella when the time came. I looked to the leader of the bowmen. "At your discretion, Hamish," I said.

"Aye, sir," he replied.

"To the walls of Jerusalem!" I ordered to the rest of the men. The company lurched forward as one entity, Taliesin leading the way.

TWENTY-THREE

No war cry rang out in this leg of the march. We marched on in determined silence. Within moments the first enemy arrow struck the forward most ladder, its flame-lit head sticking mere inches from Henry's hand. "Shields up!" I yelled. Those with shields complied, raising them up flat to the sky over their heads in protection of the nearest ladder bearer, themselves and whoever else may fit underneath. No two shields were alike, as none were of regular military issue. They were all the personal armament of the individual soldier. Some were long and rectangular and three quarters of a man's width and height, others were small and round or square, but effective nonetheless in offering at least some protection from the rain of arrows that was sure to come. With our shields in place I looked back to Hamish and our bowmen. Even as I was turning my head to see them, Hamish was giving the order to his fully loaded, bow-stretched archers, hand raised in the air.

"Loose!" he commanded with a swift downward stroke of his raised hand. The unison *thudding* sound of many bowstrings being released at once rushed to my ears as a barrage of small missiles flew from our bows. No sooner had the arrows been loosed then Hamish gave the next order. "Bowmen up! Advance the line!"

As the line of bowmen quickly got to their feet and advanced closer to our position, now only some thirty yards from the wall, the arrows they had released were finding their marks on the enemy. More than one agonized scream was heard from the top of the wall nearest our position. One Muslim soldier suddenly toppled from the wall, landing in a bone-crunching pile in front of us, two arrows protruding from his upper body.

I turned and looked at Henry who yanked the burning arrow from the ladder with his free hand and tossed it to the ground. Several more enemy missiles hit the ground in front of us, falling just short of the men. *Odd, that*, I thought. Surely their bows had the range to strike us where we now stood.

"Final position!" Hamish barked. I watched as within only an instant of time our line of bowmen dropped to one knee, notched an arrow to their bowstrings, took aim at the wall's top and pulled the sinew string taught, ready to shoot. "Loose!" commanded Hamish with the same chopping motion of his hand as before.

At that same instance I gave the final order. "Advance! Double it!" I yelled. The company ran forward as one, doubling their pace as I trotted alongside atop Macha.

"Agh!" cried one of the shield men near Henry. The man fell to the ground clutching his right knee, an arrow shaft sticking out from the joint. The man's large, oblong shield dropped to the ground as well, exposing two other men; Henry and a fellow soldier. The fallen shield bearer had been between Henry and the other soldier who had been on the outside of the group as a whole. The exposed soldier now darted toward Henry in an effort to gain protection near the larger group.

But he then stepped in front of Henry. That step proved to be fortunate for my friend Henry, but fatal for the other soldier. The distinctive and gruesome thump-sound of an arrow biting deeply into a man's upper torso told the soldier what had happened even before he looked at his chest. The man, and indeed the whole company, continued to move forward as his eyes grew wide with the shock and realization that he was about to leave this world. With a terror-filled gaze he then looked at his chest and the arrow shaft protruding from it. Helplessness crossed his face as blood began to trickle from a corner of his mouth. I looked at Henry, who starred at the man with a surprised, yet knowing look on his face; that arrow would have struck him had the soldier not stepped directly in front of him. What happened next took place so rapidly that it was completely unavoidable. The arrow-struck man's now limp body stumbled forward and collapsed to the ground, but in doing so it caused a chain reaction. Henry tripped over the man's body, dropping his end of the long and heavy ladder, thus causing the others carrying his ladder to topple in turn. The soldiers in the closest proximity now fell over them, most of them ending up on the ground, but some falling on top of the ladder itself.

Yells and screams of confusion filled the air, as did another sound for a brief instant; a snapping sound akin to a dry wood branch breaking, intruded upon the ears. "Aghhhh!!" cried someone who was obviously in stomach-churning pain. I looked to the fallen men and saw one in particular whose legs had been caught under Henry's ladder. "The devil be damned!!" the man screamed in a fierce but pain-filled, cracking voice. It was then I realized that the snapping sound had been one of the caught man's legs being broken underneath the ladder. Chaos reigned for a time.

Yet, even amidst the chaos my men kept their heads. The ladder was quickly picked up, the man with the broken leg was dragged to safety by a friend, and the rest of the company made it to the wall in short order in complete control of mind and body as evidenced by the determination on their faces and purposeful execution of their body movements. Ladders began slamming upright against the aged stone barrier. My men immediately jumped onto them and ascended. I pulled on Macha's reins, halting and spinning her to face the rest of the men, nearly knocking down Alhasan in the process. My Arab friend stood before me, mouth agape. Next to him stood the toothless Franc sergeant, Lafeit——whom I was unaware of as being company until that moment——also with a mouth wide open in surprise, even shock. "Mon Dieu!" Lafeit exclaimed.

"What, by the God, is the matter with the two of you?!" I said, suddenly infuriated at this distraction and perhaps feeling just a little naked by the way these two stared.

"Sir Masoud has Allah's favor!" said Alhasan.

It was then I realized that it was not me they were gawking at. It was the spear I held. I noticed something different about it even before looking at it; the weight of it. It suddenly felt much heavier than it should have. Slowly, I raised the spear and looked at it. To my astonishment, the spear's shaft was riddled with enemy arrows. On one side and all up and down its length arrow shafts stuck out of it like the quills of a porcupine. I had not felt nor seen any one of these arrows come so close.

"'Tis true, just as they say!" said LaFeit. "The power of Christ All Mighty is within the great Spear of Longinus. It has drawn certain death away from you!"

Before I could respond, howls of pain and outrage came from one of the ladders. Five ladders had been placed against the wall, several men now scrambling up each one, a couple of them nearing the top which landed only a foot or so from the top of the wall, some thirty-five feet off of the ground. One of the ladders with a man nearing the top was being dowsed with a dark liquid from the wall's summit. It was black and had the consistency of thin mud. It also steamed, indicating that its temperature was hot, very hot. Pitch. The liquid was a vile substance known as pitch; sticky, boiling oil mixed with water, dirt and excrement. *The Devil's Diarrhea* some called it. The substance was poured from caldrons atop the walls. The liquid was not completely unexpected, as pitch was often used by defenders of a walled city under siege. But, one could never be fully prepared for it or for its nauseating stench. Some with shields had ascended the ladders first, shields raised——as much as possible while climbing the rungs of a ladder——to help protect other climbers below from raining arrows and whatever else may be hurled down at those assaulting the walls. The shields did little now, however, to protect against the disgusting liquid. Horror filled my being as I watched the men on the one ladder inundated with pitch. Immediately, they fell, plunging backwards to the ground in the throes of searing pain. More than one man's face and hands broke into dark blisters when the foul, hot liquid came into contact with their body. Those that survived the fall to the ground wailed and writhed in ungodly torment as the pitch stuck to the skin.

Anger coursed through my being. I shook the spear violently, loosening all of the stuck arrows and sending them to the ground. A trail of pitch ran down the wall from the caldron above. The large, round iron caldron——which was big enough to hold three men——was still tipped on its front, its lip barely hanging over the wall's top edge, the dark liquid still spilling out from it, but now barely a trickle. The momentum of all the liquid that had been inside was now gone with only a few drops creating a trail down the wall's outer side directly in front of the ladder which had been its target. My anger crested. In my mind's eye I imagined a bolt of lightning come forth from the sky and setting alight this dribble of Devil's Diarrhea. It would burn well. So great was my focus and intent with this image in my mind that my body began to shake with the real feeling of it happening.

Then, it did. It came not from the sky, but from the spear in my hand, from the Spear of Longinus. A bolt of blinding white lightning shot forth from the spear's blade, striking the dribble of liquid Devil's Shit. I suddenly realized I had just broken the pact with Salah al-Din. But it was too late for regret. A flame burst out and trailed up the pitch staining the wall. The enemy at the top saw what was happening. From what I could see, there were seven of them. Five of them disappeared from sight, apparently cowardliness getting the better of them, judging by the tone with which their comrades yelled at them. One of the two remaining Muslim defenders motioned for the other one to man a side of the heavy caldron. Together, they attempted to shove the huge iron pot over the wall. But even if they could have pushed it over they were not fast enough. The flame ran quickly up the trail of pitch, onto the caldron's lip and into its interior. The large pot ignited and exploded, spewing out a flaming fireball. The caldron itself shot backwards from the exploding pressure within it, knocking the two defenders down, one falling out of sight, the other falling off the wall to the outside. He landed near Macha's feet, his dead eyes staring emptily up at me. For a brief instant, our section of the wall was clear at the top, no enemy fighters or defenders could be seen and for that brief moment I thought we might be able to rapidly breach the wall. But at least ten more Muslim defenders suddenly appeared at the top of the wall, most of whom had bow and arrows.

"Roo-hah!" came the battle cry to my left and above. Henry. It was Henry and he was yelling at the top of his lungs wielding his sword while standing on the top of the wall. Three enemy fighters were locked in combat with him, trying to cut Henry down with their scimitars. But it was Henry who had the upper hand. He spun and ducked and weaved with his sword in a deadly dance with the enemy, cutting each of the them down in turn, chopping the sword hand from one, spinning and nearly cleaving a second in two. Henry appeared his former, fearsome self, for the moment at least. He had managed to scale his ladder and breach his part of the wall, thereby creating a hole in the enemy's defenses. I was proud of him. But, as with the nearby section of wall from where the pitch had been dumped, the breach was quickly sealed as Muslim fighters swarmed to fill the gap.

I looked along the rest of the wall as far as I could see. The whole of our crusader army had begun the assault and was meeting a similar difficulty as my men and I were here. They were being repelled on ground and wall. I looked back up to where Henry was. He was there no more. In fact, he was nowhere in sight; not on the wall, nor on a ladder, nor on the ground. One of the ladders was being pushed over by Muslim defenders using the butt of two spears. They succeeded. The ladder fell backwards with at least seven of my men still on it.

"Commander, use the power of the Great Spear of Longinus again!" someone shouted.

I held the spear aloft and impulsively grabbed the King's Sword from its sheath on my back. The blades of both spear and sword glowed with a green hue, a soothing sight quite opposite to the tension of our present situation. I held both weapons aloft for all to see.

"Yes!" shouted someone else.

"Praise the All Mighty!" yelled another.

Cheers began to ring throughout the entire army as one by one they all saw the glowing weapons.

"Destroy the walls, Sir Masoud!" yelled still another soldier.

I attempted to focus my mind on just that; the walls crumbling before us. But doubt was in my heart. I felt it. And nothing happened. I shifted my focus and sought to destroy those on the walls, rather than the walls themselves. More doubt crept into my being and with it, anger at my inept use of this power. Or perhaps it was guilt over breaking my word with Salah al-Din that I would not use the spear and sword so. Regardless, nothing happened.

Arrows, rocks and more pitch began to assail us from the wall's top.

"Now, sir, or we're doomed!" said the same soldier who had last spoken.

But no bolt of lightning or other display of power came forth from either weapon. In fact, the glowing on the blades was beginning to fade.

"Look!" said Taliesin, who now stood at Macha's side. He pointed to a spot on the wall's top to our left and some fifty yards away. A blue flame shot forth from an object held by someone standing atop a turret on the wall. The object seemed to merely be a piece of wood as tall as a man. But then I saw who held the object and knew the object for what it was. The one who held the object was Rashin and the object was a piece of the rood. The blue flame, or rather, a blue flaming ball, shot forth from the rood and sailed into the midst of two centuries of Christian soldiers and crusaders near where Rashin stood above them. It exploded violently. Most of the two-hundred men were killed instantly. Incinerated. But the rest, or at least most of the rest, were set ablaze.

"No!" I shouted impotently. I spurred Macha hard and galloped off in the direction of Rashin at a break-neck speed. My outrage grew as I approached the carnage. I looked up at the turret from where Rashin had hurled the destructive power through the rood. Rashin was gone. "Rashin!" I yelled angrily. I pulled Macha to a halt in front of the base of the wall below the turret, craning my neck to see the turret and the now empty spot where Rashin had been a moment before. He seemed to have simply vanished into the air. I looked to the field around me. Moans and cries filled my ears. A sea of death and suffering lay before me. Grief, confusion and emptiness washed over me. Though these men lying before me had not been in my company I felt that I, he who wielded the Spear of Longinus and King's Sword, should have been able to thwart this. I suddenly felt less than inadequate as a leader. I was a pretender, not at all qualified to have men under my command. Holding both the spear and sword before my face I silently cursed the situation I was in. "Show me the way," I pleaded to the objects in my hands. They said nothing. And, they no longer glowed at all.

A loud hissing sound flew past my right ear, then another. The palm of my right hand suddenly stung as something collided with the spear's shaft directly opposite of my right palm. Another enemy arrow had struck the spear. I then felt something hit the King's sword in my left hand, a metal clanging sound rang in my ears as an arrow bounced off of its blade. Another one hit the sword's hilt, nicking my thumb in the process. I instinctively let go of the sword and instantly regretted it. The Kings swords hit the ground with a metallic ringing.

Before I had time to react and retrieve the weapon a flash of pain coursed through my head, then another. I felt warm liquid ooze down my face. But it was not pitch from above. I touched the side of my face with my left hand and discovered the liquid to be blood; my own. I looked up toward the top of the wall just in time to expose my face to the next stone that was being hurled at me from the top of the wall. The large-fist-sized rock smashed into the top of my forehead at the hairline. The last thing I remember as I fell from Macha's back was the erroneous inner thought of, *why? Why has the spear's power abandoned me?*

Its power is your power, came the response in my mind. *You have simply begun to lose faith, to forget, to doubt.*

My body hit the ground in a painful heap. Then, all went black.

TWENTY-FOUR

"Remember, Myrriddin," said Moscastan, my mentor, "you are always connected to the Source, always. It is your awareness of It, and especially your *feeling* of It, that creates a condition desired. Doubt, lack of Faith, destroys the condition sought and renders the circumstances you are *feeling*; in this instance, states of doubt and lack of faith and their corresponding conditions, however that may appear to you. What you are Truly *feeling* is always what will appear before you as your circumstances."

"I understand," I heard myself, my Myrriddin self, say.

"You must awaken now," Moscastan said in an odd voice and in a strangely accented tongue. Yet, I knew these qualities of voice. Not as Moscastan's, but...but...

"You must! You must to awaken now, Masoud!" said the voice urgently.

My eyelids felt heavy. It seemed to take all of my effort to open them. When I did I found I was Masoud once again, lying on the ground on my stomach, my right cheek in a small puddle of my own blood. The smell of smoke filled my nostrils along with the stench of death. Slowly, I rolled over and sat up, my forehead throbbing, and stared into the face of Alhasan. Taliesin was next to him as was Sir James, grave concern plastered across their respective faces. Beyond them I could see that the bulk of our army had pulled back, retreated, leaving the dead, their corpses littering the field and Hill of Skulls. The sun appeared at its zenith. Midday. "We've retreated?" I asked to no one in particular.

"Yes, lad," replied Sir James. "You've been out most of the morning."

I noticed then that I was nowhere near the wall were I had been struck down, some three-hundred yards away from my estimate.

"We pulled you away as soon as we could," explained Alhasan.

I nodded in understanding. My head suddenly throbbed worse than it had a moment before and for a time I gave into the pain, hanging my head in silence and willing the pain to vacate my skull. I touched the area of the injury with my right hand and felt the wet bandage which someone had dressed onto the wound. My attention shifted to the rest of my body in an attempt to assess whether or not I had any other injured regions. I did not. *The King's Sword*, I thought suddenly, for its weight was no longer on my back. I remembered. It had been knocked out of my hand by an arrow! And the spear; I must have dropped it when I was struck in the head. *Certainly, someone retrieved them!* I thought. I forgot about the pain in my head for the moment and looked around the ground near where I sat, expecting to see them resting nearby. They were not there. A panic began to run through my body as I turned my head to view my immediate surroundings in a frantic attempt to look for the sacred weapons. "Where are they?!" I asked, hearing the cracking of fear in my own voice.

The three men before me exchanged a look, a look that told me they had certain knowledge but were loath to share it for how I may react. "They've gone, lad," said Sir James at last, "taken by the enemy."

"I don't understand," I replied, dumbfounded.

"They came through the wall when you fell, Masoud. They took your King's Sword and Great Spear, but not you," offered Alhasan.

"But," I said as I tried to recall in my mind's eye the exact location I was in when struck down, "what do mean they came through the wall? Do you mean a gate? I was not near a gate when I fell," I heard myself babble.

"There are passages, you see, blocks in the wall that open," said Alhasan.

I sat in silence for a moment, feeling shame for the fact that I had lost the sacred instruments. "Your Sultan has them both now, does he not, Alhasan," I stated as a foregone conclusion. "Punishment for a broken promise," I whispered under my breath.

"He does not!" exclaimed Alhasan, clearly insulted that I would even think such a thing. "He knows they are connected to you. He could have taken them already and long ago had he wished, but he is not dishonorable! It was not by his order your spear and sword were taken, but by Rashin's, I am sure of it."

I thought for a moment. What Alhasan said made sense. "You are probably correct, my friend. And your Salah al-Din *is* honorable. Still, we, I must get them back."

"How, commander?" asked Taliesin with the gleam of adventure-to-come in his eyes.

I looked to Alhasan. "You said there are passages in the wall, blocks that open."

"Yes. That is how Rashin's men snuck out and stole your weapons," answered Alhasan.

"And you saw them?" I asked.

"No," he admitted. "But it is the only explanation."

"Do you know where these passages are?"

"Not the certain one that was used to take your weapons," Alhasan said. "But I do know of one. I can take you correctly to it."

"Why did you not tell us of these passages before?" asked Sir James in an accusatory tone.

"As I said, I only know of the one. Useless to know of only one. Can an entire river rush quickly through a tiny hole without detection? I think not," said Alhasan. "And, I had forgotten about them until this time, you see."

"Umph," was Sir James' cryptic response. "I say we find the one that they came through to steal the sword and spear."

"Commander, you or I could search for days for that one particular movable block and never find it, so well are they concealed," said Alhasan.

"Then we will go through the block, the passage that you know of, Alhasan," I said. "Will you lead me?"

"Of course, Master Masoud," he replied.

"I do not think..." began Sir James.

"I am going, Jonathan, Sir James," I said forcefully, hearing the desire for redemption echoing in my voice. "Strip me of my new command and title for abandoning duties if you wish, but I am going to take these holy instruments back."

Sir James smiled. "I was simply going to say that I do not think you should go alone, is all."

"Perhaps," said Taliesin, "we could sneak in many men after all and…"

"No. That will not do. Alhasan was right; one small passage would not be enough to stage an invasion," said Sir James.

"Aye, But be just one of us to get to the gate from within…" replied Taliesin.

"They are not the gates of your experience," said Alhasan. "They are on machine lift-cranks and hinges. If you do not know how to work them, they will not open. In addition, they are too fortified, you see."

"There it is, then," I said. "Alhasan, you will lead us in. Sir James, will you accompany us in?"

"Honored to, lad."

"And I be at your side, Sir Masoud," Taliesin declared proudly.

"I would prefer that you stay here with the men, Taliesin." I hated to thwart the man's desire, but he was too valuable an asset between me and the soldiers. "They respect you and listen to you," I said.

He hesitated, disappointment playing across his face. "If it be your wish."

"Aye, it is. And this undertaking must be kept between the four of us," I insisted.

"Agreed," said Sir James.

"Yes," said Taliesin.

Alhasan simply nodded.

"So be it. We will go in tonight," I said hoping my redemption would be waiting for me.

مـﻴ   مـﻴ   مـﻴ

The air was cool, the moon one-quarter and just rising, cresting the walls of Jerusalem and silhouetting the city, bathing it in a heavenly glow. Night had fallen some five hours past. Silently, we made our way along the wall's base near where

Rashin had stood on the turret earlier in the day. Alhasan led the way followed by myself and Sir James. Sir James and I had discarded our crusader tunics for plain brown travelling togs that denoted us from no particular country, no particular political and religious persuasion. We could be slaves. As much as I had wanted Commander Sir James with me, I thought initially that he would be ordered to stay with his men. He would then have to decide whether it was worth the risk of accompanying me in the hopes of getting back before anyone was to notice that he had gone missing. Yet, my commander only answered to General Horatio Blackthorn. And, as it turned out, the lilac scented general had not been heard from nor seen since the day's main battle. Presently, our dead and injured had been cleared from the field of battle. Blackthorn had not been accounted for. Some speculated that he had been captured, taken prisoner. But according to eye witnesses, only those who had made it to the top of the walls, as Henry had, were taken prisoner. Blackthorn had certainly not been one of those. Regardless, Blackthorn's absence left Sir James in his place. With only two other generals to command the army presently in the immediate region, Commander Sir James' sense of duty nearly precluded him from joining me. But in the end, he delegated his duties temporarily to a subordinate under the admonitions of silence and it being a mission of biblical importance.

My thoughts drifted to Henry. So much had happened to us since arriving in this land. Neither one of us were the same people. I could only hope that he had indeed been captured. At least then he would be alive and I might even be able to help him once inside.

We traveled quietly in the darkness along the wall for some time. Finally, Alhasan slowed our pace and felt along a given section of the wall with his hands. "Here," he whispered as he placed his fingers into a crack in the stone wall. The crack was about two feet in length, at chest height and ran perpendicular to the ground. At first glance, it did not look like anything but a line, a cosmetic blemish on the aged stone wall. He dug the fingers of both hands into the crack and gave a tentative pull.

"Wait," Sir James whispered. "We can't just stroll through the door there."

"There is, how you say, an antechamber on the other side of this stone door.

Then, another door leading out into the city, or still another one leading to a nearby building, I forget which, you see," explained Alhasan.

"And no one on guard in this antechamber?" Sir James asked.

"These passageways and moving blocks are a secret and only used by the Hashishim Knights," answered Alhasan.

"You mean they *were* a secret. I doubt those were Hashishim Knights that snuck out of the passage and stole the spear and sword," I said. "The knights of the Hashishim Order I have encountered would not have performed such thievery, knowing my connection with the weapons as they did," I concluded, trying to convince myself.

"As I have stated, Rashin gave the order to take the Great Spear and King's Sword, I am sure. I am also sure they were Hashishim Knights," said Alhasan with confidence.

"How can you know that?" I asked indignantly.

"You are alive. Out of respect for you, your Templar stature and your brotherhood with the sacred weapons, they did not kill you, you see," he replied matter-of-factly.

A slight chill ran up my spine. "Yes. I do see."

"Come," said Alhasan, indicating the crack. "I am in need of your help." Sir James and I wedged our fingers in the crack and pulled. Slowly and with a slight scraping sound, the stone block hinged open toward us. We opened it just enough to squeeze through one by one.

The antechamber, as Alhasan had called it, was small and dark. There was a damp and musty smell to it that suggested the tiny room never saw the light of day. Alhasan pulled the stone block-door closed behind us by what looked to be a leather strap attached to the door's inside. The stone door closed with the slight scraping sound again, as well as a gentle and quiet thud, plunging us into a near complete darkness. "Now what?" I asked.

"To prayer!" said a muffled voice speaking in the Arabic tongue. Though I could not yet speak the language myself, I found that I was understanding more and more of it. It took but a moment to realize that the voice was coming from the other side of the antechamber's wall, the city's side. The voice was joined by another, also speaking in Arabic, but inaudible. By the fading sound of the voices, they appeared to be moving off.

"Come," whispered our guide, Alhasan. As my eyes adjusted to the room's dark interior, I could see Alhasan standing in front of a short, wooden door. It had a small window in the middle of it which was in the shape of a crescent moon, a sliver of light leaked through it and spilled onto the room's dirt floor. The door itself stood only four feet high and was curved at the top. Alhasan pushed the door's splintered handle down and slowly opened it inward, toward himself. Cautiously, he peered out. Apparently satisfied that the way was clear, he slipped out of the room, motioning for us to follow.

Our small group emerged onto a darkened street, its clearly Roman built stone slates long since cracked and crumbled. We had come through what was called the Second wall of Jerusalem and emerged near what had been known as the old Gennath Gate, now, judging by its appearance, dilapidated and sealed with stone and mortar. Torches cast poor shadows onto the street from their sconces along the city's wall, but there was enough light from them and the ascending moon to show that the street and immediate area were all but deserted.

"Where is everyone?" I asked.

"Prayer?" offered Sir James.

"Yes, but no. I believe the defenders of Jerusalem think they have won," Alhasan replied, "that they have defeated you. But not all of Allah's soldiers rest and pray," he said, pointing up to the top of the wall.

I looked to the top of the wall and saw figures patrolling there and watching the outside of the city. Alhasan moved forward and we followed, pacing ourselves cautiously along the wall we had come through which was on our right. We had walked quietly for only a few moments when we came to a bend in the road and yet another stone wall. This new wall met the wall of our emergence at a forty-five degree angle and went off to our left for as far as I could see in the dimness of the night. What I could see of this new wall——new to us, that is——was that it had many sections in need of repair; holes and gaps abounded. I touched this wall and a curious sensation began to radiate from within my spirit. It was an inner warmth. Just as a warm drink on a cold day warms and soothes the body from within, so too did this sensation warm my spirit. The spear was calling to me. I felt the connection swell in my heart, in the seat of my soul. This wall was an important link in retrieving the Spear of Longinus and the Kings Sword. I felt it. "We go through this wall?" I asked, eager to move on. But something in my heart immediately told me that going through this new wall at this juncture would be premature.

"No," said Alhasan, confirming my feeling. "Do not lose the prize for haste in obtaining it. This wall was the First wall of the city and we will follow along it. It will lead us to what was called the Antonia Fortress. It is where Salah al-Din is as well as Rashin. I believe there is where you will find your sacred weapons."

My heart began to race and my soul to smile. Alhasan spoke the truth, I felt it. I also knew that the ancient fortress hugged the First wall, as Alhasan had called it, in the northeastern quarter of the city. According to Sir James, General Blackthorn had commanded the host of crusaders and Christian soldiers which was to breach the section of wall nearest the Antonia Fortress, between the *Golden Gate* entrance to the city and the Mount of Olives. His troops had been annihilated and the lilac general had disappeared. From what Alhasan had just said, we would be approaching the fortress from the opposite side and from within the city herself. "How far is the fortress?" I asked.

"Approximately under one mile along this wall," replied Alhasan.

"Lead us," I ordered.

"As you wish, Master Masoud." The three of us crept on, with Alhasan and the First wall as our guide. We had travelled nearly a quarter of a mile without incident, looking through the various gaps in the wall along the way. At one point there were several Muslim soldiers on the other side of the wall, roaming or patrolling what had been known in the time of Christ as the Upper City area.

Something entered my mind, then, something that was in opposition to what my heart had indicated only a short time ago. "Alhasan, the turret upon which Rashin had wielded the power through the Rood," I began, "that was near where we first entered the outer wall or the Second wall as you called it..."

"It was the Tower of Hippicus upon which he stood, lad," answered Sir James in Alhasan's stead. "That was its name at the time of our Lord."

"Interesting, commander, but..."

"It was close to Herod's Palace," he continued, apparently intent on giving the unsolicited history lesson, "and on opposite sides of the city from the fortress. Herod's Palace; now *that's* a place that has more than a few secret passages!"

I knew Sir James had been to Jerusalem on campaign before, but I was surprised by his apparent intimate knowledge of parts of the city. However, I set that aside as being fodder for conversation at another time. "Then why would Rashin leave the tower or Herod's Palace for the fortress?" I asked.

"Sultan Salah al-Din wishes his close advisors to be close at hand," answered Alhasan.

"Especially the ones he trusts the least, eh?" Sir James commented wryly.

"This is perhaps the truth of it," replied Alhasan.

We moved silently onward toward the fortress, ducking in the shadows of the wall when patrols came to near.

Curiosity got the better of me and I decided not to wait for some other time in conversing with Sir James regarding his knowledge of Jerusalem. "You've been stationed to this region before, Sir James, I know," I whispered, "but you seem to know quite a lot about various regions of the city, especially, given that we've not occupied it of late."

"Herod's Palace and her secret passages, you mean?" he replied. "Anyone could find out these things. The historian Josephus wrote about them."

"You are not just anyone, and you implied a much deeper knowledge, based on experience I'd say, than your words indicated or some historian might write about," I said.

"Did I now!"

"Aye. Well, at the very least, I sense that you know a lot more," I replied.

"Indeed."

We continued on in silence for a few more moments and I was beginning to think that he would say no more. I was wrong. "I know the intricacies of Herod's Palace and a few other important spots, yes," Sir James continued. "I know them as a Templar, just as Alhasan knows them as a servant of the Hashishim Order, is that not so Alhasan?"

"Yes, yes. Many rituals and ceremonies together here, you see," replied my Arab friend, albeit somewhat cryptically. "No doubt you too will participate in them quite soon, Sir Masoud."

I still did not understand how our two factions——the Order of Templar Knights and The Order of Hashishim Knights——worked together on certain, deeper fronts, yet warred with each other on the outer fronts. Regardless, that was not my concern at the present. "Right now all I care about is getting back the spear and the sword," I replied.

"And so you shall," assured Alhasan. He suddenly stopped and crouched, startling Sir James and I and causing us to instinctively do the same.

"What is it?" I asked. My head wound throbbed from the quick drop and my hands flew to my head in a vane attempt at keeping the pain at bay.

"Masoud, Liam, are you well, lad?" Sir James asked.

"Yes. It will pass," I replied. The pain throbbed for a moment more and subsided. "Why did you stop, Alhasan?"

"We are here," he said, peering around the corner of the wall we had crouched near. I peered around Alhasan and the wall's corner. It turned out not to be a corner at all, but a large chunk of the wall jutting out and over the section of wall we had been moving along. Upon further inspection, it was clear that the portion jutting out was actually a patchwork of wall laid or built over the main wall, as if it were a large patch covering a hole in the this particular section of the wall. Following Alhasan's lead, we moved out and around the patched portion and could see that the main wall stretched on for at least another one-hundred-and-fifty yards, and to my surprise, immediately in front of our position began a steady and gradual increase in height, ending at a near seventy feet in the air by my estimation. It also culminated in at least one huge turret or tower. We had arrived at the fortress. But my heart sank. From our position the wall and tower looked formidable, impenetrable even from this side which was technically inside the city proper. Yet, I refused to give in to despair. "There has to be a way in," I declared, "a gate perhaps."

"This *was* the gate for this section of the wall," said Alhasan, indicating the jutting patchwork of wall which we had just come around. "It was sealed some century ago, you see."

"Why?" I asked.

"I do not know," he replied matter-of-factly.

"Even if the gate were still here, lad, would you have us simply walk right through unnoticed by any of the enemy?" asked Sir James sardonically.

"Your point is taken, commander, but the underlying question remains; how do we get in?" I said. In near unison, Sir James and I looked to Alhasan for the answer.

"My good Sirs, would I have led you to this point without a way of entering the desired place?" Alhasan said with mock insult. Yet, the tone of his voice gave me pause; I sensed that his reaction of a mock insult was more of a cover for an inexplicable nervousness than anything else. Sir James and I exchanged a glance. He had clearly heard the uncertainty in Alhasan's voice as well. I looked back to my friend, my *servant*. "Alhasan..." I said, letting my voice trail off as if calling out the deceit of a small child.

"La, la! No! Sir Masoud. I have plan! Truly," he said defensively.

"Well then, what is it?" I asked. "Surely you..." my head began to throb again with intense, searing pain. But the origin of the pain this time was not my head wound. It was something else entirely. The spear, something was happening with the spear! I felt it. I closed my eyes. In my mind I saw a darkened stone room. Inside this room stood several hooded figures standing in a loose circle. In the circle's center stood Rashin, hooded as well, but face exposed. Upon his face danced an unearthly red glowing light. The source of this light came from three objects in front of him, each on its own makeshift stone altar. The objects were the Rood of Christ, The King's Sword and The Spear of Longinus. Power was arcing through these sacred objects in the form akin to lightning in the sky. The power was clearly being directed by Rashin, each object magnifying the power through the other. I then noticed yet another hooded figure step from the shadows near Rashin and come to stand next to him. The arcing power also coursed through this individual, through Rashin and subsequently through the objects. Though I could not see the new figures face I instantly knew who he was, for the scent of lilacs suddenly filled my ethereal nostrils. "How can this be?!"

"As to your general, I cannot say. Each makes his own choices," said a nearby voice. But the voice did not come from Sir James or Alhasan. I turned my head and looked directly in to a pair of gold-colored eyes. I was stunned into silence. "But the objects have become a conduit," he continued, "a conduit for the Power of the One that flows through each of us equally yet is only expressed to the degree of the individual's understanding of it."

"How did you..." I stammered, finding my tongue at last.

"The law of the One knows only to respond to the belief of the individual," the ancient, golden-eyed priest continued, oblivious to my partially posed question. "According to the individual's belief, the objects will act as a multiplier, again, if that is what he believes. You knew all this at one time, but are in need of reminding."

"But they have to be stopped!" I said, ignoring his last apparent jab at the accumulative knowledge of my soul.

"Masoud!" said Alhasan in a reprimanding tone.

"Go to the last gate," said the ancient priest in my mind as he faded from my mind's eye.

"Who were you talking to," asked Sir James.

"Where is the last gate?" I asked Alhasan, ignoring the commander's query.

"The last gate?" replied Alhasan, confused. "That would depend upon which gate you're start from counting."

"Sir Masoud..." began Sir James,

"I saw Rashin in my mind's eye using the spear, the sword and the rood as a conduit for bringing Power here I believe for purely destructive purposes," I explained. "And that is not all; Blackthorn was with him."

"You saw this in your mind, Liam. It doesn't mean it was actually so," replied Sir James none-too-convincingly.

"Then the gold-eyed...the voice I heard said, 'go to the last gate,'" I continued, ignoring Sir James' reply.

"There is not a last gate in distinction, no first gate and subsequent last gate, you see," said Alhasan.

"Not in distinction, but in passing," noted Sir James.

Yes. I understood. We all three understood. The three of us looked to the *last gate* we had passed, sealed now. Or, so it appeared.

"It has to be *this* gate," I said, but not knowing where to begin looking for an opening or way through the patchwork.

"Begin at the bottom," said the priest's voice in my mind.

The priest's name came to me then. A name from my spirit's distant past. "Thank you, Father Pretorius," I whispered knowing that to be the golden-eyed, disembodied priest's former name. I stepped to the patchwork segment of the wall and began looking around its base.

"What do you look for, Master Masoud?" asked Alhasan.

"I'm not sure. I just know to start here and it will be revealed," I replied. I began to run my hand along the base of the wall where it met the earth, digging my fingers into the dirt. Nothing but sand and dirt and hard stone met my efforts. Until, that is, one of the base blocks moved ever so slightly, as if it were balanced on the point of a deeper stone below it. The patched section of the wall had been constructed with what appeared to be rough blocks of stone approximately three feet tall by two feet wide and laid unevenly atop one-another and overlapping each other. Little mortar appeared to have been used to seal the blocks together, thus creating more of a balanced wall of stacked blocks than a solid, cohesive one. Consequently, at least one block was bound to be loose and of no particular anchoring quality. Once I was confident that the moving of this loose block would pose no threat of the entire patchwork wall section tumbling down upon us I began to dig dirt from its base, and continued to do so, Sir James and Alhasan joining my efforts when they perceived the stone block was indeed loose. As dirt and debris loosened around the block, a two inch gap appeared at the top of it. Putting my hands beneath the block as if I were cradling a babe, I pushed up once, twice, thrice. The stone lifted slightly, loosening the rest of the dirt and sand that had lodged itself between the block and those next to it. "Help me pull it free," I said to my companions.

"Perhaps the whole section of wall will fall should we free this stone," said Alhasan.

"Not likely," replied Sir James as he examined the wall section. "I'm no engineer, but judging by the way they all overlap, this one stone, if removed would present no threat," he said, echoing my earlier assessment.

"Come then. Help me," I repeated. The two men knelt beside me, wedging their fingers in the now visible gaps around the loose stone block. "Pull." We pulled and wriggled the stone block toward us. The block, though heavy, turned out to be atop other smaller, round stones which effectively acted as ancient rollers. Slowly, it became looser and looser, sliding out of resting place ever so begrudgingly. "One more effort, now," I said. Our obvious success thus far inspired us to heave our backs and legs into it with even more vigor. Soon we could nearly wrap our arms around the block to gain more of a grip and were surprised to find that the block just seemed to keep coming out of its slot, so long it was——long in the sense that it extended through the wall from our side to the other some five or more feet. The stone block was heavy, but with a gallant effort and the aid of the ancient roller-stones beneath it, we three were able to finally pull it out completely.

As soon as the block was free I got on my hands and knees and peered through the opening now at the base of the patched section of wall. A small and short tunnel greeted my eyes. The moon was higher in the sky and looking through the tunnel I could see that the ground on the other side of the wall was bathed in soft moonlight. Without preamble, I lay flat on my stomach and pulled myself through the tunnel.

TWENTY-FIVE

Upon closer inspection of the fortress and its walls and towers, it was quite obvious that my initial awestruck assessment of the fortress as being impenetrable and formidable had been severely misplaced. Though two of its towers and most of its walls still stood, the fortress itself was very unimpressive. I could imagine that during the time it was built it had been a most functional and, perhaps, formidable structure; part fortified city, part palace. Presently, however, it was a partially destroyed, crumbling shadow of its former self. I came to find later that it was named Antonia Fortress after the famous Roman Triumvir Marcus Antonius, or Mark Antony as he was also known, and was partially torn asunder by Rome herself a few centuries earlier. No wonder it was currently so un-noteworthy. It was also the place, according to some, wherein Jesus had been put on trial.

Unlike most of our journey this night, many Muslim soldiers were now about. The moon had risen and though it was a quarter waning, it still gave off enough light to find one's way to the fortress proper, as well as view the quantity of Arab troops we came upon. Sir James and I had wrapped our heads in the Arab manner. Alhasan led us and we followed in a way that denoted us as his servants; walking slightly behind him with our heads bowed respectfully and eyes averted so as not to look directly at our *betters*, as it were. We moved rapidly through the court and the ancient temple, or what was left of these structures, and arrived promptly at the remains of the fortress itself. Alhasan led us through one of the walkways and to a rampart leading up into the center part of the main structure. The rampart took us into a very large, high ceilinged room with four passages leading off in different directions. Though the room was partially lit by many torches in wall sconces, it was still dark and foreboding, foreboding because the large space now more resembled a huge cave than the large, well-built room of a fortress. I looked to the passages before us as we walked on. They appeared to be dark openings to dark tunnels beyond. Until, that is, one of them on our right caught my attention. It looked no different than the others, but something about it *spoke* to me on the deepest of levels as being the passage through which my task would be accomplished. "Stop!" I barked, my two companions halting cold in their steps and both staring at me in a reprimanding way, *keep your English speaking voice down, you fool!* spoke their look.

A troop of Arabic guards was walking nearby, heading out in the direction through which we had come. I looked out of the corner of my eye at them and saw that two of the men had clearly heard the non-Arabic word I had uttered. I ignored them, drawing my attention back to the passage on our right which had called to me. The calling was a feeling in the center of my heart; a feeling that told me, compelled me, to take the passageway. My heart pounding, I took a step toward it.

But as I did, a hand grasped my arm, stopping me. "La, Masoud. I believe Rashin to be in another part, not that way," said Alhasan gently, quietly.

"I do not know why, but my sense is to follow this passageway," I replied, "and I trust my inner sense more than ever."

"I understand, but..."

"Who are you?!" demanded a strong voice in the Arabic tongue. The two Arab soldiers that had looked at me a moment ago now stood before us. Though I did not raise my eyes to look at them directly, I did, nonetheless, peer at them from beneath my brow. They looked at me in an accusatory manner, and the hands of both men rested on the pommel of their as of yet still sheathed scimitar. "Who are you?! Answer!" demanded the one man again.

"I am," began Alhasan, drawing at least one of the men to look at him rather than me, "servant to Salah al-Din and these two are my servants."

The Arab soldier who had spoken and who also still stared at me now turned to Alhasan. "This one," he said, pointing at me, but speaking to Alhasan, "spoke in the crusader tongue and you answered him in it. I will ask but once more, both of you; who are you?"

"And I will answer you but once more," Alhasan blustered in an arrogant tone. "*I* am personal servant to Sultan Salah al-Din and these two men serve me," he stated indicating Sir James and me. "Do you not think that a great leader such as our Sultan would have those near him who speak the enemy's tongue? Salah al-Din himself speaks the crusader tongue or are you too dim to understand the intricacies of leadership or even what I have just said?"

Rather than back down, the Arab soldier became angry and took a threatening step toward Alhasan. Though Sir James and I both carried standard issue, sidearm crusader swords——beautiful weapons that were part long dagger, part sword—— beneath our tunics we dared not draw them lest we give ourselves away and bring re-inforcements for the Arab soldiers and certain death for us. Fortunately, that point was rendered moot as the Arab soldier's comrade proved to be of a more amenable disposition and thought. "Come, Abbas," he said, gently taking the arm of his hot-headed partner. "Leave them. They are unworthy and I for one do not wish the wrath of the Sultan on my head should we bring harm to his property."

Screams and yells of confusion suddenly assaulted our ears from within the city near the fortress and diverted all of our attention from the immediate situation. A fraction of a second later the fortress rocked with an explosion, causing dust and dirt from the ancient stones above us to sprinkle down upon our heads. More yells found their way to us. All at once, four more Arab soldiers ran by us heading out of the fortress. "Come! We are assaulted!" one them commanded to Abbas and his comrade as he ran past with the others. The two before us did as they were bade, the belligerent Abbas giving me a look of utter contempt and spitting at my feet before joining his fellow soldiers.

"What is happening?" I asked, addressing no one in particular when the oth-ers were gone.

It was Sir James who answered. "Catapults, I should imagine. They and the siege engines finally arrived just before you woke up. I suspect fireballs of pitch and wood are being launched over the walls and at the gates."

This news was completely unexpected as was the realization that came next into my mind. "Why did we not wait until they were in place before attempting the assault yesterday?!" I asked, appalled. "Countless lives might have been saved!"

"Blackthorn did not want to wait, said he didn't trust the runners' reports that they were on the way," replied Sir James in a tone of disgust. "Blackthorn's a fool. I doubt very much if the catapults and siege engines are going to help now. We've not enough men left."

"Blackthorn is appearing more and more a wretch," I said.

"Aye," was all Sir James could muster as a reply.

I then looked at the passage still to our right, the one I was about to head into a moment before. I took a deep breath and silently asked my inner sense. The feeling was stronger than before; this was the passage to follow. My feet were moving of their own accord, carrying me in the direction of the passageway's mouth, some forty feet away.

"Masoud!" said Alhasan. But he was not going to stop me this time. I entered the passageway just as another explosion shook the fortress, striking even closer than before and nearly knocking me off of my feet. I looked back briefly and saw, with relief and satisfaction, that Alhasan and Sir James were now following me.

The passageway or corridor was dark, barely lit by a scant three sconce torches which were spaced very far apart, approximately every twenty yards or so. The corridor was wide, by some ten yards across, but low in height, a mere six feet high at most. Another surprising thing; the remnants of the fortress appeared tall from the outside, with the tower appearing to be at least seventy-five feet or more tall. Since we had entered at the ground level I had expected these inner passageways and corridors to incline upwards. The one we were in, however, inclined downward and became steeper with every step.

We rushed on for a moment in silence until we came to the last of the lit torch sconces, at which point I stopped us for a moment. "I still protest, Master Masoud," whispered Alhasan urgently. "I believe we should be going to another part of the..." he was cut off by yet another explosion, jolting all of us. This one obviously had been a direct hit onto fortress.

"No. I'm sorry, Alhasan, but I still believe I need to go in this direction and down this passageway," I replied. Yet, a moment of doubt splashed into my mind as I looked ahead and saw nothing but darkness. Regardless, I ran on. A moment later, however, my feet suddenly went out from under me and I was falling. But before I could voice my surprise and fear, I hit solid ground again in the form of a profoundly steep incline. Landing on my rear with a thud, I then began to slide and roll downward in the darkness.

I heard my companions land behind me with an equally hard thud and begin their own slide and roll into God only knew what. Finally, I went airborne again. A few seconds later I landed in a soft pile of what I took to be straw or hay by the feel of it. The smell of stale urine filled my nostrils. "Allah!" Alhasan exclaimed as he apparently went into the final freefall. It suddenly dawned on me that I was going to be his landing cushion if I did not move quickly. I did, scrambling out of the way just in time to feel Alhasan land in the straw beside me. Unfortunately, Alhasan was not so lucky. Before he could react at all, Sir James plummeted in, landing directly on top of him, at least by the sound of it in the complete darkness.

"Agh! Commander!" cried Alhasan.

"My apologies, Alhasan," said Sir James as he rolled off of Alhasan. "Liam, are you here?"

"Yes, sir."

"What the devil have you gotten us into?!"

"I'm sorry, I don't know why I was led to this point," I said lamely.

"And just where is here?" asked my commander.

"I was hoping one of you could answer that," I said.

"La. I know some of this fortress, but little," said Alhasan.

"That's just..." began Sir James. But he inexplicably stopped in mid sentence. I was about to ask him why, when I heard the reason; voices, faint voices were wafting to our ears. But from where?

"You hear that," he asked in the darkness.

"Yes," I replied. But there was something odd about the voices. They seemed distraught, but there was something else, a quality that seemed out of place in the middle of this place of battle. "Children?" I asked, horrified at the prospect of any child being in this place.

"La. Not children," answered Alhasan. We sat in silence for time, listening. We could not discern what was being said or who the voices belonged to, though I still felt that it could be children. "Look!"

"What?" I replied, confused. "Look at what? It's black as pitch in here." But then I saw it; a sliver of light on the ground nearby, some ten feet away by the look of it. Slowly, I crawled toward it, bumping into two objects along the way which impeded my progress. I decided that I did not care to know what the objects were. Thus, I made my way around them and kept on moving toward the sliver of light. I reached out and touched the line of light and it became quite apparent what it was. "There's a door here," I said. "The light is coming from underneath the door at the bottom."

My friends crawled over to my position and for the first time in a few harrowing minutes I was able to see their faces from the soft bounce of light beneath the door. "You are correct it appears, Masoud. It is a door." Alhasan felt up the door's center-left side until he located what turned out to be a leather strap or handle. Giving a tentative tug the door easily opened inward.

TWENTY-SIX

We all three stood and looked out into a gloomy but lit hallway. This hallway was nothing like the dilapidated one we had initially come through, however. This one was pristine, complete with dark marble-tiled floors and tapestries on the walls.

The voices still came to us in a muffled and distant manner, but were a little more audible. The hall extended some forty feet and cornered left. "We've come this far. Let's push on," commanded Sir James, drawing his sword. Following his lead I did so as well, though I did not feel the need. Besides, it now felt odd to be holding any other sword or weapon than the King's Sword or the Spear of Longinus.

"Is that necessary?" asked Alhasan.

"I doubt that the ploy of being your servants will work down here," answered Sir James. "Something tells me we've truly entered the monster's bowels."

"You are probably most correct commander, though I'd not classify it as the *monster's* anything. There are two monsters at least in any conflict, you see." said Alhasan. We stepped out of the room and began our trek down the hall.

As we reached the corner, the voices suddenly went silent. After a moment, we tentatively peered around the corner. There was no one there, no one to impede our progress. We rounded the corner and continued on. Three things became apparent. The first was that this part of the hallway was extremely long.

It seemed to go on as far as the eyes could see. The second was that there were many rooms off of this section. Beginning some thirty yards ahead of our present position there was light spilling out of doorways. The third thing was something completely and utterly unexpected; the stale urine stench of a few moments ago, which seemed to follow us as we went down the hall, was suddenly replaced by the sweet but faint scent of perfume. I thought instantly of Blackthorn and his perpetual lilac scent. But that was not it. This smell was not of lilacs per se. It was distinctly perfume, decidedly feminine and intoxicating. "Ah, laddie," said Sir James as he sniffed the air. "Have you led us to a harem now?" he asked rhetorically in a tone that denoted trouble was at hand.

In my mind's eye a pair of beautiful lavender eyes stared at me. "Najeeba," I whispered.

I felt real eyes upon me and turned to see Alhasan's stern look of disproval. "I doubt very much that she is here, Masoud. Do not be distracted from the duty at hand."

"She is not a distraction," I said defensively.

"Najeeba? Who is that?" asked Sir James.

"She is niece to the Sultan. Sir Masoud was of assistance to her some time back," explained Alhasan, "and is presently, how you say, enamored with her. Quite inappropriate, you see."

"You cannot place a judgment on such things. I can't explain what I feel other than to say she and I have known one-another for centuries, daft as that may sound," I said.

Sir James stared at me for a moment. He seemed to understand. "You have become more attuned with your soul, Liam, to be sure. And I believe what you say. However, we are not here to rescue a maiden, soul partner or no. We are here to retrieve the sword and spear."

"We create what we are here to do and perhaps we will do both," I retorted, brushing past both men and slowly making my way down the hall.

"Liam. Masoud," Sir James whispered loudly from behind me.

"There is no point in attempting to dissuade him, commander. You will not succeed," said Alhasan.

"Aye. I'm more his follower now than his commander as I see it."

Ignoring my companions, I made my way to the first door and looked in. Nothing. The room was empty except for a few throw pillows and carpets. The next room proved to be the same, as did the one after that. But the fourth, the fourth was the source of the smell of perfume, for it lingered in the air as I entered the room. Throw rugs and rich accoutrements dotted the space; a gold-leafed table here, silken shawls and thick silken pillows there. "Well, they are gone now," said Alhasan from behind me, clearly relieved.

"Don't be so pleased, my friend. The night is new. We may come across her yet," I said. I turned and left the room, my companions following.

Still, the hall seemed to go on and on, bending and curving one way then the other.

"What the devil," exclaimed Sir James. "It's like a maze. We'll not get any-where like this. Think, lad. Do you feel the spear or the sword, here a-bouts?"

I closed my eyes briefly, searching my mind, my soul and saw the Spear of Longinus and the King's Sword. In my mind's eye, I saw them in the same room as before. But this time, a light from the spear reached out to me, making its way through to where I presently stood in the hall. My eyes popped open, obliterating the vision in my mind's eye. There was no light extending from anywhere and making contact with me. But what I felt next was the unseen connection with the Great Spear asserting itself on my being. The hair on my neck stood on end. A tingling sensation began at the base of my spine and ended at the area of my heart. It then gave me a tugging sensation, pulling me forward. My steps began slowly, moving me forward further down the hall.

"Masoud, it speaks to you, yes?" Alhasan said.

I did not respond for fear of breaking the connection with the spear, thus losing direction once again. I moved some thirty feet more and came to an open doorway on the left. But it was not a doorway as such. It was the entryway to an extensive, left-spiraling staircase leading down, lit only by faint light coming up from below. "Agh!" cried a woman from deep down the staircase, breaking the connection with the spear. No matter. It was clear that descending the ancient stone stairs was in order. I looked back at my friends for the briefest of instances.

A momentary crease of disapproval furrowed their brows in near unison. But for Sir James' part, it was quickly replaced by a smile of support.

"Ah, the devil be damned. If we're going to jump in, may as well go all the way, eh lad," Sir James pointed out. "Let's go then!"

Like three bolts of lightning, we descended the stairs, going round and round and down and down, nearly stumbling more than once in darkened space and on the crumbling stone steps. Finally I did stumble, catching my foot on the sharp, jagged edge of one the final steps. I completely lost my footing and flew head-long into a flimsy door at the base of the staircase, crashing loudly through it and sprawling on the floor. The crusader sword which I had been holding flipped out of my hand as the latter hit the ground hard. It clanged and slid across the floor, coming to rest under a black boot as the boot stepped upon it. I looked up and into the face of the boot's owner; the opaque-eyed soothsayer, Rashin. "I am quite impressed. Your connection to the ancient weapons is indeed strong for you to have made it this far."

Alhasan and Sir James came rushing through the door and froze at my side. I made it to my feet without pretense, forcing my embarrassment over the entry I made to the basement of my mind. The hooded figures I had seen in this room within my mind's eye were all present, all but Blackthorn, that is. But his smell was there; the faint but unmistakable scent of lilac hovered in the air.

It was then I noticed out of the corner of my eye that Sir James' sword was raised in a ready-defensive position.

"It is unwise to brandish your sword just now," said Rashin to my commander. "Do you not agree, Sir Blackthorn?" he said over his shoulder.

From the shadows behind Rashin a figure emerged. The figure threw off his cowl and revealed his face; General Sir Horatio Blackthorn, Commander of the crusader army and in that moment, traitor to his race and religion and soul. Anger welled within my being. I had not wanted to believe the vision I had earlier of this man being in the midst of those who stole the Great Spear and King's Sword. Indeed, until that very moment I had not truly believed the vision. Yet, he was here.

"You are a disgrace, Horatio," declared Sir James.

"My good fellow," replied Blackthorn condescendingly, "quite the contrary, we are merging our powers, the Order of Templar Knights and the Knights of the Hashishim Order. These weapons are *our* legacy, they are *our* birthright!" he said.

"You are mad. And, you do not speak for the Templar Order," I said.

"Am I mad? Quite the contrary, I am one of the very few who is in his complete right mind," laughed Blackthorn. "You cannot remember, though your soul knows. Your soul knows everything of your journey, Masoud. But instead of using this knowledge for your soul's advancement and incarnating as an advanced divine being on this earth, instead of incarnating as a man knowingly connected to his advanced soul as you did with your last life as a Master Merlin, you chose to reincarnate in this life as an ignorant foot soldier barely connected with his spirit's knowledge," Blackthorn said, pausing for what I interpreted as being nothing more than the drama of it.

Some of what he said made sense. Yet, my feet were firmly on the path they had always been on. Even in this life as Liam Mason-Masoud, I had been experiencing much of those lives of Longinus and Myrriddin, or rather, re-experiencing some of the moments of great learning and importance, and with each re-experiencing, solidifying the lessons and seeing them with a new layer that was not apparent before. The fact that someone else could not see this was of no concern to me. We are each of us on our chosen journey, this and every life, the purposes of which, the objectives of which, remain hidden to all but the individualized soul. To say that one soul is more advanced this time around or that time around is to miss the point of the subjective journey within the One Mind, which is this: that Mind may experience Itself, as Itself, through our individualized experiences within Itself.

"We have all been with you on your soul's journey, Master Masoud," Blackthorn continued. "All for our own purposes, of course, but there nonetheless. Yet, you were oblivious to one of the greatest Orders of Knights even as the Roman centurion who set all this in motion. The Militia Crucifera Evangelica, protector of the newly birthed Christian sect, deflector of Rome by way of deception and magic, it was they who ensured that the roots of the new religion could take hold. Do you think as Longinus you languished in the Mists with the likes of the Celts for those years all on your own? Our Orders," he ranted on, now indicating

Rashin and his men, "have been in existence since the dawn of knowledge in one form or another, ensuring that only the select and worthy know the Eternal Light and Infinite Knowledge, the Great Secrets, the True Workings of the One and The Law that governs our very nature."

"It is not for you to withhold anything," I said, angrily. "All are equal by the One and under the Law of the One, and by the Law enact experiences to the degree of their understanding," I countered, not exactly sure of where my words were coming from, but not questioning them either. "Who are you to deny them the knowledge of their very being, their very essence?!"

"You should be bowing before him, Blackthorn," snarled Sir James, indicating that the general should be on his knees before me.

"You have been keeper of the Great Spear and King's Sword until now, this is true," said Blackthorn, ignoring Sir James' taunt and my question. "And for that, we are truly grateful," he said, sounding falsely contrite. "But you have not always had it, and while some still see you as the weapons' keeper, the time has come for all of the relics to come back into the fold of the Order, the true guardians of the Eternal Light and Infinite Knowledge. We had been waiting to see if this was indeed the Great Spear of Longinus and the King's Sword and for you, your soul, to appear and demonstrate the fact. Together with the Rood, The Grail, the Shroud and the bone of the Apostle, the Power of the One can be infinitely multiplied and directed."

"If not mad, then you truly are a fool," I said, "for if you were the true guardian of the Eternal Light and Infinite Knowledge, you would know that you do not need these things to multiply and direct the Power. You need only your unwavering confidence in belief and knowingness in the very nature of your being."

"Enough of this," declared Rashin as he stepped away from us and deeper into the room.

TWENTY-SEVEN

As Rashin walked deeper into the room, I realized for the first time that the space was a large, cavernous, high ceilinged, cathedral type structure. Stained glass windows banked the walls, eerily lit from behind by torches and candles. Though we were obviously deep underground, the windows were meant to mimic the outside night's light of an above ground cathedral. Instead, in this vast underground place it appeared as more the devil's church then a Christian cathedral. It was then I noticed that the high ceiling was designed to resemble the inside of a Mosque. This place did no service to either of these great religious sanctuaries. It was a poor representation of their blending, almost a mocking.

There were no pews as in a real cathedral. In the center were the pedestals that I had seen in my vision. One contained a piece of wood——a part of the Rood——another The Spear of Longinus and still another The King's Sword. Yet, there were three other pedestals as well. One contained the Shroud of the Christ——that which my spirit recognized as the burial cloth of Jesus——folded so that His emblazoned image faced all. Another pedestal had upon it a plain wooden bowl. *The Holy Grail?* I wondered. It must be. Yet, I sensed nothing special about this bowl. And finally, one more pedestal held a small, pointed object which stood upright. It took me a moment to realize what it was; a human finger bone. I tried to approach the pedestals but was prevented by four very large, dark robed, hooded figures. They unceremoniously took me by both of my arms and led me to a spot just outside of the six-pointed configuration of pedestals. Sir James and Alhasan joined me, escorted by other hooded figures. Two other hooded figures appeared, having come from the cathedral's far end, near what would have been the area of the altar in a real church. "You did not succeed," stated Rashin to the newcomers.

"We did not, sire. She is gone," said one of them.

"No matter," said Rashin.

For the briefest of instances, my eyes darted around the whole room, trying to discern the room's overall layout, yes, but also, I suddenly realized, looking for the female whose voice we had heard from atop the spiral staircase and obviously who the men had been looking for.

The woman all but forgotten by our robed and hooded hosts, we were flanked by several of these men. My companions and I faced the pedestals while Rashin, Blackthorn and eleven other dark-robed ones encircled the sacred relics. "You see before you the power of God conveyed in these objects," stated Rashin to us. "The Rood by which your Jesus was hanged, the cloth in which he was buried, the cup with which he drank the first Holy Communion," continued Rashin, pointing to each object in turn, "the finger of Paul, one of your Prophet's great Apostles, Excalibur——The King's Sword——and finally, the Great Spear, that which you Masoud, as Longinus, used to stab your Prophet, your Anointed One while he was on the cross, killing him. Behold now the power!" he finished, taking his place near Blackthorn. Nodding to the lilac general, the...ceremony, for want of a better word, began.

In high theatrical pose, Blackthorn raised his face and arms toward the ceiling, the heavens, and closed his eyes. "Abwûn d'bwaschmâja Nethkâdasch schmach Têtê malkuthach," he intoned in a tongue that was so ancient it had not been heard in a thousand years. Yet, it was not so far removed from my mind, my soul, as to be unrecognizable; Aramaic, the language of Christ's time. "Nehwê tzevjân-ach aikâna d'bwaschmâja af b'arha. Hawylân lachma d'sûkanân jaomâna..."

"'Oh thou, Oh Birther! Father-Mother of the Cosmos from whom the breath of life comes...,'" Sir James whispered next to me, interpreting the ancient Aramaic chant as Blackthorn droned on in the background. In that moment I was not sure which surprised me more; the fact that Sir James understood Aramaic or the fact that I had the sudden realization that this was no ordinary chant. It was the Lord's Prayer, in its original form and meaning, in its original language of Aramaic. "'...who fills all realms of sound, light and vibration. May your Light be experienced in my utmost holiest. Your Heavenly domain approaches. Let your will come true——in the Universe just as on earth. Give us wisdom for our daily needs, detach the fetters of fault that bind us like we let go the guilt of others. Let us not be lost in superficial things, but let us be freed from that what keeps us off from our true purpose. From you comes the all-working will, the lively strength to act, the song that beautifies all and renews itself from age to age.'"

"Amên," finished Blackthorn.

"'Sealed in trust, faith and truth,'" Sir James said, thus concluding his interpreter's performance of the Aramaic words.

Silence filled the room. All the robed figures seemed to be in a deep state of meditation. An odd way to tempt the power of God, the power of the One through these artifacts and the ancient Lord's Prayer, yet...

A tingling sensation filled the room, making the hairs on my body stand on end. An energy entered that seemed to fill the space with a strange buoyancy. I had the sensation that I could float off of the ground if I set my mind to it. "Abwûn d'bwaschmâja Nethkâdasch schmach Têtê malkuthach," came the words again, but this time in unison by all the hooded figures present, chanting the prayer and focusing their individual minds to be of one collective mind and hence joining directly with the One Mind. The energy that had entered the room now centered itself on the sacred objects. From all but one of them came a light with an odd, unearthly blue glow, radiating the light from an unseen source. The one object that remained darkened and plain was the so-called grail. As I had sensed previously, it appeared to be a plain bowl or cup. I saw Rashin's eyes then also looking at the wooden bowl. His eyes narrowed with anger at the bowl's apparent falseness, his discolored eye watering with the emotion. By the look of his face it was all he could do to not let the anger consume him, thereby breaking the spell being cast, the power being summoned. The other five objects held the

Otherworldly glow, however. I could feel the power coming through the objects, particularly the Spear and the Sword. The power grew, building and building in intensity as evidenced by the pressure being pressed upon my body from without. It was as if a giant hand was squeezing me. I looked to Sir James whose expression told me he felt it as well. As if to further confirm the sensation, the power and the glow began to expand from the objects, taking the form of a vaporous cloud, engulfing the room, seemingly becoming too large and potent to contain, yet singular in its concentration, its locality.

"Strengthen the bonds of power!" said Blackthorn loudly to the air, to the power coursing through the objects and the room, speaking to it as though it had a conscious mind, for indeed it appeared to, directing its attention first to those near the objects and then the individuals nearby. The power, the energy, while engulfing the room we were in also localized itself into a stretched, oblong vaporous sphere with one round end that seemed the head of the thing. It was as if the power, the energy, was looking at all with unseen eyes, assessing, even asking, *who dares call me forth?!* It was directly in front of Blackthorn when the general had said the words. It now moved around the circle of hooded and robed figures, and came to Sir James, Alhasan and myself, stopping in front of me.

It hovered before me and my first instinct was to fear it. But I did not. There was nothing to fear from a power that is from the One Source, for it was my power, everyone's power. Nothing but peace and devotion, happiness and abundance is what I held in my mind. And, within a heart's beat that is what I felt from it, this mass of power-filled energy. Overwhelming feelings of warmth and comfort, prosperity and peace and yes, love is what radiated back to me. I was receiving what I was giving and to a tenth degree more. It was the most wonderful sensation, as if I was in the lap of God and, of course, I was. Right there and right then, I was. I also knew truly that we are always in this presence because it is us. It only appears missing, absent, when we turn our intention and realization away from It.

"Death! Destruction! Oblivion to the enemies of the Eternal Light!" Blackthorn yelled at the powerful sphere of energy in an enraged tone.

In that moment I pitied the lilac scented general for he had absolutely lost his way. He was no knight of the Templar Order. He was displaying everything the

Templar Order was not. As with the knights of Arthur's legendary round table, those who were among our predecessors, the Templar Order stood for truth, justice, service and protection of those less fortunate. We were the keepers of the Light and Sacred Knowledge, yes, but not to the exclusion of others. In fact, it was for the preservation of these things that they may be taught to all and held by all to be the right of all that we kept them safe and out of the hands of those who would seek to control the populace by keeping the knowledge for themselves. Blackthorn had truly lost sight of that.

"Oblivion to the enemies of the keepers of Infinite Knowledge!" yelled Blackthorn.

It is done unto you as you believe, said the voice in my mind, the voice of the golden-eyed priest, reciting the great Truth.

The sphere of power turned and floated back to Blackthorn. "Direct your power to them and destroy the enemy!" he commanded of the sphere. The sphere of power complied, giving Blackthorn what he was giving it. The sphere stretched itself and embraced Blackthorn, wrapping itself completely around his body in a slow, near sensual manner. He was lifted off of the ground to the astonishment of all present. Instinctively, everyone took a step back and away from the oblong sphere. "Aaaggghhh!!!" screamed the general in utter agony. A rumbling sound began to fill the room, growing in volume as if thunder were approaching. The next sound was that of a horrific crunching sound, bones being crunched within the body of the floating Blackthorn. The rumbling grew louder, the large room began to shake, sending chunks of the stone and tiled ceiling plummeting to the floor, striking three of the robed figures in the head——two of whom were the men who had searched for the female——and killing them instantly. The remaining figures panicked, including those guarding Sir James, Alhasan and myself, dropping the ceremonial pretense and bolting for the door I had come through. Another rumble and shaking of the room brought down more of the ceiling and some of the wall, blocking that door. Hoods now flew off of our former guards and their eyes darted back and forth seeking another way out but clearly not knowing of one.

Now was my chance. I lunged forward toward the pedestals, intent on removing the relics from their resting place. I tossed the Rood to Sir James who enfolded it in the extra cloth of his tunic and slung it on his back. I then gently wrapped the Finger Bone, Bowl and Shroud in the spare cloth of my own tunic for safekeeping. Finally, I took the Spear of Longinus and the King's Sword from their pedestals. The sphere of power dropped the limp body of General Blackthorn on top of Rashin, who appeared to be stunned, in a complete state of shock by the events. The building shook again, more crumbling ceiling fell but struck no one this time. The sphere of power then turned toward me. I held the Spear of Longinus and the King's Sword aloft to it, not in a threatening manner, but in a manner of victory. *You will be led to freedom,* said the golden-eyed Priest's voice in my mind again. But this time, I knew the voice to be coming from the sphere of power. But how? Was it truly the priest I had known as Pretorius in my previous existence? Or was it the One appearing in a given form? Or Both?

"Where to go, Masoud?" asked Alhasan standing next to me. "Our previous way is now blocked."

"You will die before I let you take these things!" yelled Rashin as he tried to push the dead Blackthorn off of him. "Do not let them escape!" he yelled to the remaining robed figures.

"This way!" I said, not knowing exactly where to go, but realizing we could not stay here. I ran to the far end of the large room, the large pretend cathedral, toward where an altar would be if this were an actual church, the direction from which the two men had returned from while apparently searching for the escaped female. Unless she was hiding in the cathedral, she must have escaped out of some opening on the altar side of the room. Two heavy wooden doors were there on either side. I crashed hard into the one on our right, presuming it would give way and I would fall into another room or hallway. It did not. I might as well have flung myself into a solid stone wall. It would not budge. The next door proved to be the same. It became clear that like the stained glass windows, the doors were there for appearance and not function. I began to lose patience, and allow fear to creep in. Another thunderous rumble jolted the room. A large wall near where we had been standing with the pedestals broke free, crushing three more of the robed figures and the pedestals and nearly crushing Rashin. Rashin was free, standing near the remaining robed figures and pointing at us.

"La, here!" said a female voice from our left. I looked in the direction of the tender but urgent voice and saw a darkened archway. In the archway was silhouetted a petite and slender figure. Her face was in shadow but an arm extended from the figure and into the light, beckoning us into the archway. "Quickly," she said in Arabic accented English. "There's no too much time."

In spite of myself and our situation my whole being smiled. I could not help but look at Alhasan, who, also recognizing the voice, could only give a look of resignation.

TWENTY-EIGHT

Immediately, I began to walk toward the shadowed figure.

"Wait," insisted Sir James.

I halted briefly and looked at my commander.

"This is Najeeba, I presume? What's she doing here? This could be a trap," he observed.

I looked back at Rashin and his remaining robed men, now gathered in a group and heading toward us. "I'd say we're already trapped, commander."

"Aye," Sir James admitted, seeing Rashin and his men as well. "On with ya, then, but be on guard!"

"Always," I said as I turned and dashed toward the darkened archway.

Najeeba stepped into the light just as we arrived, her lavender eyes bright in spite of the gloom of this place. I froze at the sight of her beauty, nearly losing sight of our need to escape. "Follow," she said in hushed but urgent tone. She turned and ran back through the archway. We did as she bade and followed. She was fast, running down a darkened corridor as if she knew every step. It was all we could do to keep up. Though my spirit soared at the sight of her, I could not help but expect others, perhaps her keepers, to jump out at any given moment and apprehend us. I chastised myself for such thinking. *Trust. Trust,* I kept telling myself. We had no choice, as it was anyway. We could hear Rashin and his men entering the corridor behind us from the pretend cathedral. They were not far behind.

"Here," she said, ducking into a room. We followed, ending up in some kind of small storage closet, Alhasan closing the door behind us. We were as cramped together as wrapped fish. Yet, for a moment I was glad of it. I was pressed up against Najeeba, could smell the lovely scent of her hair, so close was I. I could barely see any of her features, so dark was the closet. What scant light was there came through cracks in the closed wooden door. But it was enough to reveal half of Najeeba's face. She turned that lovely face to mine and our eyes met in the semi-darkness. There was a kindness and depth in those eyes. I also felt a connection with her that truly spanned time itself. Sir James had referred to her as my *soul partner*. Indeed, I sensed the truth of it in that moment. But there was no time to revel it. We heard Rashin and his men run past the closet, could see their shadows pass us through the cracks in the closet's door. We remained in the cramped silence until the footfalls receded.

Slowly, quietly, Alhasan opened the closet door and stepped back out into the corridor, the rest of us followed. "They will come back, I believe," observed Alhasan.

"Yes. And they will bring Sultan's men," said Najeeba.

"Where are your women," asked Alhasan sternly, suddenly switching to Arabic.

"Are you so ungrateful as to insult me?" asked Najeeba, replying in Arabic. It was all I could do to follow their conversation, and it became obvious that Najeeba did not yet realize that I could understand her language.

"You take great risk," Alhasan continued in his native tongue. "Your women and watchers have been negligent.

"All other women have been sent East. I am here at my request, as are two other of my woman friends. My uncle can never say no to me, danger or no." Najeeba said, displaying none of the demureness I noticed at our first, actually our second, meeting. "I have no *watchers* as you call them. I am here now to aid Sir Masoud," she said turning her eyes to me, but continuing to speak to Alhasan. "He saved my life, my very soul, as you know, Alhasan. I do this now because of that and because of...because of..."

"Say it," urged Alhasan with quiet irritation.

"Because of love," she admitted as she still stared at me.

My heart swelled at the hearing of it, yet I gave no hint that I was following their conversation in Arabic, let alone understood what she had just specifically said. Though I wanted to embrace her passionately I simply held her gaze instead. After a moment, I looked to Alhasan who had the look of a crestfallen school boy.

"Love?" he finally said.

"Yes," she stated, now looking back at him. She saw his look and knew it for what it was. She stepped to Alhasan and stood before him. "You have served my uncle and me well, Alhasan. You are as a brother to me, but you know I've never had feelings for you beyond that, nor would it have ever been appropriate for me to."

"These revelations are all quite interesting," Sir James said in clear Arabic, quite irritated at the distraction. He had been pacing the immediate area, patrolling and guarding, making sure no one was yet coming back after us. "But we need to leave before none of us get the chance to discuss it further. Now?!"

Najeeba was obviously surprised by the commander's use of the Arabic language. She suddenly looked at me with an expression that was a mixture of questioning realization and embarrassment. I read her look instantly. *Do you understand my language too?* she seemed to ask silently.

"I understand enough," I said in English.

She held my look for a moment longer before getting back to the matter at hand. "This way," she said as she turned and headed back toward the cathedral.

"But, we just came from that way!" I said.

"Follow!" she said as more of a command than a request.

I looked to Sir James who simply shrugged and began to follow Najeeba. A moment later, we found ourselves back in the pretend cathedral.

The thunderous rumbling had ceased, the sphere of power was gone. Yet, there was still an unmistakable energy to the air, a tangible sensation of infinite possibility. Najeeba led us past the bodies of the robed figures and Blackthorn. Sir James paused and stared at the general's body.

"We should keep on move," said Najeeba in broken English.

"Would that we could take him back for a proper rite," said Sir James, ignoring Najeeba for the moment.

"I understand," I replied. "He lost his way, but was still a servant of the Light."

"A great one for a time. What led him astray?" wondered Sir James aloud. "Ah, impossible though, to take him back, I mean."

I looked at the face of General Horatio Blackthorn and did something impulsive. I reached out the spear and touched its blade gently to the general's bruised and battered forehead. All went dark around me as I turned my sight inward intending on blessing the general and his service up to his wayward turn, but even still blessing that too, for it was all of The One. However, my intention notwithstanding, what happened next shocked me to the core of my being. In my mind's eye, I saw General Horatio Blackthorn in all his fine Templar regalia on a younger day, the day of his installation as a Grand Master of The Knights Templar many years earlier. His face conveyed an idealistic vigor that shined with divine purpose. The general seemed to look directly at me and I saw into his soul, saw all his former selves. I had known the general in previous lifetimes but had not recognized him, his spirit until that moment. His face changed, shaped into a familiar from my time as Myrriddin. He was, had been, my mentor, Moscastan. The shock of seeing his face now brought emotion and memory to the surface I had not anticipated; nights and years of tutelage under my beloved Master Moscastan, observing the wizard becoming the age and persona of his desire at will in any given moment, for example. Or, the carrying of his bones to be placed within his crystal sanctuary, which had become my place of solace as Myrriddin the elder. His appearance shifted again and he became his soul's expression before Moscastan; my beloved mentor and friend Jacobi during my life as Longinus! How had he come back to this earth as a wayward general and knight from such two previously lofty, advanced soul's incarnations?!

The words then echoed in my mind; *to say that one soul is more advanced...is to miss the point of the soul's subjective journey within the One Mind, which is this: that Mind may experience Itself, as Itself, through our individualized experiences within Itself.* It seemed some lessons must be repeated. "Blessings to you, my old friend," I heard myself saying to the image in my mind's eye. "And may your soul's journey be swift and effortless." The image of Jacobi/Moscastan/Blackthorn faded from my mind. I opened my eyes and was fully and completely present in the Devil's church, the pretend cathedral once more. I removed the spear's blade flat from the general's forehead and stared at the body before me.

TWENTY-NINE

"Come," said Najeeba, "No more time!" She took three steps toward the entrance Sir James, Alhasan and I had originally come, only to see it was blocked by rubble. Undeterred, she then darted to the left, and came to a crumbled section of the room's wall with ceiling debris and rubble piled at its base. She began to remove some of the rubble, clearly looking for something. Rather than waste time in questioning her, Sir James and I left the dead general's side and began to help her, pushing aside debris near the base of the wall. "There!" Najeeba said as Sir James uncovered what was a four foot in diameter dark hole near the base of the wall.

"A ventilation duct," Sir James stated.

"La, no." replied Najeeba. "I believe it to be an escape tunnel. This place was once used as prison."

"How do you know of these things?" asked Alhasan with a mixture of awe and dismay, as if to say, *a woman should not know of these things!*

"I venture to explore," she said with pride.

Sir James took one of the nearby torches out of its sconce on the wall and entered the small tunnel on his hands and knees. Najeeba went next, followed by Alhasan and myself, tucking the sword in the cloth belt of my under-tunic thus leaving one hand free as I hung onto the spear with the other. I pulled some of the debris back over the opening as I went in concealing the whole from Rashin or anyone coming after us.

Once again, darkness engulfed us, save for the torch that Sir James held at the lead. The tunnel we now found ourselves in was cramped, barely enough room to crawl forward on hands and knees in a single-file line. On and on we went, the tunnel bending to the right and then the left and then returning to a straight course, all the while making a steady, gradual incline toward the surface. After a time, the air became stale and thin, making it difficult to breathe, as it became apparent that there was not much air ventilating through this tunnel. I began to think that rather than escaping we may have entombed ourselves, never to see the outside world again or breathe fresh air. Each of us began to cough as smoke from the dying torch flame swirled back on us with nowhere to escape, and I put part of my tunic cloth over my mouth and nose in an effort to help my breathing and filter out the smoke. The others were doing the same. Sir James extinguished the torch in the dirt of our tunnel floor. We would continue on in utter darkness. But a better idea impinged itself upon my mind. No sooner had the torch gone out when I began to fully concentrate on the spear and sword, holding the image in my mind that they both were leading us in light, their blades glowing to show the way. So fully was the conviction of my desire and intent that almost instantly the spear's blade began to glow a soft green. I removed The King's Sword from my tunic's belt. It too glowed a soft green and in the same hue, in harmony with the Spear of Longinus. And, to my astonishment, after a few seconds I was able to breathe with less difficulty. It was as if the spear and sword were providing enhancement of our air, producing the necessary qualities in it for our sustentation. "Sir James, take the King's Sword as it will illuminate the way," I said in a raspy whisper, passing the instrument forward. As I did, each of my companions audibly breathed easier.

"Allah be praised," sighed Alhasan.

"Amazing," said Sir James.

We continued on, our hands and knees becoming raw with the effort of the crawl. The hours passed by as if time itself crawled. We travelled for what felt like several hours, though in my mind I could not believe that it was so long. Suddenly, our journey began to become more difficult, not because of a thinning in the air around us again, but because the tunnel had begun a steeper incline, much steeper than any before this point. Also, the tunnel passageway had become narrower. We were all on our stomachs pulling ourselves forward. "Here's something!" Sir James finally declared.

Each of us suddenly emerged into the ruins of a large, high domed ceilinged room not too dissimilar in configuration than the pretend cathedral we had left below. Blessedly, though, this one was obviously above ground. Bright light, sunlight streamed in through the upper window openings on the dome. I breathed deeply and nearly started to laugh, so pleased I was to be in a large space and above ground.

"The day has dawned," exclaimed Sir James, noting the wonderful light entering the room from windows. We apparently had indeed been in the tunnel for several hours.

"The tunnel. We were in the tunnel for very, very long," observed Najeeba. "It took longer than last attempt."

"'longer than *last* attempt?'" Alhasan asked horrified that she had made the journey through the tunnel before.

"Yes."

"But, how? Why?! I, la, la. I do not wish to know," concluded Alhasan.

"Listen," ordered Sir James, as he held his head high to hear the sounds of our surroundings. But there were none, no sounds. All was silent; no sounds of soldiers urgently running to their task or even simply going about their duties, no sounds of nearby battles, no sounds of catapulted fireballs exploding and the chaos they bring.

"What has happened?" I asked.

"The battle is won by the Sultan?" Alhasan asked Najeeba.

"Yes," she replied, firm with the knowledge of it. "Not many are presently present."

Were it not for my sudden sense of isolation I may have smiled at Najeeba's use of English, so endearing it was at times. But the matter was grave if she was correct. At least, it was grave for Sir James and I. "How can you be sure the battle's won?" I asked.

"It was so before coming to you," explained Najeeba. "I wanted you not prisoner. I desired to escape you out. The Sultan and his men are now talking with prisoners at your army's camp. He is most merciful. But others will demand *your* head, for you control those," she said pointing to the spear in my hand and the sword in Sir James' hand, "and that you lead Templar Knights."

"But..." I began in protest.

"You said, 'I escape you out,'" Sir James said to Najeeba. "Escape him or take him out to where, to here, to the Sultan?"

"Commander, I should as well to leave him down below as to that," she replied. She then turned to me. "I take you to freedom, both of you," she said, addressing Sir James for the last portion.

I looked to Sir James and saw a personal battle waging across his face. His sense of duty was no doubt at war with his desire for freedom from this place. My own sense of duty and honor reared up from within. *Am I to leave this place and return home, or should I rejoin my men and fellow soldiers and crusaders?* I wondered. At the thought of joining my men, Henry came into my mind. What had become of him? "Where would prisoners be in this place?" I blurted out.

"No, Masoud. You must not. You must not search for your friend!" said Alhasan, understanding my meaning.

"But I told you where prisoners were," said Najeeba, ignoring Alhasan's outburst, "where I led you from was prisoners' place. They are gone now." she said, obviously confused by my question.

"But I thought you meant it was *originally* a prison, not that it had been made into a type of holding room," I said.

"I aided to some of men there, cleaned wounds. It is why it looks like your churches and our mosques," she said. "Sultan, my uncle, is most merciful, allowing all to worship as they wish, even as prisoner. I believe some made and escaped through tunnel we came through. The rest taken to your camp."

"Perhaps your Henry is still alive then, Liam, Sir Masoud," said Sir James. "But now you are charged with a higher duty," he said, handing me the King's Sword and the Rood. "It is your duty as Templar Knight and Guardian of the sacred relics to take these items, all of them, to safety, to the safety and protection of our Order in our homeland. I order you to do that. Go with Najeeba," he said looking at Najeeba, but speaking to me. "Something tells me her uncle, the great Salah al-Din had a hand in planning this, your escape." He smiled, then. To Najeeba's credit she kept her face impassive, giving nothing away.

"And you, Sir James, Jonathan?" I asked, not wanting this to be our parting, but knowing it to be so.

"I will remain here in hiding for at least a few hours so as not to draw attention to you," he explained. "I'll then make my way back to our men, come what may. Go now and discharge your duty, lad."

"I...I...yes, Sir. Thank you for everything," I stammered.

"Come, this way," said Najeeba, as she moved off. I followed tentatively, Al-hasan behind me all but prodding my back to go. I looked back one last time at my Commander Sir Jonathan James. He was already gone.

EPILOGUE

"I have not been unwise in the discharge of my duty, have I, my love?" the old man asked.

"La, you have not, Masoud," replied the aged woman with lavender eyes. Though many years had passed since their first meeting on a crusader battlefield, beauty still lived in those eyes and in that soul. Indeed in the soul of Liam Arthur Mason, renamed Masoud all those years passed, resided the very soul of Longinus the Centurion and first keeper of the spear, and Myrriddin, Guardian and keeper of the Spear of Longinus and the King's Sword. The soul of Masoud, Myrriddin and Longinus were one soul and had never strayed too far from this Earth, this plane of existence.

But the time had come for this soul to sojourn on another plane. "It is time, father," said the voice of Aiden Alhasan Mason.

Masoud and Najeeba turned to see their firstborn, handsome son standing before them in the full regalia of the Grand Master he was. His hair was as dark as his mother's and his eyes were hers too; lavender. His skin tone was a mixture of the people of the Isles of Britain and the Arab nations. Standing near Aiden were five Master Templar Knights, also in the ceremonial robes of the high Templar. They filed past Masoud, each bowing in respect to the aged Master, then slipping through the portal into the secret, darkened Temple beyond. Two servants came to stand next to Aiden, one on each side, each holding the sacred relics of Christ wrapped in silk cloth.

"Unwrap them," said Masoud. It was not a request. He would not see the new dawn. His soul's journey was to continue elsewhere, at least for a time. "I will behold them one last time, before charging you for their safe-keeping, Aiden."

"As you wish, father," Aiden replied, nodding to the servants next to him to do as his father bade. One by one, the relics were unveiled. Masoud stood on hobbled legs and gingerly shuffled across the antechamber to the servants. He touched each relic in turn, pausing long enough to feel their energy. At last he came to the Spear of Longinus. "Wood and metal you be, old friend, but keeper of the Divine too, yes?" he whispered to the thing. He reverently kissed the spear's blade. He then turned to face the Temple doors which opened for him. The small procession then entered the Temple for the rite of passage, including Najeeba. Unprecedented, this was, for a woman to be allowed into the inner sanctuary of the Templar Knights. But this was to be no ordinary rite, but a rite of the transference of Templar Power and Guardianship of the Sacred Objects. It was also to be the rite of Transition of The Soul or in this case, of two souls; Masoud's and Najeeba's. It was their choice to leave this plane, together and on this night.

All took their places within the Temple's darkened interior. The servants, lead by Aiden, walked Masoud and Najeeba to their place of honor in the middle of the Temple. They sat, side by side, in the west-facing high-backed plush reclining chairs. The drink was given to them and the ceremony begun. They sat hand in hand, did Masoud and Najeeba, as they began to drift in mind and spirit to the threshold of the Otherworld, to the chorus of chants and rites being read. Drifting, floating, was Masoud. He began to see things of his soul's journey, from its past, though time in this state was rendered nonexistent. They flashed by his mind's eye, and he relived each in an instant. Finally, a place, a time, a persona came into view. He settled there for a span and enjoyed the cool mists.

The mists rolled across the headlands as waves across a shoreline. Masoud walked down to the edge of the lake on this moonlit night and stared across the water at the Isle of Mystery and the ancient temple ruins thereon; the very place where he, as Myrriddin, had found the Spear of Longinus all those many years past. A part of him remained at One with the mists now, calling them and keeping them here as a comfort the way one clings to a blanket in childhood.

"Masoud, Myrriddin?" Igraines said as she approached him from behind. Her voice was still as sweet as a summer robin's song. Though they were both well aged and long in the experiences of living even in this place, his passion for her had never waned no matter in what form. Indeed, the more experience his soul received the more he lived in that passion and the more he allowed it to carry over from life to life. He turned and looked into Igraines' eyes—and hence the soul of Irena, his love during his embodiment as Longinus—now turned a brilliant lavender. *But...how could that be?* he wondered. *They had never been lavender before.* And then it hit him. Myrriddin/Masoud, was not just dreaming the dream of his soul, reeling from the continuous thread of his existence from one life to the next to the next, and the overlapping of his partner souls, the good ones and the challenging ones, that he moved with through eternal existence and growth and expression. He was crossing to the next expression of his journey, leaving the persona of Longinus, Myrriddin and Masoud behind and parting, for now, from his partner soul of Irena, Igraines and Najeeba. His soul had chosen this place and his Myrriddin self through which to exit.

"Myrriddin, my dearest," she said staring back at him.

"Yes, my love, my queen," Myrriddin said. She stood next to him. He looked deeper into those lavender eyes and took comfort in them as he took comfort in the mists. Her face was still lovely. "'Tis near time for me, Igraines, near time to travel on."

"Do not speak so, Myrriddin," she said sadly.

"You have never been afraid of the truth before, my love. Do not fear it now," I replied. "Besides, I have done all I can here."

"You have been of great service, 'tis true. But, what of us? We missed so much of each other because of our duties. We've only just begun spending more time in each other's company," she lamented. "One lifetime is not enough."

"We each answered a greater call. Yet I have no doubt that we will have the opportunity to be with each other again and again and again if we so choose," I said.

"I do so choose, Myrriddin." She stood on tip-toe then and kissed his lips. He returned her kiss with the lost ardor of youth, their youth.

Their lips parted and something shifted within his being. He knew the time had come. She must have seen it in his eyes, for she simply nodded in understanding, in acceptance, a tear of sadness rolling down her cheek. *Attachment is the root of our sadness at loss.* He suddenly thought. *With no attachment there is no loss. That is not to be understood as indifferent detachment, however. Compassionate non-attachment is an aspect of unconditional love.* Such were his thoughts in that moment. He looked once again to the Isle of Mystery across the Lake and stepped onto the lake's surface. With one foot after the other, he walked on the surface of the water all the way to the Isle's shore. Looking back in the direction he'd come, he gave one last wave of his hand to the lone figure of Igraines still standing on the opposite shore. She waved back and turned, walking away and fading from sight, continuing on the journey of her soul. He then turned and walked toward the ancient temple ruins to say farewell to his lives as Longinus, Myrriddin and Masoud, knowing that though these figures are gone they may be forever revisited at any time and in the blink of an eye. He knew too that his soul's journey was just beginning. A soul's journey is always just beginning, for it is never ending, always present in the eternal moment.

You Are What You Love
By Vaishāli

You Are What You Love is the definitive 21st century guide for Spiritual seekers of timeless wisdom who have hit a pothole on the way to enlightenment and are searching for the answers to the big questions in life: "Who am I?" and "Why am I here?" Author Vaishāli explores mystic Emanuel Swedenborg's philosophy of gratitude and love. She expands this wisdom by associating it to traditional sources including Christianity and Buddhism. Through storytelling and humor, the focal point of the book "you don't have love, you are love" is revealed. A compelling read to deepen your understanding of Oneness.

Paperback, 400 pages, ISBN 978-0-9773200-0-4, $24.95

You Are What You Love®, Book on CD
By Vaishāli

Also available on CD an 80-minute condensed and abridged version of the 400-page book counter part. Read by the author.

CD, ISBN 978-0-9773200-2-8, $14.95

You Are What You Love Playbook
By Vaishāli

You Are What You Love Playbook s a playtime manual offering practical play practices to invoke play into action. Included is step-by-step guidance on dream work, a 13-month course in how to practice playful miracles, and a copy of the author's lucid dream diary. The perfect companion to You Are What You Love.

Paperback, 124 pages, ISBN 978-0-9773200-1-1, $14.95

More Books By Purple Haze Press:

Wisdom Rising
By Vaishāli

Sometimes wisdom is best served up like M&M candies, in small pieces that you can savor, enjoy and hold in your hand. So it is with Vaishāli's new book, Wisdom Rising. It is a delightful, sweet, and satisfying collection of brilliant articles and short stories, that like gem quality jewels, are a thing of beauty, and a joy to behold.

It doesn't matter what your background is there is something to appeal to everyone in this book. Vaishāli's trademark "out of the box" sense of humor and wild woman perspective runs rampant throughout the book. Whether she is talking about the Nature of God or simply poking fun at our own cultural insecurities and hypocrisies, Vaishāli raises the bar on laugh out loud Spiritual wisdom. The entertainment as well as the wisdom rises flawlessly together, inviting the reader to go deeper in examining and showing up for their own life.

Everything about this book from the cover to the cartoon illustrations that punctuate every story, screams playful, fun, witty, and what we have seen Vaishāli dish up before, which is the unexpected . . . no wonder she is know as "the Spiritual Wild Child."

Paperback, ISBN: 978-0-9773200-6-6 $14.95

Wisdom Rising, Book on CD
By Vaishāli

This 4-CD set is the condensed and abridged version of the 285 page book counter part. Read by the author.

CD, ISBN 987-0-9773200-9-7 $19.95

LONGINUS: BOOK I OF THE MERLIN FACTOR
by Steven Maines

Longinus follows the tale of Gaius Cassius Longinus, the Roman Centurion who pierced the side Jesus with his spear while the condemned one hung from the cross.

After that fateful day, Longinus escapes Rome and the priests who want to take the spear and its supposed power for themselves. Longinus follows the Centurion's life from his love for the prostitute Irena to his mystical studies with the Druids of Gaul. But it also reveals Longinus' profound spiritual awakening through his Druidic studies and the spear that speaks to him with the voice of Christ.

Paperback, 241 pages, ISBN 978-0-9773200-3-5 $14.95

Longinus: Book I of the Merlin Factor
By Steven Maines

This abridged audio version of the critically acclaimed novel, follows the tale of Gaius Cassius Longinus, the Roman Centurion who pierced the side of Jesus with his spear while the condemned one hung from the cross. Abridged Audio Book (3 CD). As Read By Mark Colson

CD, ISBN 978-0-9773200-7-3 $19.95

MYRRIDDIN: BOOK II OF THE MERLIN FACTOR
by Steven Maines

In *Myrriddin: Book II of the Merlin Factor*, it is the 4th Century A.D. A young boy has found sacred relics of the early Christians in the ruins of an ancient Druid temple on the Isle of Mystery in Old Britain. For reasons beyond his immediate comprehension, the lad connects with one item in particular;the Spear of Longinus, the very spear that pierced the side of Jesus and allegedly holds the power of Christ. The boy's name is Myrriddin. The world would remember him as Merlin, the greatest Druid and Wizard of all time.

Paperback, 217 pages

ISBN 978-0-9773200-4-2 $14.95

Myrriddin: Book II of the Merlin Factor, Book on CD
By Steven Maines

This 4-CD set is the condensed and abridged version of the 217 page book counter part. Read by actor Mark Colson.

CD, ISBN 987-0-9773200-8-0 $19.95

More Books By Purple Haze Press:

Masoud: Book III of the Merlin Factor
by Steven Maines

Follow the tale of Liam Arthur Mason as he struggles with the reawakening of his spirit and hence the ultimate advancement of his being. Experience his reawakening through his sacred initiation into the Knights Templar and his partnership with their Muslim counterparts, the Hashishim Knights, as well as through his passion for the woman Najeeba. And, finally be with him as he comes to fulfill his true destiny with the Spear of Longinus and Great King's Sword. Liam Arthur Mason was his Christian name. Masoud is who he would become.

Paperback, ISBN 978-0-9773200-5-9 $14.95

Geraldine Goodkitty
by F.J. Kercher

The author experienced a curious dream about a stray cat with the odd name Geraldine Goodkitty and her three kittens. She decided to write about each of the characters in the dream in order to probe its meaning. Geraldine's story began to expand, and the author continued to write. The story grew into a composite inspired by the wonderful animals that have graced her life and lent their names, personalities, and physical appearance to most of the characters in the novel. Geraldine's tale is told primarily from a feline perspective. However, the animal and human stories interweave at various points and eventually converge.

Paperback, 236 pages, ISBN 978-1-935183-05-1 $14.95